ESCAPE
FROM
ROME

ESCAPE
FROM
ROME

Marleen Kunze

Tate Publishing *&* *Enterprises*

Published by Tate Publishing & Enterprises, LLC
127 E. Trade Center Terrace | Mustang, Oklahoma 73064 USA
1.888.361.9473 | www.tatepublishing.com

Tate Publishing is committed to excellence in the publishing industry. The company reflects the philosophy established by the founders, based on Psalm 68:11,
"The Lord gave the word and great was the company of those who published it."

Book design copyright © 2009 by Tate Publishing, LLC. All rights reserved.
Cover design & Illustrations by Jeff Kunze
Interior design by Joey Garrett

Published in the United States of America

ISBN: 978-1-60799-607-1
1. Fiction / Christian / Historical
2. Fiction / Historical
09.08.31

DEDICATION

This book is dedicated to the memory of my father, Gail Clayton, who loved to write and who always enjoyed a good story.

ACKNOWLEDGMENTS

I would like to thank my family for encouraging me to write, especially my mom, Marjorie Clayton, and my husband, John, who are my biggest fans. I would also like to thank my six adult children, Mike, Jeff, Krissy, Mark, Stacy, and Kerry, for being my inspiration into family dynamics, and thanks to Jeff, for designing the map and the cover of the book.

CHAPTER 1

Argus, Felix, and Maximus were the sons of Nolan, the manager of the Coliseum. They had been following their father around since they were little tots, and they knew every meeting room, storage bin, and eatery in the Coliseum, from the rooms underground to the walkways of the upper level. But they were never allowed to watch a performance of any kind, and they were not allowed to go near Gate 40 or Gate 80. They knew that Gate 40 was the emperor's entrance and that Gate 80 had something to do with dead people and animals.

The year was 90 a.d., and Emperor Domitian was in power and in control of the entire Roman Empire, which extended all the way around the Great Sea. His rule was filled with violence, and most of the citizens in Rome spent their time socializing and watching bloody shows at the Coliseum. The day was the first of August, and the time was noon. The Coliseum was packed with forty-five thousand fans.

The sky was alive with flashes of lightning and

rumblings of thunder. Manager Nolan grabbed two of his sons, Argus and Felix, and shouted, "The awnings. Hurry and find the sailors. The emperor is going to get wet, and we'll all pay the price for that."

The boys knew that the sailors were probably hanging out downstairs, having a midday meal. They went charging into the room and found them sitting around on cushions, eating cakes and drinking tea.

"The awnings!" shouted Argus, Nolan's oldest son. "Hurry, a storm is coming, and Father says the emperor will get wet."

Argus and Felix gasped for air as they followed the sailors round and round up the many sets of stairs. When they reached the top of the Coliseum, the wind was blowing so hard that everyone had to hold on to keep from falling over the handrail.

"We can help, if you want us to," yelled Felix.

"Grab those lines and pull, hand over hand. Watch us and do just what we do!" a sailor shouted. The boys pulled and pulled, and they were amazed as the bright red, blue, yellow, and green sails came across the top of the place and provided the audience shelter from the rain. The boys and the sailors each grabbed another rope and pulled more awnings across, sheltering the spectators below. But what would keep people in place with all the wind and lightning and thunder? The boys looked below and realized that an event was taking place.

Then the sailors returned to the café, and the boys decided to stick around and peek down from their perches. The entire floor of the arena was decorated with large groups of trees, shrubbery, and vines. As they watched, five rhinos were released into the arena. The animals seemed very aggressive, charging the entire distance across the place and then back again, dodging trees and each other, to the cheers of the crowd. The storm was whipping the sails, and the sky was ablaze with lightning, but the crowds cheered on. Suddenly, a man in hunting clothes entered the arena. He had nothing with him but a bow and a quiver full of arrows. The door was slammed shut behind him.

"Please don't tell me he's going to kill those beautiful animals!" shouted Felix.

"What? Are you kidding? Rhinos have thick hides. You saw them yesterday. The hunter doesn't have a chance," responded Argus.

The hunter was a skinny guy, and he ran and hid behind a tree to prepare his bow. A rhino saw him and charged straight at the tree, which exploded into a mass of plaster and other materials, and the man was plowed down like a pancake. Argus and Felix were in shock, but the crowd cheered and laughed and chanted, "More, more, more, more …"

Two more hunters entered the jungle, and once again the door was slammed behind them. They headed for a small hill covered with bushes, and a rhino charged them. It trampled the shrubbery and descended the other side of the hill, but the two hunters split up, and the rhino stormed straight between them. As one of the hunters ran through the fake jungle, he saw the first hunter's flattened body covered with blood and debris. He knelt down for a better look, and he, too, was trampled by a rhino. The crowd went crazy, laughing and cheering. The other hunter climbed a tree.

Felix shouted, "Look out! Those trees aren't very strong."

"He can't hear you from way up here," Argus said.

It was difficult to see what the hunter was doing, but they could only guess that he was getting an arrow ready. Finally two rhinos went charging past the tree, and an arrow hit one of them in its backside. In its fury, it began knocking down trees, and suddenly it plowed into another rhino. With a gory wound on its side, the second rhino joined the rampage, destroying the beautiful trees and shrubbery. Another arrow was shot out of the tree, and a third rhino was wounded.

The boys watched in horror as the rhinos leveled every bit of scenery the stage crew had erected except for the tree that the hunter was in. The hunter had released other arrows, but only two of them met their marks.

"That guy is dead already. I don't want to see it," said Argus. "Let's get out of here and never watch again."

"Hold on," shouted Felix. "Remember the crane we use to move the heavy materials into the arena? It's out of the way right now, but if we went down there, we could slide it straight out into the arena, turn it to the right, and that hunter could grab the chain. Do you think he would grab the chain?"

"If we get caught, we will be in big trouble," said Argus. "But I like it."

The boys hurried down the steps, raced through the corridors, and came to an area roped off for equipment. The crane was mounted on a track, and the boys had watched many times as the crew pushed it out to the arena. They did not expect it to be so heavy. They pushed together, straining with all their might. Finally it began to move, slowly at first, and then at a decent pace. The boys forgot to peek out into the arena from their location to see if their plan was possible, and now it was too late, for the crane suddenly appeared for all of the audience to see. The boys were hidden from view, but they could see the tree and the hunter and swung the crane straight for him. They practically knocked the hunter out when the heavy chain hit the tree, but the man quickly wised up and grabbed the chain. Argus and Felix swung him back to the front and began pushing the crane backwards with all their strength. An unrecognizable sound filled the place, but the boys continued the push. Once the hunter was inside the walls, Argus grabbed his arm and pulled him deeper into the room.

"Do you hear that sound?" asked Felix. "They are booing us. Let's hide."

They looked around and remembered a place they had hidden in the past to get out of work. It was down the corridor, two rooms away. They ran there, opened a closet door, and squeezed in. The three of them were panting so hard they were sure to be discovered. The crowd continued to boo, and now they were stamping their feet, too.

"What were we thinking?" whispered Argus. "Those people are really angry. If they find us, they might kill us."

"So this is the reason Father doesn't allow us to watch the performances," said Felix. "The audience is ruthless. They want people to get hurt."

Argus cupped his hand over Felix's mouth. "Shhh," he whispered.

They could hear men shouting and running down the hallway. Felix could feel the poor hunter shaking violently on one side of him and Argus's stifling presence on the other side. The three fugitives stayed quiet for a long time and listened as the crowd went from angry to quiet to cheering and laughing.

The room next door to the closet was used to house costumes, so the three of them went in there and quickly disguised themselves to look like rich foreigners with turbans on their heads and long colorful robes flowing around their ankles. They simply descended the stairs gracefully and walked out into the busy city streets, where sidewalk vendors were shaking the rain off tarps and uncovering their sales items. Behind them they could still hear the laughter of the fickle crowd.

"Are you all right?" Argus asked the hunter, who had not said one word.

"I think I will be," said the young man, "once I stop shaking. Do you think they will recognize me and make me go back in there?"

"They will never recognize you in that disguise. Do you hear the crowd? Something new has captured their attention," said Felix. Then he turned to his brother. "Argus, promise me you'll never tell anyone what we did."

"I never will," said Argus. "And I'll never watch another show at the Coliseum."

"I won't either," said Felix. "And now we must say goodbye to our new friend."

"You leave me?" questioned the hunter man. "I have no place to hide. They will kill me."

"Well, what did you expect?" asked Argus. "What are you doing playing a hunter for crowds in the Coliseum, anyway? That was not very smart."

"I did not have a choice. I was a prisoner of war, brought here by a bunch of Roman soldiers. Those men killed were my friends. One of them was husband to my sister," said the man.

Argus looked down at the ground, sorry for the insensitive things he had said to the young man who was in so much pain.

"Please forgive me. I did not know," Argus said.

Felix couldn't say anything. He was ashamed that he had watched the performance when his father had always forbidden it, and he was also sorry that Argus had scolded a man who had lost his home and his family. The three of them walked silently through the city streets.

The boys reached the point where they needed to turn toward their home.

"I wish there was something we could do to help you," Argus said. The young man looked so helpless and scared.

"Let's hide him in our tree house," suggested Felix. "We can sneak food and water and clothes to him, and then we can help him escape the city."

"I will be most grateful. I will try to pay you back someday. My name is Ravi, and I came from Egypt."

The boys and the young man named Ravi shed their costumes in an alleyway, and Ravi stripped down to his waist so he would not be recognized as the hunter. They immediately sent Ravi up in the tree house and instructed him to pull the ladder up, making it impossible for anyone to go up and discover him. They promised to bring food and water soon.

When the boys entered the house, they were surprised to see their younger brother, Maximus, sitting on a sofa between their mother and their sister, Claudia. Maximus was sobbing, and they were trying to comfort him. They could see that their mother and Claudia had tears in their eyes as well.

"What's wrong, Mother?" Felix asked.

"Maximus just ran home from the Coliseum," she said, "where Cadogan and Kendrick saw their father killed in the arena by rhinos."

"Their father was killed? I don't understand. He works for the emperor with Father, doesn't he?" asked Argus.

"Someone helped a hunter escape from rhinos and ruined today's show. Since their father was in charge of security and comfort of the visitors, he was killed in the hunter's place as a punishment for not being in total control of the place," said Maximus. "The emperor insisted that his boys watch. I think they are in shock. I helped them walk home, and they had to tell their mother."

Argus and Felix looked at each other. Felix wiped the tears from his eyes, and Argus looked away so he wouldn't cry.

"Does Father know?" asked Felix.

"He knows," said Maximus. "He's the one who told me to walk home with the boys, and he told me not to say a word about it when I go back to the Coliseum. I don't ever want to go back there."

Just then, Nolan came home. He looked very serious, and he went straight to the servants and told them that the family would be having a picnic that evening in the backyard of the villa, and that they would have five visitors.

"A picnic!" said Sabrina. "This is not the time for a picnic after what happened today."

"This is the perfect time for a picnic. Lavinia and

the children will be joining us. Will you prepare the tables at the back of the yard, my dear?" asked Nolan.

"Father, what's going to happen?" asked Maximus.

Nolan said not to discuss anything until later. He looked around at the family, and they understood that they must not talk around the servants. Soon the family and friends were sitting around tables loaded with food in the back of the yard, and the servants were told to return to the house and stay there. Once alone, both families began to cry.

Nolan let everyone cry for a long time. Sabrina threw her arms around Lavinia, attempting to comfort her, but Lavinia continued to cry, and the twin babies cried along with their mother. Finally Nolan stood up to talk to everyone.

"It has been ten years now that I have worked for the emperor, and I know that although he depends on me to keep the place running smoothly, my life could end at any time. I have seen him order the death of a man for simply tripping on the stairs and another for not laughing at his joke. Lavinia, your Frederick did nothing wrong. The emperor was angry that the crowd was displeased, and he insisted that someone pay. I am so sorry that the boys were there and that they had to watch. I promise you that I will take care of you and the children. Am I right that you have no one else?"

Lavinia and the children sobbed for a long time, and Nolan waited patiently. Finally she said, "We have no other family here. Remember that Frederick married me and brought me here. My family lives far, far away in the land of Britannia. It would take a long time to get there. I know that I will never see them again. I gave up on that a long time ago."

"What about Frederick's family?" asked Nolan.

"We keep the children away from them. They are crude and disgusting. They watch the killing at the Coliseum and love it. They probably are laughing that Frederick was killed," said Lavinia. "Oh, what will happen to us? The girls are just babies."

"For some time now, I have been planning our escape. Sabrina knows of these plans, but this is the first time I have mentioned it to the children," announced Nolan. "I feel the time has come to share this with you all, to give you hope. This is no place to raise a family. I have been looking for a place to go where the Roman army has little influence. Lavinia, do you think Britannia would be safe?"

"No, the Roman army is definitely in control there. Frederick was in the army, and they let him carry me off as his bride. My parents were going to move to my grandparents' town in Mide, on the island of Ireland, but they waited too long to save me. At that time, the Romans weren't interested in Mide, probably because it was small and because it was farther away. I hope my parents went there," said Lavinia.

"Do you think we could all go to your grandparents' town?" asked Nolan. "I want to raise my family without danger."

"That is more than I could ever hope for. It is a dream," she answered.

"I'll see what I can find out. In the meantime, I think it's best to keep our boys away from the emperor and away from the Coliseum. Tomorrow I am sending a hunting party off to Africa to bring back lions for the emperor's birthday celebration. I want Argus, Felix, and Maximus to go, and I think Cadogan and

Kendrick should go, too. I am afraid the emperor will be watching for them after today. A trip like this will give him time to forget all about them."

"Will they be safe?" asked Lavinia. Sabrina looked worried, too.

"My friend Titus will lead the party. He is like a brother to me, and I trust him to take care of our boys. Hopefully our sons will be building strong cages and hunting for food to feed the lions and the hunting party as well. Titus will teach them how to live off the land, how to set up tents, how to defend themselves, and how to travel inconspicuously. His son Flavius will be going along. Titus is the best. They will have a company of soldiers along for protection, of course. Sabrina, what do you think?" Nolan asked.

Sabrina looked at her precious sons. At seventeen, sixteen, and fifteen, the boys were tall and built strong. They had dark hair and dark eyes, and they were very handsome. "That sounds like good training, and, at least for now, it will keep them out of the Roman army. Boys, do you want to go hunting lions in Africa?" she asked.

The boys all said that they would go, but Sabrina noticed that Argus and Felix hesitated and looked at the ground.

"You two don't seem like you mean it. Is something wrong?" asked Nolan.

The boys couldn't keep their secret any longer. They started crying.

"It's our fault. Because of Felix and me, our family is in danger," said Argus.

"What are you talking about, Son?" Nolan asked.

"Today at the Coliseum, it was Felix and I who saved

the hunter. I'm so sorry. We didn't know the emperor would kill Frederick."

"You boys saved the hunter? Where is he?" asked Nolan.

"He's up there near the villa in our tree house," said Felix. "Will you forgive us?" The boys looked at Lavinia and her boys with tears streaming down their faces.

"You did a good thing," said Lavinia, "when you saved a life. It is the emperor that we hate. He's the evil one. There is nothing to forgive. And yes, my boys will go along hunting. It is the kind of training they need." Kendrick got up from the table and hugged Argus and Felix and said he wanted to go hunting. Cadogan stayed in his seat and frowned as he watched his brother give comfort to the ones responsible for his father's death.

"Argus, go get the man and bring him here at once," said Nolan.

While Argus was gone, Nolan summed everything up. "Here is the plan. I will continue to save money as I have been doing for ten years. I will send a party of men to Britannia and Mide in search of Lavinia's parents and possibly her grandparents. You must give me the details," he said to Lavinia. "Perhaps they will find a safe place for our families to settle, away from the empire. Meanwhile, our boys will be in training with my friend Titus, and they will be away from the emperor. When they return, we will go from there."

Argus brought Ravi to the backyard. He was short with dark skin, and he looked very skinny in just his shorts. "This is Ravi, the hunter that Felix and I rescued today," he said.

"How old are you, Ravi?" asked Nolan.

"I am nineteen years old, and I have been away from my country for one year now," he answered.

"I see," said Nolan. "Tomorrow our boys are all going to Africa to learn hunting and survival skills. I also am sending a team to Britannia. You need to get away from here immediately. Which way would you like to go?"

"I would like to go with the hunting party. Perhaps I can keep going all the way back to Egypt and find my family," Ravi said.

"Very well. Boys, after we eat, you must go in and pack a few clothes and snacks and be ready to leave by morning. Find some clothes for Ravi to wear," said Nolan.

"Lavinia, I am sorry, but I cannot take care of your household and ours and still save money to leave," announced Nolan. "Would you bring the babies and live here at the villa? There is a small building just over there where I think you could be comfortable and safe."

"Oh, please come," said Sabrina. "We can comfort each other because we will miss our boys so much. And I can help take care of the twins." Lavinia agreed to move there for now and to let her two servants go.

Finally everyone realized they were hungry. As they ate their picnic dinner, Nolan reminded everyone that their plans were secret and if the emperor or his men found out, they could all be lion bait in October.

Lavinia and her family went home to pack, and they agreed to return at dawn the next morning.

After they left and the boys took Ravi in the house to pack, Sabrina had a talk with her husband.

"Nolan, there is another problem that we have not

discussed. Lately a man has taken an interest in Claudia. All I know about the man is that he is probably wealthy since he wears fine purple clothing and that he goes by the villa every day and watches for her. I'm fairly worried. Claudia is totally disgusted. The man must be forty years old."

"He looks old enough to be my grandfather. Yuck!" Claudia said.

"This could be a problem if he has any influence," said Father. "Claudia is fourteen now, and many girls are given in marriage at that age. If he approaches the emperor, we might have no choice but to give in. What can we do?"

"I could act like a twelve-year-old," suggested Claudia.

"Well, you look more like a seventeen-year-old, dear," said Sabrina. "Would you like to go stay with your grandparents for a while?"

"I would rather wrap my chest and cut my hair and go hunting with my brothers than stay with Grandmother and Grandfather," said Claudia. "They treat me like their own personal slave when I'm there."

"We'll keep you hidden until we think of something. If we move far away, I want you unmarried so you can go with us," said Nolan. "Now I must go back to the Coliseum and find Titus and inform him that he will have six young men accompanying them, and that he will be giving them instruction and training along the way. He will put together his best men for the job, and he will tell me what the boys need to bring."

❦

Later, inside the house, the boys were packing to be gone for a long time.

Sabrina walked into the boys' room with a pile of clean blankets.

"I get the blue one," said Argus, and Felix reached out and grabbed the green blanket. Maximus looked at Ravi and let him choose his blanket. Ravi took the dark red one, which left Maximus with the brown blanket, as usual.

Maximus pulled an old piece of birch bark out from under his bed and sat down and looked at it.

"Well, are you taking your letter along on the hunting trip?" asked Argus.

"What letter?" asked Sabrina.

"Well, a long time ago, I found this piece of a letter. This letter tells me that there is a real god out there, one who gives us life and who cares about us," said Maximus.

"He gets that little piece of birch bark out almost every night and reads it," said Felix.

"Can I see it?" asked Sabrina.

Maximus carefully handed her the letter, and she read it aloud.

> And we know that in all things God works for the good of those who love him, who have been called according to his purpose. For those God foreknew he also predestined to be conformed to the likeness of his Son, that he might be the firstborn among many brothers. And those he predestined, he also called; those he called, he also justified; those he justified, he also glorified. What, then, shall we say in response to this? If God is for us,

who can be against us? He who did not spare his own Son, but gave him up for us all—how will he not also, along with him, graciously give us all things?[1]

"That's very interesting," said Sabrina. "Let's keep it here. If you take it with you, it could get ruined. Someday maybe we will learn more about God and his Son."

Maximus took the letter and put it back under his bed. "I'm going to miss you so much, Mother," he said. "We're going to be gone a long time, aren't we?"

Sabrina put her arms around her son and hugged him close. "I'm afraid so. Your father wants you away from the Coliseum. After today's events, you boys know just how dangerous and unpredictable the emperor can be. There are things you boys need to learn to get along in life, and I hope you will work hard for your father's friend Titus."

"Mother, look at my pack. I got everything in it," said Felix.

"Are you sure that you want to take all of that?" asked Sabrina. "You have to carry it a long way."

They all looked at Ravi and started laughing. He was wearing Felix's clothes, and he was swimming in them.

"Ravi, I think we can do better than that. I have a bag of Maximus's clothes from last summer that I was going to give away. I'll go get them for you," said Sabrina.

Claudia was sitting on Felix's bed the whole time, crying as if it were the end of the world. She was very devoted to her brothers.

Suddenly, Nolan came charging in. "The good news is that Titus was able to put together a very capable group of men to go on the African lion hunt, and we were able to secure passage on a ship leaving tomorrow. But there is bad news. The man who has been eyeing Claudia has already been married two times. No one knows exactly what happened to his first wife, but it is common knowledge that his second wife, a girl of just fifteen years old, was so distraught that she took her own life. He is very rich to be sure, but he is not a nice man. We need to get Claudia out of here immediately."

"I'll send word to your grandmother," said Sabrina.

"No. I won't go. They are mean to me, and they don't have indoor plumbing. They made me empty the chamber pot. I actually threw up when I did it." Claudia began to cry.

"It's better than marrying a rich old pervert," said Argus.

Felix jumped up and grabbed Claudia's arm. "She can come with us. I'll take care of her. I won't let her out of my sight."

Claudia smiled and said, "Remember my idea to cut my hair and wrap my chest and wear boy's clothes? I could do it. I want to be with the boys."

Sabrina put her face in her hands as if she were really struggling for an answer. Finally she said, "If I had to choose between staying at my parents' house or going on a rugged, dangerous lion hunt, I would choose the lion hunt, too. My mother and father can be terrible. I couldn't wait to get married."

Nolan looked at Claudia for a long time. Finally he said, "Well, I think it will be right for you to dress like a boy but only to fool the strangers you will be around. I will tell Titus and the men the truth."

Claudia laughed and jumped up and down with her brothers like they did when they were little kids. The boys all assured their parents that they would take very good care of her. Sabrina took Claudia into another room and cut off her long, beautiful black hair, making her resemble her brothers. She had Claudia dress in layers to cover up her curviness.

"Maybe that old coot will find a wife while you're gone," said Sabrina. "If that happens, then this will all be worth it."

"But what will you tell the emperor if the rich man appeals to him, Father?" asked Claudia.

"I'll tell him that you went far away to care for your ailing aunt," said Nolan. "That should do it."

CHAPTER 2

Early the next morning, Nolan and Sabrina's four children were dressed and ready to travel, and so was their visitor, Ravi. Lavinia's two boys, Cadogan and Kendrick, arrived at their house with heavy travel packs.

"Mother said to thank you for getting us away from here," said Cadogan. "She wanted to see us off, but the twins weren't cooperating. She didn't want to make a scene by going through the streets with two screaming babies."

Kendrick knew Ravi from the night before, but he stared at Claudia with a very puzzled look on his face. "Who is this?"

"Why, this is our little brother, Charles. You know him, don't you?" asked Felix with a smile.

"No, I don't think we ever met before," said Kendrick.

The boys couldn't stop laughing. "It's Claudia," said Cadogan. "I recognized her right off, but I would like to know what's going on."

"I can explain when I tell the others," said Nolan. "Here comes our hunting party."

Coming down the road was a huge group, including a dozen Roman soldiers for protection and a wagon pulled by horses to carry tents, tools, traps, cages, nets, food, and medical supplies to be loaded onto the ship. The party included many men who looked excited to be on such an adventure.

Titus was smiling broadly and ran ahead to greet Nolan and his family. "This is my son Flavius, and today is his seventeenth birthday," said Titus. It was obvious that Titus was very proud of his son. "Son, this is my faithful friend, Nolan."

Flavius had red, shoulder-length hair, a handsome face, and an athletic build. He was very excited as Nolan introduced him to the family. "These are my sons, Argus, Felix, and Maximus, and this is our stowaway, Ravi, who hopes to go into Africa with you and then try to return to his home in Egypt."

"Ah, the elusive hunter who caused quite a stir at the Coliseum yesterday," said Titus. "And are these the clever young men who saved his life?"

Nolan smiled. "Yes, that was the work of my two sons, Argus and Felix. And these two young men are the sons of my friend who paid the ultimate price for Ravi's freedom. Cadogan and Kendrick, meet Titus and his son Flavius." They greeted each other warmly, and Titus expressed his sorrow at their loss. Then all eyes turned to Claudia. "And this, believe it or not, is my daughter, Claudia, who is much too beautiful and captivating for her own good. It seems that an exceedingly rich and ruthless merchant with ties to the emperor has set his sights on her, and we all decided that she would be safer around wild lions and tigers. Claudia wants you to call her Charles and to treat her like one of the boys. All of the men on the hunting party are to know that she is a girl and give her plenty of help and privacy, but when you are among strangers, please pretend that she is a young man. One of her brothers is to be near her at all times."

Flavius's face turned a bright shade of red as he reached out for her hand, and he said that he would try to make her journey a pleasant one.

"Well, that's about all. Come here, my children, and give me one last hug," said Nolan. He hugged each one a long time, as if it could be the last. Felix and Claudia both cried as they said goodbye to their father. "Their mother planned to come out and see them off, but she couldn't stop crying; you can see her there in the window."

The children all waved to their mother, gave their father one last look, and walked toward the rest of the party.

Titus looked at Claudia and asked, "Would you like to ride in the wagon? This is going to be quite a hike."

"If I get tired, I might like that. Thanks," said Claudia.

The group reached the others and moved close to the front of the procession, just behind six of the Roman soldiers leading the way. They walked at a brisk pace that would get them to the Great Sea by the middle of the afternoon.

Flavius moved to Claudia's side and matched her pace. "My father tells me that your family plans to secretly move far away to escape the emperor."

"Well, it won't be a secret if we talk about it around all these people," whispered Claudia.

"No one is around but your family. The others are pretty far back. I think we can talk safely," he said.

"My father told us that if the wrong people find out about our plans, we could become lion bait at the emperor's birthday party in October, so let's at least talk quietly," Claudia said.

"Well, why does your family want to leave so badly?" Flavius asked.

"Why do you think? Do you know anyone who wants to be told who to marry or what army to fight for?" she asked.

"Well, I guess my family feels the same way," said Flavius. "My father takes me along on the hunting trips, but we try not to think about what happens to the animals once we take them to the Coliseum. He won't let me go to the shows either, and many of my friends go all the time."

"How does that affect them?" Claudia asked.

"They aren't the same as when we were little. Now they are crude and loud and kind of callous. Not everyone, though; some of the guys don't go to the shows either," said Flavius.

"For years, certain things make Father very angry. For instance, he gets furious if someone beats their slaves or if a man mistreats his wife," said Claudia. "He always treats Mother and me very well."

"I don't blame him," said Flavius. "Tell me more about your father."

Claudia didn't know if Flavius was really interested in her father's ideas or if he just liked watching her talk, but she went on. "He hates idols. His mother and father have gods sitting all over their house, so we are not allowed to visit them. He thinks it is silly to think that an object that someone made could actually help us in any way. Oh, and the emperor has astrologers advising him about everything, and Father thinks it would be nonsense to have our lives revolve around the stars."

Up ahead of Flavius and Claudia, Argus noticed that there was something wrong with Kendrick. His face was white, and he was cold and shaking all over.

"What's wrong with him?" Argus asked Cadogan.

"He can't get rid of the image of the rhino goring and killing Father. He doesn't want to think about it, but he can't stop. I think he's in shock. I don't feel too well myself," Cadogan confided.

Argus put his hand on his shoulder and said, "Hold on. I'll talk to Titus about it."

Argus ran up to Titus and described the situation. "I thought it was kind of sudden for them to leave their mother and the security of their home to go traipsing through the jungle, but your father thought that their lives could actually be in danger," said Titus. "He said the emperor got a great deal of pleasure watching them suffer as their father was gored and trampled. I think sleep is the best thing for the boys. Let's put them in the wagon and cover them with blankets. If the sun comes out, they could get too hot. Someone should probably keep an eye on them."

"I'll take care of it," said Argus.

Argus explained the situation to his brothers, and both went along to get the boys in the wagon. Cadogan and Kendrick used their packs as pillows, covered up with their own blankets, and had a long drink of water. Maximus decided to ride for a while and keep them comfortable. He asked them if they would like it if he played a few songs, and they both said they would. He pulled a flute out of his pack and began to play very softly. He played song after song, and he noticed that the boys fell asleep and after a while, Kendrick stopped shaking. Maximus wished he had his letter with him. He tried to remember it and spoke very softly, "If God is for us, who can be against us? And what was that about him not sparing his own Son?"

Cadogan still had his eyes closed, but he asked, "What is that you are talking about?"

"Oh, sorry," said Maximus. "I didn't know you were awake. I didn't mean to bother you."

"No. Please. I found it very comforting. Is there more? Where does it come from?" asked Cadogan.

"A long time ago, when I was only nine or ten, I was walking along the road with my father when I saw a piece of white birch bark paper on the ground. I picked it up, and I realized that it was something special. It was part of a letter, and the rest was torn away. I've kept it all these years, and I read it every night. I didn't bring it along, because Mother said it could get ruined," said Maximus.

"Do you remember any more of it?" asked Cadogan, who sat up and looked much better.

"No," said Maximus. "I wish I would have memorized it instead of just reading it all the time. Now when I need it, I can't remember it exactly."

"Maximus, I was very angry yesterday with Argus and Felix. I still feel like it's their fault that our father was killed," said Cadogan.

"You saw how sorry they were," said Maximus. "They

cried and begged your family for forgiveness. I don't think I ever saw Argus cry about anything before."

"Why couldn't they just let the man die?" asked Cadogan. "They didn't know him."

"They saw someone in trouble and helped him out," said Maximus. "That's how they are; they act before they think. But I'm proud of them, just the same."

"Well, I guess they didn't know Father would get hurt," said Cadogan.

"I wish I had my letter along to read to you," said Maximus. "Thinking about God always gives me a lot of comfort."

The driver of the wagon spoke for the first time. "I'm sorry, but I couldn't help hearing you boys. There is a story that my grandfather used to tell. Would you like to hear it?"

"I would like to hear a story," said Maximus.

"I would, too," Cadogan said.

"Well, when my grandfather was a boy, he was a shepherd. His whole family raised sheep, and sometimes they were gone for many weeks at a time, watching their sheep. One night when they were out in the hills, an angel appeared to them, and the area around them was shining so brightly that they were terrified."

"What did the angel do?" asked Cadogan.

"Oh, first of all he told them not to be afraid. Then he told them that a child was born, nearby in Bethlehem, and that it was Christ the Lord. He gave them a sign. He said the child would be wrapped in cloths and lying in a manger."

"What is an angel?" asked Maximus.

"Why, it is a messenger from God himself," answered the driver.

"So they saw an angel and it spoke to them?" asked Maximus.

"Not just one. After the angel spoke, a whole company of angels appeared to them, praising God and saying, 'Glory to God in the highest, and on earth peace to men on whom his favor rests,'" he said.

"What did the shepherds do?" asked Cadogan.

"They got right up and went to Bethlehem, and sure enough, they found a baby in a manger," answered the driver.[2] "My grandfather never stopped praising God for what he saw that night. I have wanted to hear more about it all these years. I wonder if the baby in the manger is the same one mentioned in your letter, the son that God did not spare. What do you think, boys?"

"I think that it could be," said Maximus. "Are you going all the way to Africa with us?"

"Oh no," he answered. "I'm just going as far as the ship. Once I have helped load this stuff on board, I will head back to the city. They will have to hire another wagon when they land."

"But how can I find you when I learn more about God and his son?" asked Maximus.

"Bless you, boy. Just ask your father where to find his favorite wagon driver, and he will send you directly to me. Your father takes good care of me and my family, giving me plenty of work to do," answered the driver.

Way up ahead, Titus was directing the entire party of travelers off the road and into a large shady area. Titus came back to check on the sick boys and was happy to see Cadogan sitting up and smiling. "We are pulling off the road to have some lunch. We have another hour of traveling, and we will need every minute of it to digest our food. We don't want to get seasick, do we?"

"No, I don't want to get seasick," said Cadogan.

"And how is our patient doing?" Titus asked Maximus.

"He's sleeping, and I think that is just what he needs. He's not cold or shaking anymore, and he's breathing evenly. He's probably better," said Maximus.

"Good. Let's let him sleep. If he doesn't wake up before we finish eating, pack him a lunch and save him some water," said Titus.

Cadogan and Maximus got down from the wagon and joined the others. The driver parked the wagon in the shade to protect Kendrick, and after watering his horses, he ate his lunch nearby to keep an eye on the sick young person.

The twelve soldiers ate their lunches by the road to watch for marauders who might see the party and want to rob them. Those men worked directly for Nolan, who treated them very well. They were always careful to follow directions exactly, for they did not want to be assigned anywhere else.

Most of the men in the group ate together, laughing and teasing one another about other trips they had shared. The teenagers ate their lunch very quickly and were soon playing a game of stickball in a nearby flat area. Felix brought his favorite little ball along, and they all found their own sticks.

"I think Cadogan, Ravi, and I could give the brothers Argus, Felix, and Maximus a hard time," said Flavius.

"What about me?" yelled Claudia. "I can play stick-ball as well as my brothers."

"Oh, sorry, but then the teams won't be even," answered Flavius.

"I can play," shouted Kendrick.

"He is better," said Cadogan. "Don't you think you better eat first?"

"No. I'll grab something after the game," said Kendrick.

Maximus looked at the wagon driver, who smiled and nodded at him, so Maximus said, "Sure, Claudia will play on our team, and you can help save the others."

"Charles!" shouted Claudia. "You need to call me Charles."

"Look alive, Charles," shouted Flavius. She saw the ball coming and whacked it back to the other side.

The ball got by Flavius and he shouted, "Oh, no, outflanked by a girl. I'm losing my flair for the game."

Cadogan had been observing Claudia for many years, and he admired far more than her beauty. "Don't underestimate Charles, there. Their team has the advantage."

They played stickball for a good half hour while the adults rested. The teams were very well matched, for although Ravi was small and wiry, he was quite athletic. Kendrick looked much better and said that he could walk with the others now. The wagon driver insisted that he sit in the back of the wagon long enough to eat his lunch and drink some water.

After a good lunch and a time of socializing, the group was in good spirits. As they walked along at a brisk rate, Felix got his little harp out of his pack, and Maximus pulled out his flute, and soon everyone was learning silly Greek folk songs. They sang and laughed and enjoyed the sunshine and flowery breeze of a perfect summer day. Before they knew it, they reached the docks of the Great Sea. There were many ships around, but Titus pointed to the largest one, the Sea Traveler, and said that was the ship that would take them to Carthage, then to Oea, and then to Cyrene, and finally to Alexandria, where they would find a ship to take them back to Rome.

Titus handed the paperwork to the ship's captain and paid him the fees for the passage. Then the men loaded everything onto the ship from the wagon. The wagon driver waved goodbye and took right off, because he wanted to get back to the city before dark. Finally the passengers all boarded and were sent to their sleeping quarters to store their packs.

Titus led all of the teens to their room down below.

"We're sleeping in hammocks!" shouted Felix. "This trip is going to be wonderful." He jumped in one, and Maximus jumped in another, and they rocked so hard they bumped into each other.

"I'm putting all of you young people in here," said Titus. "I figure you'll talk or wrestle half the night, and this way we adults can get some sleep."

"Father, are you going to be next door?" asked Flavius.

"No, but don't worry. There will be two soldiers guarding your room at all times. They are taking two-hour shifts. And during the day, you are to have two soldiers with you at all times. Try to stick together."

"Are we in some kind of danger?" asked Argus.

"I don't really know," said Titus. "The crew and passengers on this ship seem safe enough, so far, but ships on the sea are notorious for dangerous crews and mysterious passengers. Please stay together, and stay with your soldiers."

Felix grabbed Claudia's arm and led her to the hammock in the very corner of the room, farthest from the door. "You make your bed here," he said as he threw his blanket into the hammock next to hers.

"I'll be right here in front of her," said Maximus. He looked expectantly at Argus, who grabbed his pack and moved to the bed next to him, forming a protective arc around Claudia.

Suddenly the room shook. "Did you feel that?" asked Flavius.

"I think we're on our way," said Titus.

"Can we explore the ship now, Father?" asked Flavius.

Titus nodded to the two soldiers at the door and addressed the group. "We have our own common room upstairs, near where we came aboard. We will be dining there very soon, so make your tour a quick one." Titus left to check out the accommodations of the other men and to find a hammock for himself.

The teens and the soldiers all stood at the railing and watched as the ship sailed away from the shore.

Claudia jumped up and down in excitement. "I can't believe I'm actually going," she said.

"We were this close to the sea, and our parents never brought us here," said Codogan. "We could have watched the ships coming and going."

"We aren't just watching," said Felix. "We are heading for Carthage right now. Our soldier said we will be stopping at all kinds of places on the way and on the way back. This is our chance to see the world."

The teens all marveled at the sound of the birds, the smell of the sea, and the rocking of the ship. Ravi had been quiet through all the excitement, so Argus asked him if he was all right.

"The first time I was put on a ship," said Ravi, "I didn't notice the beauty of the sea. I was a prisoner, and I was so unhappy that I don't even remember the ship rocking."

"And how is it now?" asked Argus.

"Now I am a free man, heading for home," said Ravi. "I am bursting with joy, and I notice all kinds of sights and sounds."

The teens were called inside to dinner. Meals on the ship were very simple, each consisting of fresh seafood, in-season fruit, and bread. The lamps were lit, and after the meal the group sat and socialized. Titus and the men spent the first night discussing the course of the ship, the stops, and the route to the intended jungle area in Africa once they docked.

The teens sat around the table trying to think of something they could do in such a small area. They decided to arm wrestle, and the first two to compete were Argus and Flavius. After a long time, Flavius had a very red face, and Argus had sweat dripping down his forehead. Finally Argus won, but he knew his arm would hurt half the night. Several more of them arm wrestled, but they were soon bored with that.

"Hey, Flavius," said Felix. "Didn't I hear something about this being your birthday? How old are you, anyway?"

"I'm seventeen now," Flavius answered.

"Seventeen, huh? Did you hear that, everyone?" Felix asked.

Argus, Claudia, and Maximus all smiled and instructed all the young people to pull their chairs into a big circle.

"What's going on?" asked Flavius.

"This is what we call 'the spanking game,'" said Felix. "You have to run inside the circle while we try to hit, slap, spank, or kick you seventeen times. I'll give your father the hourglass. When the sand runs out, we have to stop, and as you come near us, we can lean in, but we can't step forward." The adults were all watching the young people and smiling.

Flavius soon figured out that he was safest around Claudia, Ravi, Maximus, and Kendrick, so he spent more time near them. He received some solid blows from Felix and Cadogan, but he never went near Argus. He was up to ten strikes when Titus announced that time was almost up. He headed straight for Claudia, smiling as he went in close. Suddenly her fist went straight up and she nailed him in the chin. Flavius bit his tongue hard, and he stopped and bent over. When he came up, his eyes were full of tears. Everyone in the room roared with laughter, including the soldiers.

Claudia felt so bad that everyone thought she was going to cry.

"I am so sorry," she said. "I didn't think I could hit that hard." She cupped his chin in her hands to comfort him.

"I bit my tongue, but I'll be fine. Don't worry about it," said Flavius. Once again, his face turned bright red, embarrassed that a girl gave him the blow that hurt him. He did like the feel of her hands on his face, though.

"That's enough play, children," said Titus. "Now

off to the bathrooms and get yourselves ready for bed. The rest of us will be along when you're finished." He pointed to two of the soldiers, who jumped right up, grabbed their weapons, and followed the teenagers out of the room.

After getting their packs from the sleeping quarters, they all went to the bathroom area, a large room with many open salt-water showers. The boys all sat down against the walls in the hallway outside of the bathroom and let Claudia enter alone. When finished, Claudia waited in the hallway with the soldiers, while all the boys went in at once. She had to laugh at the sounds coming from the room, yells and laughter and a great amount of splashing.

In the bedroom, Claudia lined her hammock with her blanket, jumped in, and was soon sound asleep. The boys got in their hammocks as well, some using their blankets and some without. Felix began a discussion as he addressed Ravi.

"Will you tell us, Ravi, how you came to Rome and how you ended up fighting rhinos?"

"Yes, I will tell you," said Ravi. "One evening, my friends and I were walking to the bath house, and it was closed to us. It was taken over by the occupying Romans, for their own use, and we were to walk to the next town when we needed a bath. Well, we made a big scene outside of the place, and the local governor had us arrested, thrown on a ship, and sent off to Rome. We didn't have a nice place to sleep like this but were tied together in a room down below to ride for days and given only bread and water occasionally. We were taken to Rome and placed in a prison to wait until called for. We were there for many months. Yesterday some men came and got us, poured water over us to clean us up, and made us dress in the hunting costumes. We were taken to the Coliseum, as you call it, and given a bow and a quiver of arrows. We weren't told anything. My sister's husband, Marjan, was sent into the arena first. My friend and I heard a lot of yelling and cheering, and then we were sent in and found ourselves running for our lives. I climbed up in a tree and actually hit two rhinos, but the arrows only made the rhinos angrier. I was sure that I was a dead man, and then I was knocked senseless by that chain. I didn't know what it was for, but I knew I didn't want to climb down the tree or have it smashed by rhinos, so I grabbed the chain. You know the rest. By the way, did I ever thank you and Argus for saving my life?"

"No, I don't think you've had time," said Felix with a smile.

"Well, thank you both. I would not be alive if it weren't for the brave thing you two did," Ravi said. "And I am sorry about the consequences that you all suffer for my sake." He looked over at Cadogan and Kendrick. "I am sorry that your father died in my place."

"The emperor is mean and ugly, and I hate him," Cadogan answered.

Kendrick did not answer, and he looked like he was going to cry.

Argus asked Ravi, "Will you dare go back to your home?"

"I have been thinking about that all day," Ravi said. "I will go to my cousins' house. They are a whole day's walk from our city. I am not even sure the Romans occupy their small town. I will stay with them and tell them all that happened, and they will send someone to tell my family that I am still alive. I feel so sorry for my sister, because she lost her husband, Marjan, and thinks she lost me, her favorite brother. She and Marjan were only married for a few months."

"When you get to Egypt, how will you get from the stop in Alexandria to your cousins' home?" asked Felix.

"I'll think of something. Maybe I will ask the God of hope to help me get there," said Ravi.

Maximus sat right up in his hammock and asked him, "What are you talking about when you say the God of hope?"

"I don't know," said Ravi. "It was something I heard one day in Rome when I was in prison. Some people came for a visit and gave us a nice dinner and some fresh water. One of them said, 'May the God of hope fill you with all joy and peace as you trust in him, so that you may overflow with hope by the power of the Holy Spirit.'[3] There was more, but that is all I can remember."

"Please. If you remember any more, will you tell me?" Maximus asked.

"Of course I will," said Ravi.

The boys were fairly quiet for a while. Ravi was praying to the God of hope, and Maximus was saying the new verse over and over to himself so he would never forget it. Kendrick was sniffing, and Cadogan figured he was crying.

"Are you all right?" Cadogan asked.

"Did I hear that Mother and the girls are leaving the house?" Kendrick asked.

"Yes. Remember, Mother has no way to pay for our

household now. Nolan said that she and the family can move into a small house at their villa. You saw it. We'll be fine," said Cadogan.

"I miss the girls, and Mother needs me to help take care of them. Do you think she's doing all right?" asked Kendrick.

"Argus's and Felix's mother is probably helping her," answered Cadogan.

"Do you think she will remember to take my rock collection?" asked Kendrick.

"Mother will certainly take those rocks," said Cadogan.

"It's just so much to understand," said Kendrick. "Father is dead, and we are on this trip because the emperor enjoyed watching us suffer yesterday. Is that right?"

"Well, not just that," said Cadogan. "I like to think of this as an opportunity to pick up a few skills and see the world. When we get back, the emperor will have forgotten all about us."

"It's just a lot to lose all at once," said Kendrick, "and now we have to stay away from Rome."

"We'll just stay away from the Coliseum. We can go anyplace else," said Cadogan.

CHAPTER 3

The day after all four of her children left, Sabrina sat in her chair, drinking some tea and wondering what to do with her time. Nolan walked in and kissed her.

"Lavinia is having a hard time preparing to leave her home," said Nolan. "Do you want to go help her? I sent my wagon driver over with the wagon to load stuff up, but she could use a lot more help."

"Why didn't I think of that?" asked Sabrina. She jumped up and asked, "What should I take along to help?"

"Maybe some baskets to move the smaller things," Nolan answered.

Nolan walked his wife over to Lavinia's house and then went back to his work. Lavinia and Sabrina took turns. Sometimes Lavinia packed while Sabrina played with the twins, and sometimes Lavinia watched the girls and Sabrina packed. The driver had been carrying things to the wagon all day, and he was almost finished.

The driver came back to the house carrying a basket. "I don't think I should pack this in the wagon," he said. "Nolan won't let you move in with these gods."

Sabrina walked over and looked in the basket. "He is right. Nolan and I both agree about gods. We won't allow an idol of any kind in our home or any place near our villa."

"Well, I guess they never did anything good for me," said Lavinia. "Should I just leave them here? I paid a lot of money for them."

"Go ahead and leave them here. We can come back later and sell them. You will probably need some money later," said Sabrina.

They left the basket of gods inside the house, and they all climbed into the wagon. Lavinia held Heather and Sabrina held Harmony while the driver guided the wagon and horses through the streets.

Just as the wagon approached the villa, Sabrina told him to stop. She could see three men approaching their front door. They were all dressed in purple and dark blue robes, and Sabrina had the bad feeling it was the ruthless rich man who was interested in Claudia. He probably had a lawyer or two with him to intimidate them. They waited a long time, and finally the men reluctantly walked back toward the city.

"I am hoping the man will get interested in someone else before Claudia gets back," said Sabrina.

"I hope this never happens to my two sweet little girls," said Lavinia. "I don't want some rich old man to come calling on them."

"Maybe by that time we will have a society where young men and women can fall in love and get married and no one will interfere," said Sabrina.

"That was the way it used to be in Britannia before

Rome took us over," said Lavinia. "I was in love with a boy my own age. He was so cute and funny, too. He made me laugh all the time. I wonder what happened to him after I was taken away to marry Frederick."

The driver guided the wagons around to the back of the villa to the small house, and he stayed and helped move everything in.

"Please don't tell Nolan this," said Lavinia, "but I'm not as sad as I should be right now. I mean, it's hard leaving my home and letting the servants go and having to depend on you kind people, but I never was very happy with Frederick. I kept my feelings a secret from the boys because he was a good father to them. But he was mean to me, and he completely ignored the twins. He just thought that men are better than women."

"Probably nine out of ten men at the Coliseum right now feel the same way Frederick did about women, like they are inferior to men," said Sabrina. "But my Nolan is not like that. He's so good to me, and he loves and respects Claudia as much as the boys. That's why she's so well adjusted. I wonder how she's doing with all those boys on the trip."

❧

The group went to their assigned common room, and their breakfast was waiting for them—fish as usual.

Titus came in and asked, "How would you young people like to make yourselves useful?"

"I would," said Felix. "What can we do?"

"Well, you could help catch our lunch," he said.

Titus and the cook led them to the side of the ship and gave them each a pole. He showed them the bait and the way to store the fish once they caught them, and then they left them alone.

"Want me to put the bait on your hook, Claudia?" asked Maximus.

"Charles," she said. "Call me Charles. And no, I can bait my own hook."

"Shall we have a fishing contest?" asked Argus.

"How about Argus, Ravi, Cadogan, and Maximus against Claudia, Kendrick, Flavius, and me?" suggested Felix.

"That sounds great, and I think we are going to lead," said Argus as he pulled a large fish out of the water.

As they worked, Flavius got to know Felix and Claudia. He enjoyed the way they teased each other, and he felt sorry that he didn't have a sister. Felix splashed fish water on Claudia, so she reached up and shook a little fish over his head. Felix laughed at her fish and asked if he could use it as bait.

The group fished for a couple of hours, and everyone caught at least one fish. Argus's team won, because he and Maximus had such a knack for fishing and also because on the other team, Flavius wasted time flirting with Claudia while Felix and Claudia tormented each other. When Titus turned the fish in to the ship's cook, he was very happy and made them a special treat for lunch: fig cookies.

❧

The teens became expert fishermen over the next few days and were enjoying their great adventure. The cook continued to reward them with desserts. Finally the ship docked at Carthage, and because they were told not to get off the boat, the teens all went to the railing on the upper deck and watched the action. The Roman soldiers that were guarding them were getting so comfortable around the teens that they almost forgot their weapons.

As they were watching, a large number of elephants were led onto the ship. The elephants were not in cages and were pulled, whipped, and pushed aboard by a bunch of slaves. It was obvious that two men were in charge. The two leaders wore crisp, clean white robes, and they constantly yelled at the slaves to hurry up and to whip the elephants harder. One of the elephants got very angry and charged one of the men in white. First, the elephant knocked the man down, and then it rolled him across the deck of the ship, and finally it leaned its head down hard on the man, crushing him to death. The other man in white yelled for them to spear the elephant, and the teens all yelled not to kill it.

Finally one of the slaves coaxed the elephant off the man, talking softly to it. Ignoring the man in white, he led the elephant down a ramp to the rooms below that were prepared for holding the animals. Other elephants followed, and the teens counted forty-five elephants. And they kept coming.

"I'm so relieved they didn't spear the elephant. Aren't you, Flavius?" asked Claudia.

"Oh, I don't know. I think if I was a beautiful, wild elephant, I would rather die here in my own country than be taken across the world to Rome to be slaughtered in the Coliseum," Flavius answered.

"What are you talking about? Won't they just perform some kind of animal show to thrill the audience?" she asked.

"The only thrill the audience at our arena will tolerate is to see the animals killed or to see the animals run down some poor person chosen to die a humiliating death. Our assignment to hunt wild animals for the Coliseum is not an honorable one, but we must do what we are told, or we will be the ones suffering a humiliating death," said Flavius.

"I know that Father hates most of the things they do at the Coliseum," said Claudia. "I just found that out."

As they watched, more and more elephants were loaded onto the boat. They had the feeling the ship was sitting lower in the water. They could hear some trumpeting of the elephants and a lot of commotion below. Two of the slaves came charging back up the ramp, followed by an angry elephant. One of the slaves headed for the walkway where they entered the boat, squeezed by the oncoming elephants, and jumped over the railing into the water. The other slave was running across the deck of the ship with the elephant right behind him. He jumped up on the railing, and the elephant charged right into him, sending him flying off the ship and onto the pier below. The side of the ship was damaged. The elephant continued to pace around the deck with workers and sailors running for their lives. The ship's captain was notified, and he began yelling from the upper deck to get the elephants under control.

Felix had some experience at calming down wild animals from working at the Coliseum. He ran down the hall and came back with his little harp. He began to play a very soothing tune that he had used before for the same purpose. Finally the elephant went back down the ramp, and the last of the others followed it down. A few cargo items were loaded onto the ship, and then they set sail for Oea.

That afternoon at lunch, Cadogan managed to sit next to Claudia. "So how are you enjoying the ride so far?" he asked.

"Actually, it's been pretty exciting, with the elephants and all," she answered.

"You look kind of cute with that short hair," Cadogan said. "But you still look like a girl to me."

"Well, when we're around more strangers, I will try to lower my voice and walk more like a boy," she said.

"I hope your father's plan for the future works out for all of us," Cadogan said.

"I hope so, too, but I hate to leave all my friends," she said, and she looked around and smiled at Flavius.

"Oh, I see how it is," he said.

"Oh, no," said Claudia. "I will miss lots of friends, like our neighbor friends and my friends from school."

"And Flavius," said Cadogan. He looked kind of angry and turned and began talking to Kendrick, who was on the other side of him.

Claudia wasn't even surprised, because it was always that way at school. Boys liked her, and they would get jealous of one another. The other girls used to flirt and giggle and try hard to get the boys' attention, but the boys seemed to prefer Claudia, who had a natural way of talking to guys that came from being around three brothers. *I don't need any drama on this trip*, Claudia thought. *Why can't they just treat me like one of the guys?*

Felix, who was on the other side of Claudia, got up to get more fish, and Flavius slid right into his seat.

"Hi," he said, smiling shyly. "What did you think of all those elephants?"

"I thought I was going to pass out when the elephant killed that man. Did they take the man away? Do you think his family knows about it?" Claudia asked.

"They put him in a box to take back to Rome, just like the poor slave who got knocked off the ship by another elephant. He landed head first on the pier and died instantly. Both men were from Rome on a hunting expedition like ours. I just don't understand why they didn't make an enclosed path for the elephants to follow into the boat. Then the animals wouldn't have gotten out of control," said Flavius. "My father says we are always very careful to keep the animals in close quarters and completely out of reach of people. We don't take any chances."

"Do they have the elephants tied up securely?" asked Claudia. "I don't want them visiting us in the night."

"We have the soldiers standing guard, and I'm sure they will take good care of us," said Flavius.

❦

The days that followed were rocky. The winds on the sea were unusually violent, causing the waves to roll and the ship to rock. The elephants were agitated, pacing back and forth, adding to the rocking problem. The first day out, the captain ordered a huge pile of wood to be placed before the ramp that led up to the main deck, making it impossible for the elephants to escape the lower level. Although it helped the passengers relax and it kept the ship's crew safe, it created a nightmare for the slaves who were ordered to feed and care for the elephants. After several days of chaos, with a slave trampled each day, they decided not to clean up after the elephants until they were unloaded, and to only give them food and water each morning.

One evening during dinner, Argus noticed that there was a serious discussion among the adults, and then Titus stood up to address everyone in the room.

"We seem to have a change of plans, and I hope that you will all be flexible and patient. In a few hours, we will be landing in Oea. We have been notified by the ship's captain that the elephants are a very difficult and heavy cargo and he is not willing to make the five other scheduled stops before returning to Rome. He is giving us a credit to board the next ship that is coming along, first thing in the morning. We have a choice. We can unload all of our cargo and supplies and set up camp at the edge of town. Or we can move our cargo next to the pier and camp out very close, without setting up tents but just lying on our packs and sleeping under the sky. The first choice involves a great deal of carrying heavy loads and setting up and then reversing the entire procedure in the morning, all for about four hours of peaceful slumber. The second choice involves only enough work to unload tonight and load again in the morning, but we will have no privacy and no protection from the elements. It could rain tonight. But we wouldn't have the time pressure. Talk it over for a few minutes among yourselves, and then I will give you an opportunity to express your ideas."

At the teens' table, there was a big difference of opinions. Half of the boys thought they should move to the edge of town and set up a camp, and the other half thought they should stay close to the boat dock, to make sure they didn't miss the ship in the morning. Claudia kept quiet and didn't express any opinion.

Finally Titus stood up and said, "Well, I guess we all know the pros and cons of the choices, so let's just go ahead and take a vote. How many of you adults think we should spend the night on the dock and sleep under the open sky?"

Almost all of the adults raised their hands, choosing to do less work and have less shelter. Titus seemed relieved and said, "Well, it's decided then. As soon as we dock, we will start immediately, since the captain wants to get going. We will begin with the cargo and get our packs when that is finished."

The ship docked in Oea in the early evening, and they headed for their cargo. Flavius caught up with his father and said, "What about Claudia, Father? Do you think she will be all right outside all night?"

"If you are worried about her, loan her your blanket to help keep her warm," he said.

Everyone, including Claudia, carried the equipment out to the dock. Each person only had to make about five trips out to the waiting area and back again, and then they took turns going in to get their own personal packs. As soon as they were finished, the captain gave the signal, and the ship took off.

Since there was an hour of daylight left, the group decided to walk into town and check out the marketplace. Half of the soldiers and some of the adults stayed behind and guarded their stuff. The marketplace was bustling with activity. Everyone was delighted with the beautiful blankets and rugs. Flavius noticed how longingly Claudia looked at one of the blankets, so he talked his father into buying it for her, saying he would pay him back with lots of work.

Claudia loved it so much that she almost cried, and she said, "I would give you a big hug, but since I'm supposed to look like a boy, I had better not do it."

"I will be glad to wait until a later time," said Flavius, smiling at her.

Cadogan was following behind them, and he was wishing that he had some money to buy Claudia a pretty bracelet or some other jewelry. Well, he didn't have any, and now he didn't have a father to buy things for him. Feeling very sorry for himself, Cadogan kicked a rock on the road, and it hit a man on the leg. The man turned and yelled at the boys and asked who kicked the rock. Cadogan looked like he was about to cry. Titus came running up, listened to the man, and told him that it was probably an accident.

The man looked angry, but he turned and walked away.

Then Maximus saw it. He came to a stand in the marketplace that was run by a very old man. There were all kinds of hand-drawn pictures, maps, and scrolls on display, but only one item captured his attention. The scroll was bound with a wide red ribbon, and on the ribbon was written "The Word of God." Maximus stood there as if in a trance. The price on the scroll was more money than he had.

Argus noticed his expression and asked, "Maximus, is something wrong?" Maximus stood there speechless, so Argus searched the merchandise to see what could have such an effect on his brother. "Wow. That's what you have been searching for your whole life. What are you going to do?"

Maximus finally answered, "I don't have that much money. Do you?"

"No, and Father would never approve of us asking any of the adults for a loan," Argus answered. Then he looked at the owner and asked, "Sir, do you have another copy of this, perhaps one that is not as nice as this or not as complete? We do not have that much money."

The man answered, "That price is not negotiable, and I do not have an inferior copy. Go and make some money and come back another time."

Argus grabbed Maximus's arm and guided him away. Felix found an item for sale that he never saw before. It was a round, wooden object attached to a string, and Felix knew that he just had to have one. He looked through his pouch and counted out enough coins to pay for the toy. As they walked back to the dock, Felix put his finger through the loop and let it roll toward the ground. To their delight, it rolled back up. In no time at all, Felix was very good and sent it flying through the air toward Argus, Maximus, and Claudia. Annoying as it was, it made the four siblings feel at home, because that was the sort of thing that Felix did every day.

Before the group left the market area, they came to a public bathroom of sorts, and they all took turns inside. They weren't going to get to wash up tonight. The sky was clear, and the temperature was dropping rapidly. Back at the dock, everyone decided to lie side by side in a circle around the cargo. The soldiers stuck to the same schedule of guard duty that they followed on the ship. Claudia was snuggled in between two of her brothers with her two blankets wrapped around her, and she was soon asleep. Maximus tossed and turned, trying to think of a way to make some money before morning.

Kendrick went to sleep right away, but some time in the night he woke up with the feeling that something was crawling on him. It was very dark out, but he sat up and felt his arms and knew that there were little bugs on him. He started screaming, standing up, and shaking his arms and legs. The guard lit a torch and came running over. Sure enough, there were ants all over him.

"Were you eating anything since you went to bed?" the guard asked.

"I ate my fig cookie that I saved from lunch," Kendrick answered. Cadogan helped him wipe all the ants off his skin and the crumbs off his clothes. They stamped out the trail of ants on the ground, shook their blankets off, and decided to go sleep on the other side of the cargo pile. Everyone was restless the rest of the night, certain that they had ants crawling on them. All around the circle, people were slapping themselves or standing up and shaking out their blankets. Finally, just before dawn, they heard the horn of an advancing ship. They went in two groups to the bathroom area to splash water on their faces and prepare to load the cargo.

Titus was the first to board the ship and talk to the captain. "Captain, as you can see over there on the dock, we have a very large hunting party. Our first ship experienced a serious problem and had to return to Rome."

"What sort of problem?" asked the captain.

"Elephants," said Titus. "They had too many discontented elephants on board."

"I see how that could be a problem," said the captain.

"Here is the letter of credit for our passage," said Titus. "Could you get us as far as Cyrene?"

"Fitting you on the ship is no problem," answered the captain. He looked over at their travel party. "I just don't have enough food and water for that many people. There aren't even any beds available."

"Well, we slept on the dock last night. I guess we could sleep with our cargo on the ship," said Titus. "We have food and water for our hunting trip. We could dip into that for a few days."

"Then come on board," said the captain.

Titus was relieved when no one complained about the accommodations but happily settled into the cargo area.

They ate dried fish, dried fruit, and dried bread, and they drank their stale water. They were all hot and bored.

The teens decided to play a game of "answer or die." Flavius went first and asked Claudia if Argus ever had a girlfriend.

She answered, "No way."

"You didn't have to answer so fast," said Argus. Everyone laughed.

Claudia went next. "Ravi, do you have a girlfriend back home?" she asked.

"I did have a girlfriend," Ravi answered, "and I hope to find out very soon if she is waiting for me."

At this point, they stopped playing the game. Titus asked Ravi what he planned to do next, and he said that he would like to stay on board the ship and get off in Alexandria, Egypt, because that was very close to the home of his cousins, where he was planning to stay. Titus said that he would arrange that with the ship's captain.

The group laid around on their packs, resting for a while until they heard some excitement out on the ship's main deck. The teens and their guards went out to have a look, and there were acrobats performing all kinds of jumps and tumbles. The teens became the audience, and they cheered and clapped and whistled at each trick. This continued for a long time, and finally the performers went over and began visiting with their audience. The acrobats told them that they were treated very well by the Coliseum manager, but they were very happy that the emperor finally got tired of their act and sent them home. They asked if the horror stories were true about the performances that go on later in the day at the Coliseum. Felix told them about the first time they watched a performance and all about the rhinos and their rescue of Ravi.

Ravi spoke up and said that he was alive because of Argus and Felix. Then they told how the emperor had Fredrick killed in the arena in Ravi's place and how he made Cadogan and Kendrick watch. They explained that most of them were along on this trip to get away from the emperor for one reason or another.

The teens showed the acrobats their sleeping accommodations, and they couldn't believe it. The acrobats decided to share the bathroom with them, letting them know when they finished each morning and night. They also decided to take double portions of food and give the extras to their group.

The trip vastly improved after that. The dinner that the acrobats shared was a bit skimpy but much tastier than what they would have had from their own supplies. The cleanup time went fine, and everyone was in much better spirits with a clean body. They made up their beds and enjoyed warm southerly breezes.

CHAPTER 4

The group arrived in Cyrene around noon, after the acrobats had shared a light lunch with them. They thanked the acrobats for all they did for them and left Ravi in their care. The acrobats gave Ravi a hammock in their room and promised to see that he arrived in Alexandria without any problems.

Before they left, Ravi cornered Argus and Felix and said, "I must take a moment to say farewell. When you saved my life, you put your own lives in danger. I will never see you again, but I will always pray for you."

Maximus joined them in time to hear Ravi, and he got very excited.

"What is it?" asked Argus.

"That just reminded me of something. When we get home, we can find the prison where Ravi stayed, and then we can find the people who took the meals and comfort to the prisoners. They can tell me where to find the verse they told Ravi about," Maximus answered.

"I hope you find what you are seeking," Ravi said.

"Promise me that you will seek God too, Ravi," said Maximus.

"I promise," he answered.

The boys had to leave him then, as they were called to help. Everyone had to unload the ship, just like before. Each person made five or six trips with cargo, and then one trip to get their own pack off the ship. Titus hired four carts pulled by oxen to go with them on their expedition into the wilds of Africa.

As they were leaving town, Flavius asked, "Father, don't we need to get permission before we go into their jungles and remove lions?"

"We don't need permission because this entire region is part of the Roman Empire, and we have orders from the emperor himself to bring back at least twenty lions for his birthday performances," said Titus.

"What if we can't find any lions?" Flavius asked.

"Then we won't even bother going home," laughed Titus. "But don't worry, Son, we will find many lions once we get into the wild interior of the country."

After walking for several hours, the vegetation started getting denser. Titus told everyone to sit down and rest and have some water. They passed around pieces of dried meat to give them some energy. Several of the teens had red faces, so Titus made them drink more water before going again. As they sat there resting, Titus had his men begin teaching the travelers about the area around them. They pointed out animal tracks and droppings and even signs on the trees and shrubbery that indicated the recent passage of animals. They decided to spread out and have some of the men hunt for their dinner. Claudia had to stay with the main hunting party as they traveled deeper into the jungle.

After a couple of hours, they began to see lion tracks. A group stayed behind to assemble cages while the others separated and began the real hunt. Claudia learned how to put the pieces together in no time at all, and she assembled two lion cages completely on her own. Two of the men assembled two each as well.

Two of the soldiers never left Claudia's side. It was not their job to put cages together or to hunt for food or lions. They were along only to keep the group safe, and now they were alert to an approaching sound.

Into the clearing appeared a hunting party, carrying a very angry male lion in a net suspended between two poles. Without any trouble at all, they slipped the lion into a cage and pulled the net away. The hunters were very excited, saying that they saw the tracks of two other lions, and they must go and catch them before the lions left the vicinity. Everyone went with them except for Claudia and her two soldiers.

Before he left, Titus turned to Claudia and said, "Whatever you do, stay far away from that cage. That lion can throw its paw out and slash you with its sharp claws." He held up his hands to indicate the distance to stay away from the cage.

Claudia and her soldiers sat there for several hours, and it began to get dark. Suddenly a lion jumped out of the jungle and attacked one of the soldiers. The other soldier told Claudia to get in one of the animal cages as he grabbed the spear and stabbed the lion. Claudia did as she was told, and from inside the cage, she saw the lion growling and biting and fighting the two soldiers. Claudia knew that she was not completely safe, because if a lion can reach outside the cage, it can certainly reach into one. The lion, after receiving several injuries, retreated into the jungle.

Claudia started to get out, but the men warned her to stay inside the cage.

"No," said Claudia. "You both are wounded, and it is my turn to care for you."

Claudia's mother had prepared a container for her to carry along on the trip. In it were bandages and healing salves. Claudia rinsed their wounds with water, treated them with the medication, and wrapped them with the bandages. Both men had cuts on their bodies.

"I really thought you guys were in bad shape, but the wounds aren't so bad," said Claudia.

"See this," said the soldier who was first attacked. He held up a blanket.

"This blanket saved my life. I was going to change my robe because it smells so bad. So I put this blanket around me, out of respect for you, Miss Claudia. Before I could do anything, the lion attacked. It knocked me down, but I don't think it could find a place to sink its teeth with this blanket on me. And then you came to my rescue," he said, smiling at his friend.

"We are fortunate, all right, but we need to be prepared," said the other soldier. "He will probably come back for his friend here."

For protection and for light, the men started a fire. Several more hours went by, and no one approached their camp. Everyone got very nervous. They emptied out a cart and put Claudia in it. They piled two lion cages on top of the one she was in and tied them on securely. They were having a big discussion about how they were going to protect the oxen and what they should put on the opening of the cart to protect

Claudia completely. Finally one of the hunting groups joined them, and it was the group with Argus, Felix, Maximus, and two hunters. The soldiers told them all about the lion attack and showed them the cart they set up with Claudia inside. The two men began laughing and couldn't stop. They stuck their torches into the ground and began giving orders to everyone there. In no time at all, they set up six large tents, rigged a trap for the injured lion, and prepared and cooked a meal fit for the emperor. The other two groups returned in the night, one with food for breakfast and lunch, and the other with two more lions.

CHAPTER 5

One morning when Sabrina and a servant girl were home alone, someone knocked on the door. Assuming it was Lavinia, Sabrina ran and opened the door. Filling the entire doorway, the man in purple surveyed the room behind her.

"Would you be so kind and allow me to talk to the young woman named Claudia?" the man asked.

Sabrina was shaking violently. She tried to swallow, but her throat didn't seem to work. Finally she cleared her throat and some sound came out.

"Claudia isn't here right now. She went to Corsica to visit her aunt; I mean my aunt. Yes, she's very old, my aunt, that is. Claudia went to take care of her," said Sabrina.

"I don't believe you," said the man.

"On no, it's true," said Sabrina.

"Why didn't you go and take care of your aunt?" asked the man.

"I have a family to take care of here," Sabrina answered. The man stood there, looking in her eyes, trying to intimidate her. "I'm sure she will be gone a long time," she added. Her voice sounded weak and shaky, and she was hoping that tears would not appear until he left.

"I will return," the man said. "In the mean time, I will appeal to the emperor."

Sabrina couldn't think of a thing to say. She slowly shut the door, hoping he would leave. She stood there for several minutes, barely breathing. Finally, she went through the place and peeked out another window. The man was walking toward town, and he was with another man who was dressed in royal blue. Sabrina ran straight to Lavinia's little house and cried for the next hour. She expressed her fears and her anger. She was mostly angry with herself that she couldn't hold herself together under pressure.

"I'm sure he didn't believe me," said Sabrina. "I've never been able to tell a lie."

Later that day when the emperor asked Nolan about the whereabouts of his daughter, Nolan felt sick. He forgot which relative she went to visit and which country the relative lived in and what exactly was wrong with the relative. Nolan decided not to answer any questions about his daughter and instead to ask the emperor about the interested man.

"Please tell me, Your Excellence, the name of the man who is inquiring about my daughter," said Nolan.

"The man's name is Nuncio," answered the emperor.

"And would you recommend this man as a husband for my daughter?" Nolan asked.

"I certainly would not. The man is a pompous bore," answered the emperor, and he laughed heartily at the thought. "Shall I tell this Nuncio that your daughter will not return to Rome for at least half of a year?"

"I would be most grateful, Your Excellence," said Nolan. "And now let's discuss the plans for your birthday celebration."

Nolan could always distract the emperor by bringing up something that would bring him much attention and popularity.

"Let's see, Nolan. We have elephants, lions, rhinos, monkeys, gorillas, and tigers coming for my big week. What about the ostriches? Are you getting those?" asked the emperor.

"Are you sure you want ostriches? Do you really think your subjects will like to see those tortured and killed?" asked Nolan.

"Oh, we have to have ostriches. My advisors tell me that the people will love that," said the emperor. "The moon and the stars will be lined up in such a way that my birthday celebration will win the hearts of all the people in the empire, and I will have no enemies from then on."

"Very well, we will have ostriches. I'll get right on that," answered Nolan.

"And I will see to it that the pompous Nuncio finds a beautiful wife who is not your daughter," answered the emperor.

"You are very kind to me, Your Excellence," said Nolan.

Before putting a team together to hunt for ostriches, Nolan ran home to tell Sabrina the good news that the emperor didn't even like the rich man who was after Claudia, and that he was going to distract him with another woman.

Sabrina was very relieved. She decided not to burden Nolan just now about her terrifying experience with the man in purple, since he was no longer a threat. "Oh, Nolan, let's get Lavinia and the twins and go have a nice dinner to celebrate. I'm sure she's been very sad about losing her home, not to mention her boys being away. Perhaps this will cheer her up some," she said.

That evening, Nolan took the ladies to a famous and expensive eatery to celebrate their good fortune. Just as they were sitting down, they were approached by not only the wealthy man who was after Claudia but by two of his companions as well. Nolan looked at Sabrina, who was white as a ghost, and he was afraid she might pass out. He was mad at himself for forgetting to get his story straight with Sabrina about where Claudia was supposed to have gone.

"My name is Nuncio," said the man, "and I have hopes of acquiring your daughter as my wife. I can assure you that I can give her everything she could ever dream of."

"Oh, I am sorry, but our daughter has gone far away to care for an ailing relative. We don't expect her to be home for a long time," said Nolan.

Nuncio moved in very close to Nolan and said, "I don't believe you. I think you have her hidden someplace on that villa of yours."

Nolan stood up, looked him straight in the eye, and said, "My daughter is not in Rome, but when she returns, I don't think I want her to marry a man who would try to intimidate her loved ones to obtain her hand in marriage. Why don't you look for a wife elsewhere?"

"I have friends in high places," said Nuncio, looking at his two friends.

"I think you will find that the law is on our side," said Nolan.

"We can have your property searched," said Nuncio, looking at his friends. His friends gave him a look like he was going too far. "Well, I am certain that I can appeal to the emperor."

"You do that," said Nolan. "Now, if you don't mind, my family and friends would like to enjoy our dinner."

The twins were starting to cry, and Nolan turned his back on the three men and reached for one of the babies. "Is this little Harmony?" he asked.

The three men left, but Nuncio gave them a look as he was leaving that sent chills through Sabrina. After they left, she began to cry.

"That man is horrible," said Lavinia. "I hope he gets hit by a chariot on his way home."

"I doubt that we would be so lucky," Sabrina said. "Nolan, I should have told you that he came to see me this afternoon. I just thought that the emperor would take care of it."

"Well, I guess he didn't get a chance to do that. But we can't count on the emperor to do anything nice for us. Now, let's just all relax. If Claudia was in town, I would be worried too, but they won't be back for a long time. We did the right thing sending her away, don't you think?"

"It looks like we did. I wonder what our children are doing right now," said Sabrina.

The hunting parties went out, and they all returned by dinnertime. They had plenty of wild game to eat for dinner; plus they had an interesting animal in a cage. It was a beautiful red, green, and blue parrot to give to the emperor for his birthday. Titus had instructed them to be on the look out for an animal of some kind to give as a pet, and they thought the parrot was perfect.

Cadogan had a lovely flower that he picked to give Claudia, and he pulled it out of the top of his pack. It was wrapped in a little moss that he had surrounded with leaves, and it was as pretty as it was when he picked it. He walked up to Claudia shyly and gave it to her.

Claudia could see that Cadogan was kind of embarrassed, so she took it from him and said, "Thank you, Cadogan. It's beautiful. Do you know what it's called?" He shook his head, indicating that he didn't know, and she put it behind her ear. It was pale yellow and star-like, and it looked great with her dark hair and eyes.

Claudia helped the men prepare the meal for everyone as the different groups arrived. One hunting group brought back three lions. Argus had gone with them, and he was thrilled about their progress. He looked at Titus and asked, "We have six lions now. Does that mean we can begin the trip home?"

"Oh, no," answered Titus. "Our instructions are to catch twenty lions and transport them back to Rome. Tomorrow we will pack up all of our gear and move deeper into the jungle."

"Well," said Argus, "I don't mind. I'm really learning a lot."

"Do you think you will be catching lions a lot in your life?" Titus asked him.

"No." Argus laughed. "But I am enjoying it anyway. Thank you so much for taking me along today."

They all sat down and enjoyed another feast of meat and fresh-picked fruit. They shared stories of the day's adventures and fed the animals and gave them water. Everyone was smiling and happy except for Claudia, and the soldier who was keeping an eye on her noticed.

"Everyone, look at Claudia. What's wrong with her face?" he asked. Suddenly she opened her eyes and vomited. Her face was very puffy and red.

One of the hunters grabbed the flower off her face and threw it on the ground. "Where did that flower come from?" he asked.

"Uh, I found it in the jungle," said Cadogan. "I thought she would like it."

"Don't go picking any more of the wild flowers. That particular plant is called Star-of-Bethlehem, and it is poisonous. How long was she wearing it?" the hunter asked.

"I'm afraid she has been wearing it since we got back. It could have been two hours," Cadogan answered.

"Well, I wish I would have seen it sooner. Let's wash her skin off and make her drink lots of water," he said. "I think she should get better soon, but everyone is different."

Felix washed Claudia's face and made her drink as much water as she could handle. She vomited again. He took a cloth and wiped her face with it, trying to cool her down. All the men sat around the camp, watching

Felix care for his sister, and they were quiet for a long time. It started getting dark.

Finally Claudia sat up and said, "I think I'm going to live, but for a while I wasn't so sure. What happened?"

"That flower you were wearing on your face behind your ear was poisonous," said Flavius. He looked over at Cadogan, who was looking down at the ground.

Felix asked, "Where did it get the name Star-of-Bethlehem?"

One of the hunters, whose name was Francis, answered, "Why, it was named after the real star of Bethlehem, of course."

"What are you talking about?" asked Felix.

"Well, years ago, my great-grandparents were serving in the palace of King Herod," said Francis. "One day some men came from the East to visit the king. They were called Magi. They asked where the King of the Jews was to be born, because they saw his star and came to worship him. Well, King Herod was very upset, and a lot of other people in Jerusalem were upset, too. He called in many priests and teachers and asked them where the Christ was to be born, and they said that he was to be born in Bethlehem. Well, Herod called those Magi back in and told them to go to Bethlehem, and after they found him, they were to come back and tell him where the child was so that he could also go and worship him."

"King Herod wanted to worship the child?" asked Maximus.

"Oh, no," said Francis. "Herod was a very jealous man. He wanted to kill the child. Anyway, the Magi never went back, and Herod was furious. My great-grandmother said he was storming throughout the palace in a fit of rage. And he ordered his men to kill every single little boy two years old and under in Bethlehem and the whole area around it."

"Did they do it?" asked Felix.

"Yes, they did. I heard that those people mourned for years over all those little boys," said Francis.

"But did they kill the child who was the King of the Jews?" asked Maximus.

"I am sure they did not, at least not when he was a baby, because my great-grandparents heard stories about a special prophet who could heal people. They always believed that he was that baby who Herod tried to kill."[4]

"Did they ever go and hear the prophet?" asked Maximus.

"No," answered Francis. "They died, and my grandparents were carried off to Rome. But our family has always wanted to hear more about him, and we believe that he was more than just a prophet."

"Our wagon driver told us a story about a baby born in Bethlehem, and about a whole choir of angels who told a bunch of shepherds that the baby was Christ the Lord."

"Let me get this straight," said Francis. "The priests and the teachers told Herod that the King of the Jews was going to be born in Bethlehem, and sure enough, a baby was born in Bethlehem, and a choir of angels told a bunch of shepherds that he was Christ the Lord. I want to go home and tell my parents all of this." He looked at Titus and asked, "When are we going home?"

"Not for a while," Titus answered.

CHAPTER 6

The next morning, as the group packed everything to move deeper into the jungle, Titus reminded them to be aware of everything around them, such as plants, animals, and insects. As usual, the more experienced hunters and trackers went ahead of the group. Even though a path was cleared for the teens, sharp brambles hit them in their faces and on their arms. Their clothes were drenched with sweat.

Claudia not only had her three brothers looking after her but Flavius and Cadogan as well. With the red welts on the side of her face, she wished they would all just ignore her. In the past, she always wanted to be with her brothers, but right now, she was wishing she had one of her girlfriends along to sit and chat and giggle with. Of course, she wasn't going to complain, because this was far better than having to wait on Grandmother and Grandfather and empty their chamber pot.

After about three hours of misery, the hunters began to see fresh lion tracks. Titus divided them into four groups. Someone finally told him about the injured lion that attacked the soldiers, and he decided that in the wild, they needed to treat the soldiers the same as the teens and teach them about tracking, hunting, protection, and even the technique of setting up and taking down camp. He told one team to go east, one team to go west, and one to go south. The final team was to set up camp, assemble lion cages, and find and prepare meals. All of the teens and most of the soldiers stayed behind, plus enough of the men to make sure they were all safe and working.

One of the groups moved quietly through the jungle. The less experienced ones knew that they were to travel silently, but they finally had to ask what was wrong. Francis just whispered that they would know soon enough. At a certain point, they stopped and set a trap, using some small animals as bait. They moved away from the area and waited silently. Finally they heard the commotion and came running to find a lion bigger than they ever imagined.

"That lion must weigh five hundred pounds," said Francis. "And look at that mane. It is huge. Do you see why we were excited? Its feet are twice the size of a normal lion. I wonder if this is one of a kind or if there are others."

One of the other hunters brought up a question. "Do you think this lion will fit in the cage?"

"Not even close," said Francis. "I think we should take this one back to camp immediately, if we can carry it. We are going to have to cut down trees and construct a bigger cage."

To make poles long enough just to carry the huge lion, they had to cut down a tree and cut it in two. The strongest men in the group eased the lion down. As they began the trek through the jungle, the lion roared and tried desperately to stand up. It fought hard the entire trip, and its roar was extremely loud, but finally they reached the camp.

Comparing the lion to the cage was a joke. They needed a cage that was twice as large as the ones prepared. The four men had to support the weight of the lion the entire time as they cut down trees and constructed a new cage. Due to the size and strength of the lion, they were careful to secure it with double ropes and latches. Finally they lowered it into the new cage, secured the top, and slid out the net.

The lion stood and growled and roared at its captors, hurting their ears. They decided to go ahead and load it onto a cart, because they didn't want to carry it all the way to the coast, but when they tried, they discovered that the poles they brought along weren't long enough to transport the new cage.

The group had a short food and water break and headed back to the area where they caught the big lion. This time they took along three more strong men from the set-up camp team.

The team members who were left behind were to do their best to cut down trees and construct more large cages. They had all they needed to do the job, so they immediately set to work. It took a long time to finish the first cage, and just as they did, the team from the south came back with a lion as large as the first and just as angry. The men were very relieved to find a large cage waiting for them. They lowered the lion into the cage, and before they could secure the top, it stood up and was about to jump out. One of the trackers was prepared and poked the lion with a spear. They struggled with the lion, pushing the top of the cage down on it as it fought to get out. The tracker stabbed the lion again, this time trying to knock it off its feet. The lion dropped to its four feet, and the men secured the top. The lion was bleeding slightly from a wound on its side and one on its leg.

Everyone laughed in relief. "Can you believe the size of that animal? It took four of us just to carry it, and we could barely manage it," said one of the men. He looked and saw the other enormous lion in its cage and said, "So there are two of them. We thought this guy was one of a kind."

Their group members went over and looked at the other lion.

"I say we grab a quick meal," said one man in their hunting party. "Let's get back out there and see if there are more giants like these two."

Soon they were gone, taking another strong man with them to help carry the load.

The group left behind grasped the enormity of the job before them and decided to organize their efforts. Some cut down trees while others took the trees, cut them to the new dimensions, and stripped and prepared them. Then still others took the wood, sorted it into piles, and constructed the sides of the cages. They worked that way for hours, barely taking breaks. Finally the group realized that they had better stop and put the sides of the cages together. They were proud because they had enough piles for seven cages.

"I wish that I could stop doing this and find a way to treat the injured lion," said Claudia.

"A better use of our time is to get these put together,"

said one of the men. "And besides that, lions treat their own wounds. Look at him over there licking his injuries."

They worked in pairs and assembled the seven cages, making them very strong. Just as they finished, the teams began arriving, and with them were three very large lions, two more males and one female. They were roaring loudly, and the other eight (six regular lions caught earlier and two giant lions) joined the noise, making an unbearable sound.

Claudia's fingers were bleeding from working with so much rope. She felt very small as she sat near the fire, observing the hunters yelling and prancing around, comparing their experiences.

"Look at his mouth," shouted one of them. "Francis, your great big head could fit right in there."

"And his massive foot could squash you into the ground like a nut," said Francis.

"Look at the size of his mane," said another hunter. "And that roar. Did you ever hear anything so loud?"

The men continued to laugh and talk very loudly. Claudia didn't know if it was to speak over the sound of the lions' roars, or if their ears were damaged from such close contact with them. They wrestled with one another and made roaring sounds and ran over to the cages to marvel at their conquest. The teenage boys and the soldiers were part of the chaos, with their voices loud and low and their movements wild and ferocious.

Soon everyone was hot and exhausted. Two men arrived with some small animals and some exciting news.

"We found water!" they exclaimed. "It's a very short walk from here."

The men put the animals in some of the extra cages and then led everyone to the water. The lake was very large and surrounded by weeping trees. The men stripped down to their underwear and jumped in the water. Some of the men who could swim took off for the other side, while others were content just to float nearby.

Claudia couldn't take off her clothes, so she waded in and splashed her face with water. She turned her back on the big hairy men. *When I wished they would treat me like one of the guys, this wasn't what I had in mind. Why didn't I stay at the camp with the lions?* she thought.

It started to get dark, so they all grabbed their clothes and headed back toward camp.

When they arrived, it was obvious that something had been there. A strong, disgusting odor permeated the area. One of the tents was knocked down, and many of their belongings were scattered. The men examined the evidence and decided that they had been visited by wild hyenas. The animals had been in their food supply and made quite a mess.

"We should have left someone here to guard the place," said Titus.

"I'm really glad we didn't," said Francis. "Hyenas like to eat people as well as any other food. They probably have a den near here, and from the odor, I would say that they consider this part of their territory."

"Are we in danger tonight?" asked Titus.

"Since we're all set up, let's stay here," suggested Francis. "It wouldn't hurt to post a couple of guards though. In the morning, let's move somewhere else."

"We can go back to the lake and fill our containers

with fresh water before we leave," suggested one of the men.

"That's not a good idea," said Francis. "Did you even taste that water?"

Most of them just looked at Francis, but one man said, "I could smell it, and that's enough for me."

"Stick out your arm," said one of the men holding a torch. Titus held out his arm, and it was covered with grains of white.

"What is that?" Titus asked.

"Salt," answered the man. "I would say that it is saltier than the Great Sea. It's probably stagnant."

"Well, let's get some sleep," said Titus. "We will move deeper into the jungle tomorrow, and maybe we will find fresh water as well as giant lions."

The group did move deeper into the jungle, and for the next two weeks, they continued to hunt lions, make cages, and enjoy visiting with one another.

CHAPTER 7

The large group finally had all but one of their twenty lions, so Francis had chosen two hunters to stay behind to get the last one.

"Shouldn't we be getting close to the coast by now?" asked Argus.

"Well, I don't smell the salt water yet, and it always takes a lot longer when traveling with a heavy load like we have," said one of the men.

"And remember that on the way, we walked for a few hours before we came to the jungle," said Titus. "Let's stop and set up camp. I think we are close enough to civilization that we won't die of dehydration."

They made a big circle of the nineteen lion cages as their perimeter and set up their tents inside of that. They built a nice campfire in the center and were sitting in small groups around it, talking. Flavius was off to the side, whispering to Claudia, and Cadogan was watching them from behind his tent. One of the lions roared loudly and slashed at him from its cage. It startled Cadogan and brought several men running to see what was going on.

"What are you doing back here?" asked Titus.

"Oh, nothing, really. I was just looking at the lions," Cadogan said.

Argus and Felix looked at each other. They knew he was probably spying on Flavius and Claudia. They turned and walked away, and Cadogan felt very lonely.

Maximus joined his brothers and asked them what was going on. Very quietly, Felix said, "Cadogan was over there spying on Flavius and Claudia, and I think he got too close to one of the cages. You heard the lion. I guess it slashed at him and just missed."

"This isn't the first time two guys have fought over Claudia," said Maximus.

"That's true," said Felix, "but it's the first time she ever looked like that." They all looked over at the couple, and Claudia was smiling and flirting with Flavius.

"Which one would you rather have as a brother-in-law?" asked Argus. "I think Flavius is the better man."

"I agree with you," said Felix. "Flavius is a hard worker and strong. He's fun to be around, and he says that he will never go and watch the shows at the Coliseum."

"I like Flavius a lot, too," said Maximus. "But remember that Cadogan is not himself right now. He's haunted by the sight of seeing his father killed. He said a rhino gored him right into the wall. His father screamed and suffered and lost a lot of blood, and the boys saw the whole thing. Cadogan has been having nightmares, waking up several times each night to the sound of his father screaming. And did you know that he has been in love with Claudia his whole life?"

"He's not that old." said Argus. "Besides, we can't make Claudia like him more."

"I think it is just going to take some time before Cadogan is himself," said Maximus. "I tried to share the words from my letter with him, but he didn't want to hear them."

"Those words comforted me once," said Felix.

"Really? When?" asked Maximus.

"Just before we helped Ravi, I tried out for the Race to the Sea. I know that I am the fastest runner in our class, but for some reason on the day of the tryouts, I got a cramp in my leg, and I just couldn't get rid of it. Two of my classmates beat me, so I didn't get to compete in the race. I was so disappointed that I cried all afternoon, but then I remembered your letter. I went into your room and searched all over until I found it. When I read the part about in all things God works for the good of those who love him, I was very comforted. And it was true, too, because I am here this week while the race is going on, and it would have looked like I got scared and didn't show up."

"That's really neat," said Maximus. "Are you searching for the real God just like I am?"

"Well, I guess I am. Last night when it rained, I knew God sent it, just like God had that boar lead us to a pear tree in the jungle when we were so dehydrated. God is definitely taking good care of us," said Felix.

Just then Francis came staggering into the camp alone and asked them where Titus was. They took him to Titus, and even though he was out of breath, he tried to explain everything. "We caught a really big lion, a male, two nights ago, and we were barely able to get it in the cage. When we tried to carry it, it was too heavy for us. We should have kept at least four men to bring back that monster."

"So where are the others?" asked Titus.

"They are a very long walk from here. I am afraid if we don't go back tomorrow, I won't be able to find them," said Francis. "They might not make it."

"What do you mean? Your men know how to survive. They can hunt and find fruit, can't they?" asked Titus.

"One man strained his back and can barely walk let alone carry that big lion," said Francis, "and the other one got his head slashed. You need to send four strong men with me to help carry that lion, because I'm not sure I'm up to it. Hopefully my two guys will be able to walk back here."

"I don't have four men to spare," said Titus. "In fact, I don't have one man to spare. We are going to get up in the morning and walk three or four hours, and hopefully we will arrive at the coast. After that we can send you back for your team, along with four extra strong men and plenty of food and water."

"That is six to eight hours out of my way, and I barely made it this far. Can't you just wait here until we rescue my team, and then we will all go to the coast together?" asked Francis.

"I'm sorry, but I have to think of the safety of everyone. If you want to sit down and wait here until I send help, you are welcome to do that. But I feel that you are better off going to the coast with us," said Titus.

Francis was distraught and sat down on the ground with his face in his hands.

"How long has it been since you had anything to eat or drink?" Argus asked.

"I can't remember. When my guys went down, I left. Last night I slept curled up on a tree branch. Hours ago I came across your campfire and searched for leftovers, but there weren't any. I'm really weak," Francis said. He closed his eyes, and his body moved back and forth as he struggled to maintain consciousness.

"You boys go throughout the camp and see if anyone saved pears or meat from our meal. Hurry!" urged Titus.

The three boys divided up and soon returned with three pears and a hunk of burned meat. Francis ate the pears, but the meat was not edible. They got him into his tent.

❧

Several times the group begged Titus to stop and rest, and each time he said that he thought he could smell the sea, so they must be getting close. They walked and walked until one of the men carrying a huge lion tripped and fell. The lion cage came down on the back of his legs, and although the lion wasn't in a position to claw at him, it roared loudly, and tried to bite through the bars of the cage. Everyone set their cages down and came to help as all the lions joined in the roaring. They moved the cage off the man and rolled him over. He was unconscious, and they noticed that his face was badly scratched and bloody, and his shoulders were bleeding through his robe. They brought him water and raised him up to help him drink. He woke up and sipped the water and said that he hoped that his legs weren't broken. It was obvious that he was in a great deal of pain.

Claudia and Maximus moved to the man's side and cared for him. It was decided that now it was even more imperative that they reach the Great Sea and the villages near the sea. They put the man in one of the animal nets, and Codogan and Kendrick carried him while Francis took the man's place carrying the big lion. The group walked at a very slow pace, unable to go any faster. Soon they saw signs of civilization, like domestic animals and primitive shelters, but Titus told them that they must keep walking. The breeze off the sea was refreshing, but they knew that if they didn't stop soon, more people would fall.

When they reached a marketplace and they could see seagulls in the distance, Titus knew they were close enough to stop and set up a camp. They found a shady area to set the lion cages and put up the tents. A small team stayed at the camp, too tired to move, while the rest of them went to the eatery and then the bath house. Claudia had to clean up on the beach in her clothes with a large group of their own men standing nearby. She was thankful for her short hair and boy's clothes in a village like that.

After they were clean and well fed, Argus, Felix, Maximus, and Claudia, along with their soldiers, got money from Titus and went to the marketplace. They got water and food, and took them back to the camp to care for the ones who were too worn out to move. Claudia cleaned the face and shoulders of the man who fell, while the others gave him water and food. They looked at the man's legs and could not tell if they were broken or just badly bruised. Claudia had purchased a plant known to be a painkiller at the market, so she gave it to the man. They made a bed for him in a tent and left him sleeping soundly.

Most of the other men came back to the camp and made numerous trips to the beach and back with water to splash the lion cages until they were clean. Then they gave water and meat to the lions, and they cared for the parrot and the oxen.

Titus was planning to go with Francis to rescue his hunting team, and Flavius volunteered to go with his father. Maximus volunteered to go along and take two oxcarts, one to carry the lion, and one to carry the injured hunters. Since none of the men had volunteered to go along, Titus considered the idea and decided it could work. Titus asked Francis if they needed to wait until morning to leave on the rescue mission into the jungle.

"Well, I could use some help with the preparations," he said, "but we really should take off very soon."

Argus and Felix packed a tent, food, water, medicine, extra clothes, and weapons in one of the oxcarts and got the oxen ready to go on the journey. Felix wasn't very happy about his little brother going back into the jungle, so he tried to talk him into staying behind, saying that he would go in his place. Maximus reminded Felix that he was the same height as he was and that he wanted to go help the men. Felix even tried to talk Francis and Titus into taking him instead of Maximus, but they said that it was already decided that Maximus and Flavius would make the trip.

"The thing is," said Francis to Titus, "that I think you shouldn't make the trip and leave the large group. You are the one with the authority, and you need to stay here and protect the cargo and the crew. Felix has volunteered to go with us, and I think he could take your place."

"No," said Maximus. "Felix needs to help Argus keep an eye on Claudia. Our parents gave us that job. Surely there is someone with more experience who could go into the jungle with us."

"I'll go." Everyone looked up to see Vernon, a young soldier, standing there. "I know that I'm young, but I learned a lot from you, Francis, on our hunting trip, and I would really like to go on the rescue mission."

Titus was looking at Flavius, and he felt torn. He hated to see his only son go into the jungle without him, but he knew that Francis was right. His place was with the main part of the group, to protect them and use the authority given him by the emperor. "I'm fine with that if you are," Titus said, looking at Francis.

"It's settled then," said Francis. "Let's go."

Maximus grabbed the rope and led his ox and cart out into the clearing, and Flavius hugged his dad, picked up his pack, took the rope of the other ox, and followed Maximus. Francis nodded to Titus and took off with Vernon close behind him.

Claudia saw them leave, and tears ran down her cheeks. Argus and Felix were walking toward her, and when they saw that she was crying, they went and sat next to her. Argus knew that Felix was just as sad as Claudia, so he suggested that they get a couple of soldiers and go explore the sea coast and the village.

"I don't think Flavius would have volunteered to go back into the jungle had he known that his father wasn't going," said Claudia.

"Well, he didn't try to back out when Titus decided to stay," said Argus.

"No, but he probably wanted to," said Felix.

They looked around and noticed a gathering of angry-looking men. They were all wearing dark, raggedy clothing and had long, unkempt beards and mustaches. The hair on their heads was long and wild, and their eyes had a wild look as well. One of the soldiers said that they should casually turn around and go back.

Back at the camp, they told Titus about the group of men hanging out near the marketplace. They decided that maybe the bad men hung out there every evening since they weren't there during the day. They spread word throughout the camp that no one was to go out until morning, and that four groups of three soldiers were to be on guard throughout the night.

Claudia and Felix were curious about how the injured man was doing and found that some of the men were staying at his side and giving him more of the painkiller. His legs were very bruised and swollen, but he was able to support his weight, so they figured the bones weren't broken.

Claudia stood at the side of their tent, unable to enter, as Cadogan and Kendrick were having a discussion. She knew it was wrong to eavesdrop, but she listened anyway.

"This is my opportunity to get close to Claudia, but I just don't know what to do. If I had any money, I could buy her something, but I don't," said Cadogan.

"What was that advice Francis gave you when we were in the jungle?" asked Kendrick.

"He said that I should listen to her and be sensitive to her needs, but I don't know how to get her talking about herself," said Cadogan.

"I hope I don't have the nightmares tonight," said Kendrick. "I heard the men talking about bad men in town. Now, besides the emperor, I have them to worry about too."

Claudia joined Argus and Felix, and she was really angry.

"What's wrong with you?" asked Argus.

"I overheard Cadogan talking to his brother. Can you believe it? He's planning to get close to me while Flavius is gone," she said.

"He won't get too close with us around," said Felix.

CHAPTER 8

The parrot was startled and let out a huge squawk. The noise upset the lions, which all began to roar very loudly. The three soldiers on duty came running with their torches and could tell immediately that intruders had been there and had gone back through the forest. Titus joined the soldiers and instructed them to check on the forested side of the camp frequently.

One of the soldiers on duty brought up a point. Speaking very softly, he asked Titus, "Did you notice any Roman soldiers in the area yesterday when we arrived?"

"Now that you mention it, I don't believe there were any soldiers," Titus said.

"I have heard that every spot on or near the Great Sea has a large unit of soldiers stationed there, as well as every large city one hundred miles inland. So where are they?" the soldier asked.

"Did you hear about the congregation of evil-looking men situated near the beach yesterday?" Titus asked.

"One of the others told me about them," the soldier answered. "Do you think they have taken possession of this community? They could have killed off all of the soldiers?"

"It certainly is possible," said Titus. "In the morning, we need to gather everyone around us and come up with an emergency plan. Wake everyone up at the first signs of daylight."

Two hours later, they told everyone to quietly come out of their tents for some instructions. When they all gathered around, Titus began to speak.

"Did any of you see any signs of Roman occupation in the village yesterday?"

No one answered, so Titus continued. "I think the bad men have taken over all of Cyrene. I'm just afraid they will hurt us in order to keep their secret."

"What can we do?" asked one of the men.

"Well, I think that we are a larger group of men," said Titus. "We need to stay together and have weapons on us at all times. You soldiers are to be on duty from now until we board the ship. The rest of you have hunting knives and spears, and you need to keep them on you or next to you from now on. Now this is the part that may upset many of you, especially those who have family we are leaving behind. We are going to board the next boat that comes along today. According to this general schedule, a ship will stop here tonight around sunset. We will all be there on the dock, waiting for the ship, surrounded by soldiers. The ship will go from here to Joppa, on the east end of the sea."

"We can't leave without the others, can we?" asked Argus. Felix put his arm around Claudia, but they did not say anything else.

"My own son is on that rescue mission in the jungle," said Titus, "but if we don't leave today, our lives and theirs may be in danger. I need two volunteers to go back toward the rescue party, wait on our men, and warn them of the danger. You will wait at the clearing, and time your return to the coast for early in the day. Almost every day a ship stops here, headed east. I will give you a schedule, and you will board the first ship, go where it's going, and work your way to Joppa where we will be waiting. I don't think you will be bothered if you leave early in the day, but don't try to board at night. If too much time goes by, we will be forced to return to Rome without you."

Everyone was silent for a long time. Finally one of the biggest, strongest men, named Octavius, said that he would be willing to go back to warn Francis and the others. Benedict, a soldier, also volunteered to go along, and Titus was very relieved.

He called the two men over to give them instructions.

"I trust you with the lives of our loved ones," Titus said. "Do you remember the place where the jungle ended and the low vegetation began? It was the place where we stopped cutting a path."

"I remember," said Octavius.

"You and Benedict go and wait there for the men left behind. It may be as soon as four days, or as many as six or more, before they reach you." He handed a bunch of papers to Octavius. "Here is a ship schedule, here is your letter of passage, and here is a second letter of passage that will hopefully get you to Joppa. We will wait for a while in Joppa, but if you don't arrive in three weeks from the time we arrive, we will return to Rome without you. If that happens, you will have to travel to

Rome on your own, and I am sure you can do it if you have to."

They gave the men a pack with enough food and water for two weeks and a tent and weapons. The two men left the dock, and although no strangers seemed to notice them, the eyes of all their own people watched as they crossed the village and disappeared from view.

The big group sat on the dock in the hot sun for many hours. They didn't sing or tell stories or have any fun because they were worried about their own safety and very upset about leaving without Francis and the young people. In the early evening, just as they expected, the evil men began to arrive. They stood along the beach, around the marketplace, and very close to the dock, as if they were making a statement that they owned the town. As time passed, more fierce-looking men arrived. Finally they could see a ship in the distance. It was difficult to tell if the men were going to let them board the ship and leave without any trouble.

When the bad men noticed the ship coming, they began to shout angrily to each other in another language. Some began to move in closer, and the soldiers lowered their spears and told them to move back. Finally, the ship arrived and Titus boarded it. While he was gone, the shouting got louder, and many of the local men left their stations near the marketplace and came over to the dock. Titus came off the ship just in time and told them to start loading. As the men loaded the lions onto the ship, the soldiers stood guard.

Two of the evil men got very aggressive and challenged the soldiers with their own huge knives. There was a scuffle, and one of the soldiers had to kill a man to protect himself. The other man backed away, screaming, and tried to convince some of his friends to help him stop the people from boarding.

When everyone was on board, the soldiers backed on with their spears still pointed out. The walkway was raised and the ship pulled away. From the deck of the ship, they could hear all kinds of loud, vicious shouting from the dock area.

"Now tell me again what is going on there that made you insist that we pull away so quickly. I was planning to take on some supplies there," demanded the ship's captain.

"It appears that a group of evil men have taken over the village and the dock area. We felt that our lives were in danger," said Titus. "It is possible that they have killed all of the soldiers who were stationed there."

"I guess I owe you thanks then," said the captain. "However, we don't have enough provisions to make it all the way to Joppa, so we will have to stop in Alexandria to pick up food and water. We can also send word to Rome about the takeover in Cyrene. I'm sure the emperor will send a huge regiment there."

Titus left the captain and joined his people in the cargo area. The lions were very agitated, probably due to the rocking motion of the ship. They were roaring very loudly and jumping against the sides of their cages, and the men were afraid they might break the ropes or the sides of the cages. Felix was more afraid that they were going to injure themselves, so he had the men move their cages close together for the lions' comfort and for security, and then he got out his little harp and played for a long time. Finally, the lions rolled over and fell asleep like little kittens.

Titus had been watching Felix and approached him with a job.

"Felix. I notice that you have a special touch with the animals. Will you take the job of watching the lions and the parrot until we deliver them safely to the Coliseum? Of course, I don't want you to get close to them; I just want you to keep them calm and call one of the older men to help if there is a problem. The men will take care of giving them food and water. I will make sure that you get excellent pay for the job."

"I think I could handle that," said Felix. "Now that they have adjusted to the rocking, I think they will sleep away the time on the sea."

Felix decided to sleep in the cargo area to keep an eye on the animals, so Argus and Claudia moved their packs in there, too. Two of the soldiers joined them, and all of the rest moved to quarters on the upper deck. Cadogan wanted to be near Claudia, but he was keeping his distance from the animals.

≪≫

Back in the jungle, Francis and the other rescuers got up and packed their tent. They joked about how their friends and family were probably all lazily walking on the beach, collecting shells and watching the seagulls and the ships on the Great Sea. (This was at the same time the others were actually taking down their camp to flee for their lives on the first ship that came along.)

Travel through the jungle was getting much more difficult now. Either the old path they had cut had grown back up, or they were not on the path anymore. Francis was fairly certain they were on the right trail, but they were traveling much slower now, looking for footprints and cut branches. After about an hour of this, they had no choice but to turn around and return to the place where they lost the trail. Francis was getting very frustrated, doubting his tracking abilities. Maximus tried to encourage him since he wasn't much help at tracking. He told Francis that they probably lost the trail last night when they ran out of daylight, and he was sure they would find it again when they returned to the spot where they camped for the night. Flavius and Vernon were looking very annoyed, but they kept their mouths shut.

It was easy to follow the trail they just traveled, and finally they came to the spot where they spent the night. From there they had to backtrack even farther. Francis was walking very slowly, bent low to the ground, looking for the original trail. He told Vernon to do the same thing about six feet away from him. Vernon was looking down at the ground and commented about a pile of leaves. Francis looked and yelled for him to get back, but a snake jumped out of the pile and clamped down on his neck. Francis took his knife and sliced through the snake, and it fell to the ground.

Vernon was stunned but still conscious. Francis knew that he didn't have long to live, so he asked him if he had any last words. With that, Vernon knew he was dying. He grabbed Francis's hand and said, "Tell my mom that I love her, and give my pack to my sister. Treasure in it." He died in Francis's arms. Maximus and Flavius cried, but Francis insisted that they had to leave him there and go on.

"If we take too much time mourning, the two we are rescuing could die as well," Francis said. He returned to searching for the trail, and finally he found it. The night before, they should have stopped walking sooner when they could still see the trail. They decided to take better care of themselves from now on. They took time to eat and drink and rest occasionally. They accepted the fact that they were not going to reach the men until the next day, so when they were running out of daylight, they stopped, set up camp, and built a fire. The snake had spooked them, so now they were looking around more and listening for the sounds of wild animals.

"What kind of snake was that?" Flavius asked.

"It was a rhino viper. That kind of snake actually has very bright colors, but in a pile of leaf debris, it's invisible," explained Francis.

"Do you think Vernon was in much pain?" asked Maximus.

"I don't think so," said Francis. "He only lived a minute or two, and he was able to talk till the end."

CHAPTER 9

The first night out on the ship, Claudia cried all night. What would Mother say about them leaving without Maximus? One time when they were little, the four of them were playing near the marketplace while Mother was choosing food for their evening meal. Maximus wandered off, and Mother was angry with all three of them for not keeping an eye on him. Even though they found him happily playing nearby, Argus, Felix, and Claudia felt guilty for weeks, and Mother reminded them of it every time they went out. Even now, they knew that they were responsible for one another's safety, and they would be blamed if anything happened to Maximus.

But Claudia was missing Flavius as well. She remembered their last conversation when he told her not to worry about him, and to think about their long trip back to Rome. She remembered how red his face got when he said that the trip might be romantic. Tears ran down her cheeks as she thought about him. *What if the bad men won't let them leave the city? What if the bad men kill Maximus and Flavius? Or what if they get eaten by a giant lion?*

Claudia went to sleep when it was almost daylight, and she dreamed about lions chasing Maximus and Flavius through the jungle. When she woke up, the lions in the cages near them were restless, making growling noises and trying to stand up. She woke up Felix and asked him what was bothering the lions.

"They are probably thirsty," Felix said. "We ignored them that entire trip through the jungle. They may be hungry, too, or they might be seasick. They aren't used to this rocking like we are."

Argus and Felix notified some of the hunters, who then spent the entire day caring for nineteen lions, giving them water and food and throwing water to clean their cages. Argus, Felix, and even Claudia did a lot of the work carrying food and water to the men, and then the disgusting job of cleaning up what washed out of the cages. At first the lions were very cranky, striking out at them with their claws. By the end of the day, the lions were all asleep, the men had gone back up, and the three of them were exhausted. They were dirty, wet, and smelly.

"At least I don't have to worry about any men getting interested in me today," said Claudia.

"Well, that's for sure," said Felix. "I suppose you only have eyes for Flavius now."

"He is pretty cute, isn't he?" asked Claudia. "You guys like him, don't you?"

"He is better than that old guy back in Rome," said Argus.

"You can do better than that," said Claudia.

"He's all right, if you like red," said Felix. "Did you

notice that his face matches his hair whenever he talks to you?"

"His face is red whenever he talks about you too," said Argus.

Claudia looked in her pack, and there was the gorgeous blanket that Flavius bought her at the marketplace in Oea. "I'm really filthy," she said. The three of them took turns cleaning up. They joined the rest of the group for an evening meal while two soldiers guarded the lions. Claudia looked very pretty with her clean hair and clean clothes. Cadogan kept trying to talk to her, and two of the young soldiers were near her too, talking loudly and flirting with her. Inside, Claudia was fuming because everyone was so happy that they got away from Cyrene. They weren't worried at all about Maximus or Flavius or the others. In fact, she got the feeling that some of them were happy that Flavius was gone so they could get closer to her. Claudia and her brothers returned to the lower deck with the lions. They stood on the deck, looking back toward Cyrene, and discussed that they were getting farther and farther from Maximus and the others. Claudia wrapped herself in the blanket from Flavius and cried herself to sleep again.

Argus and Felix talked quietly for hours. They were angry with Cadogan, too, for being so happy that they got away and that Flavius was left behind.

Titus came down and joined them. He felt just like they did, and he knew that his wife would be furious about him going off and leaving Flavius behind in Africa. He was wondering if he did the right thing. *Maybe they should have waited at the camp area for the group to return. No. Someone was spying on them there and spooked the animals. It was probably the bad men. They did the right thing.* But he wondered what Flavius and the group were doing right now.

⚜

Octavius and Benedict woke up early when the sun made their tent hot. It was very frustrating for them to stay in one place and wait for Francis and the others. They had arrived at the edge of the jungle, early in the day, and just sat around for hours until bedtime. Now they were facing another day of total boredom.

"You know," said Octavius, "we could follow the trail, heading south until we meet them coming back. What would be the harm in doing that? It would just be so much more interesting than sitting here."

"I'm not sure it's a good idea," said Benedict. "What will we do if we run into lions or tigers or great big spiders? What if they don't follow the same trail back to the coast? We could end up in the jungle by ourselves. I feel a lot safer here than in the jungle."

"Think of the adventure," said Octavius.

"Don't forget that we are under orders from Titus to wait right here," insisted Benedict.

"He would thank us if we helped his son, who is out there in the jungle somewhere," said Octavius.

"You know, when we walked away from our group yesterday, when they were waiting to get on that ship, it just about killed me. I wanted to go with them, and I was wishing that I wouldn't have volunteered," said Benedict. "If you think I am going to go back into the jungle, you are wrong."

Octavius had listened to Benedict whine the whole

time they were in the jungle before, and he was really surprised when he agreed to this job.

"Why did you volunteer to come with me?" Octavius asked.

"Oh, I always open my big mouth and get myself into trouble," said Benedict.

"Well, you did the right thing," said Octavius. "But I have a strong feeling that we should follow them into the jungle, and I think we should get started right now."

"What about our tent?" asked Benedict.

"I'll carry it," said Octavius.

"Why do I have the feeling that I am really going to regret this?" asked Benedict as he walked over and started taking down their tent.

The two men walked most of the day and came to a sight they weren't prepared for. It was Vernon's body. They could see the dead viper next to him, and figured out what happened.

"Maybe we should turn around and go back," said Benedict.

"No, I'm more certain than ever that we are doing the right thing. Now they are down a man. Francis is out there with just two young kids along. Let's pick up our pace," insisted Octavius.

<hr />

Francis, Maximus, and Flavius didn't sleep very well. All night long, they woke up with a start, thinking about the viper. They decided to get up just before dawn, make a fire, and have a little breakfast. After eating, they packed up their tent and put out the fire. They began walking as soon as it was light enough to make out the trail. They had to move very slowly because the brush had grown back very quickly in the jungle. Late in the afternoon, Francis recognized the area where they had first seen the paw prints of the huge lion. He remembered that they had tracked that animal for a long time, and he remembered how the three of them struggled to get it out of the net and into the cage. He pictured his friends lying in a hot tent without food or water, suffering from their injuries.

When the boys heard how close they were, they began shouting for the men. Birds squawked and flew away, but no human voices were heard in response. Francis told them to concentrate on the path. For what seemed like an hour, they tracked the men and the lion. The boys yelled out again, and the only response they heard was an ear-splitting roar of a lion. They knew they were very close, and they assumed they heard the captured lion. They headed in the direction of the roar.

Just as they entered the clearing, an enormous male lion jumped out at them. Francis had his spear ready, and the lion came right down on it. The lion fell with its full weight onto Francis. Maximus and Flavius stood there in shock, unable to see any signs of life from the lion or any part of Francis's body. Finally they came to their senses.

"We had better get this thing off Francis before he suffocates," said Flavius.

"I'm not sure we can budge it," said Maximus.

"What if the thing wakes up while we're trying to move it?" asked Flavius.

The two boys tried to roll the lion's body onto

its side, but they couldn't. They tried to lift up a leg and look under it, but they still could see no signs of Francis.

"Are you sure he's under there?" asked Flavius.

"Where would he go? He has to be under there," said Maximus.

The boys decided to look around for some kind of stick to pry the lion up and off of Francis. They came into the clearing and could not believe their eyes. The lion cage was squashed down on a lion that seemed to fill the entire cage. The two carrying poles were standing up in the air at an angle.

"I'll get this pole and you get the other," said Maximus. "We can use them to force the lion onto its side."

The position of the cage made it very difficult to jiggle the poles out, and they were worried about the lion getting free if they changed its position at all. But they were painfully aware that the time would soon be up for them to resuscitate Francis. They decided to take their chances and were able to work together to get one pole out. They took the pole, dug it into the side of the lion, and pushed together with all their strength. The lion rolled off as they strained against it. Francis was barely recognizable due to the huge quantities of blood covering him. Maximus took off his robe and wiped the blood from Francis's face. He put his ear close to his mouth and couldn't feel or hear any breathing. Maximus remembered something Claudia had told him about blowing into a person's mouth to get him breathing, so he began doing that to Francis. He did it for quite a while until Francis struggled and took a breath on his own.

Tears streamed down the faces of both boys as Francis opened his eyes and tried to speak. The boys told him to be quiet and just breathe, but Francis wanted to tell them something.

"Julius," he whispered.

"What's he talking about?" asked Flavius.

"Julius," Francis whispered again.

"Oh, he's probably one of the guys we're here to rescue," said Maximus. Francis nodded and then passed out again.

Maximus bent low and listened to see if Francis was still alive. He was relieved to hear his soft breathing.

"Let's look around for the men," suggested Flavius. "I'm surprised we haven't seen them yet."

"Julius!" they shouted.

No one answered, so they looked around at the ground, searching for clues. They looked at the lion in the collapsed cage. Ropes held the thing together, but they weren't certain it would hold for long. The lion appeared to be uninjured, but it was in such an uncomfortable position that it couldn't roar. Occasionally it made a hissing sound, like an angry cat.

"I think the dead lion over there came to rescue this lion, but when it jumped on top of the cage, it squashed it down," said Flavius.

"I guess that's probably what happened, but do you think the big lion ate Julius and the other guy? I don't see them around," said Maximus.

The boys checked on Francis again, and since he was breathing, they decided to get rope out of their cart to reinforce the lion's cage. They soon discovered that the ropes on the cage were seriously loosened but not damaged. They fed the new rope through the spaces, because they knew that the lion would probably try to jump against the sides as soon as they straightened it out. Their method worked, but the lion kept its head down on the bottom of the cage after the side was straightened up. Maximus retrieved the pole from the side of the dead lion and replaced it in the loops made to carry the cage.

"Why isn't he getting up and roaring at us?" Flavius asked.

"He might be injured or starving or thirsty," suggested Maximus. They put some water in the cage, and the lion drank it all. They filled the container three times, and the lion drank all of that.

"Well, I guess I'll go get one of the carts," said Flavius. "Do you think it's time to move Francis? I don't want to injure him any more than he already is."

The boys brought both carts into the area. They carefully examined Francis and decided that, although he had no broken bones, he could have internal injuries. Once in the cart, Francis woke up for a few minutes. They gave him a little water and asked if he was in pain. He didn't answer them but said, "Julius."

Just then an object fell out of a tree very close to them. It was a spear, and the blade went straight into the ground. The boys looked up in the tree, and there was a man hanging over two branches with his arms dangling. Another man was in a nearby tree. A spear was hanging straight down, wedged between his arm and the branch. The boys yelled up at them, but they didn't respond.

"If they are alive, they must be dehydrated," said Maximus.

Flavius put a coil of rope over his shoulder and began climbing the tree.

"What's the rope for?" asked Maximus.

"I'm going to have to lower him down from the tree, because it doesn't look like he's able to climb down," answered Flavius.

Flavius climbed up next to the first man and decided that he was still alive. A cloth was wrapped around the top of his head, and it was dark with dried blood. Flavius tried to wake him up, but he was very hot and unconscious. Flavius carefully tied the rope and lowered him. As soon as Maximus could reach the man, he grabbed him and guided him safely to the ground. Flavius risked his life to climb up to the other man, because the spear could have come loose and stabbed him. The man in the tree began talking, and Flavius yelled down that he was delirious, and then he told Maximus to get back and he dropped the spear. Then he lowered him down, too.

The boys took water and forced it into both men. When they didn't come around right away, the boys decided to move them into the cart with Francis, who was also unconscious.

"Now what are we going to do?" asked Flavius. "It's almost dark, and we are out here alone in the jungle with three injured men and an extremely heavy lion."

"There is no way that the two of us can lift that lion onto the cart. We were barely able to roll the other one," said Maximus. "If we take the men back without the lion, then all their suffering was in vain."

"Do you think you can follow the trail back to the coast without Francis to help us?" asked Flavius.

"I don't think so," said Maximus. "I wasn't much help to Francis today. Were you?"

"No," said Flavius. "We are in trouble. Do you even know how to set up the tent?"

"No, I don't, but now that you mention it, we had better learn," said Maximus. "We can't go anywhere until morning."

"How about if you figure out that tent, while I give our patients some more water and try to get them to wake up?" asked Maximus.

Maximus gently poured water into the mouths of the three men. Francis was very weak, but he seemed relieved that Julius and the other man were still alive. He responded by talking quietly. "The back of my head hurts, and I think something hard dug into my shoulder."

Maximus looked at the back of Francis's head and it was bloody. He must have landed on something hard. The pole of the spear must have come down against his shoulder, because it left a long, nasty bruise. Maximus was more concerned about the injuries that he couldn't see.

Flavius struggled for quite a while, but he couldn't figure out how to set up the tent, and he was getting very frustrated. It was almost dark out now, so the boys decided that they would have to sleep in the other cart. They were pulling their blankets out of their packs when they heard a sound in the jungle.

"What if it's another giant lion coming to rescue the first one?" whispered Maximus. They sat there, barely breathing, and suddenly two figures came into the clearing.

"Francis. Are you here?" they called.

Relief swept over the boys as they realized that help was here.

"Who's there?" asked Flavius.

"It's me, Octavius, and Benedict is with me. We were supposed to wait for you near the sea, but we were bored and thought that maybe you could use some help."

"You have no idea how glad we are to see you," said Maximus. "We have three injured men, and Flavius and I don't know how to find our way back. We can't even set up a tent."

"Well, we're here now. Everything's going to be all right," said Octavius. "Now where are the injured men?"

They lit a torch and checked on the men. The first man that they took down from the tree, the one with the head injury, was very still. They listened for his breathing and his pulse, and they thought that he must be dead. They examined the next man, Julius, who woke up and asked for water. After drinking, he went back to sleep.

Francis was in a great deal of pain. They gave him some water and checked on his injuries. They cleaned the blood off his head and hoped that his head injury wasn't so bad. They let him go back to sleep.

Octavius set up the tent, started a campfire, and cooked them some food. The boys and men ate heartily. The men kept looking at each other across the campfire, trying to decide whether to break the news to the boys that all the others had left them here and that they had to try and catch a ship without attracting any attention from the bad men in town. The boys began talking about how scared they were that Francis and Julius would die too and that they wouldn't be able to find their way back to the coast. They were worried about snakes and spiders and poisonous plants, and the men knew that the boys couldn't handle the bad news right now. Benedict told them to get a good night's sleep, and in the morning they would head north. He promised that he would sit up all night by the fire to keep them safe.

CHAPTER 10

Argus, Felix, and Claudia spent an entire day on the back deck, looking toward Cyrene and discussing all of the things they remembered about Maximus, and a few things they remembered about Flavius. Cadogan and Kendrick tried to join them once, and later they urged them to come to the meal, but both times they were sent back upstairs.

On the evening of the fourth day since they left Cyrene, they landed in Alexandria. The ship's captain told them that they would be staying there until noon the next day and that they were welcome to leave their belongings on the ship and go into the city for sight-seeing or for shopping. Titus said that he would take a group ashore that evening and another group the next morning, with six soldiers accompanying each group.

Argus, Felix, and Claudia were chosen to go with the first group since they had not eaten a decent meal for a while. Titus took them to a fine eatery first, and after that they visited the Lighthouse of Alexandria. They climbed a circular ramp inside the tower that was so wide that their entire group of ten could walk side by side most of the way up. They continued up a narrower staircase and came to a level where they could look out and see for miles. Titus overheard the teens talking about how sad they were that Maximus wasn't along to see the massive building and the striking view from the tower.

Once outside the building, Titus purchased two drawings of the lighthouse and two drawings of the view from the tower. He gave one set to Argus, Felix, and Claudia to give to Maximus, and the other set he kept to give to his son Flavius. When Felix started to argue that the gift was much too generous, Titus reminded him that he would be paying him wages for keeping an eye on the lions on the ship, and that this was just an advance.

After touring the lighthouse, they walked by beautiful gardens and came to a Roman amphitheater that was being built. They felt sad that the evil Roman shows were coming to such a beautiful city. On their walk back to the ship, they passed many vendors selling goods of all kinds. Titus purchased a new outfit of clothes for Claudia and her brothers and one for Flavius. Of course, he had to buy boys' clothes for Claudia, who looked longingly at the beautiful robes for young women. Titus planned to buy a new gown for his wife, but he thought he would wait and buy it in the morning, when Claudia wasn't along.

They arrived back on the ship just as it was getting dark. Cadogan and Kendrick were waiting by the handrail, as well as many of the men. They showed them the drawings of the lighthouse and the view of the city that they planned to give to Maximus. They were in a good mood and were more hopeful about seeing Maximus and Flavius again. Cadogan and Kendrick went down to the lower deck with them. Claudia went over to her sleeping area, wrapped up in her blanket from Flavius, and went to sleep, but Argus and Felix stayed up and visited with them.

"What's the matter with Claudia? She doesn't seem like herself," said Cadogan.

"Well, you know. She's heartbroken that we went off and left Maximus and Flavius," said Felix.

"Oh, Flavius," said Cadogan. "I figured it was about him."

"You might get along better with Claudia if you didn't seem so happy that Flavius is gone," suggested Argus.

"Hardly anyone feels sorry for us anymore that we lost our father and our home," said Kendrick.

"We just don't bring it up, but we still feel bad about it. The emperor is a jerk!" said Felix.

"The emperor is a jerk!" said a funny voice behind them.

The four boys froze and were silent for a minute. Finally Felix stood up and grabbed the lamp. "I thought we were alone with the animals down here," he said.

He took the lamp over to where the sound came from. There weren't any humans around, but the parrot was sitting there in its cage, looking right at Felix.

"The emperor is a jerk," said Felix.

"The emperor is a jerk," repeated the parrot.

"Oh, no," said Felix. "He was very chatty this morning when I was feeding him and cleaning his cage, but I forgot that parrots can mimic what we say. He needs to forget that phrase."

"The emperor is a jerk," said the parrot.

"The emperor is a god," said Felix.

"The emperor is a jerk," said the parrot.

"We're in trouble," said Felix.

"It will be more than a month before the emperor's birthday," said Argus. "We just need to teach him some more phrases."

"Happy birthday. Happy birthday," said Felix, looking in the cage, his face close to the bird.

"The emperor is a jerk," said the parrot.

Cadogan and Kendrick laughed and laughed every time the parrot repeated the phrase. Finally they said that they were going to bed and went happily off.

"Well, at least the parrot put them in a good mood," said Felix. "That's the happiest I have seen them since their father was killed."

"Laughter is good medicine," said Argus.

"Tomorrow, let's do some fun things with Claudia, like playing games, fishing, or something else. Maximus wouldn't want her crying all day like this," said Felix.

"Didn't I see Titus give you a little money?" asked Argus.

"Yes, when he gave us the new clothes, he handed me the change," said Felix. "I know he really appreciates us watching the animals and letting the men know when they need food and water."

"Well, maybe he wouldn't mind if we walked out to the marketplace, right there beside the dock, if we have a couple of soldiers with us," said Argus. "Claudia was in good spirits this evening until Cadogan joined us and went on and on about how lucky we were to get away from Cyrene."

"A walk around the marketplace is just what she needs," said Felix.

"The emperor is a jerk," said the parrot.

⚬⚬⚬

In Rome, Nolan and Sabrina were missing their four children. The children had been gone for weeks, and they had not heard anything from them in all that time. The rich man who was determined to marry Claudia was only coming by once a week now to see if she had returned. If the emperor had found another woman for him, it wasn't working yet.

One evening there was a loud rapping on Nolan's door. He and Sabrina were concerned, because they seldom had visitors at their villa, especially late at night. The servants had all gone to their quarters, so Nolan went to the door and asked who was there.

"Nolan. It's me, Rufus. I just returned from Britannia, and I thought you might want a report on our findings."

Nolan opened the door and welcomed him in. "Have you had any refreshment?"

"Oh, no. I let my guys all go home, but I came straight here," Rufus said.

Sabrina heard and went quickly to prepare a fruit tray, a serving of cheese, and a large drink. Rufus enjoyed the refreshments and then relayed the exciting news. He had found Lavinia's parents. "I went to the street where she used to live. Her parents were not there, but the elderly couple next door told me the name of a small town in Mide where they moved. I went there, asked around, and I was sent to their very house. Lavinia's parents are still alive, and they are very happy about the prospect of getting her and the children back. They have already chosen a place on their land where they will build a home for them. They were so happy that they could not stop crying."

"Rufus, we will share this with her first thing in the morning. Please tell me, was the empire present in that region?" asked Nolan.

"They are governed by a local dynasty, and although they pay some taxes, they are free to live their lives as they please. So far, the Roman Empire has stayed away," said Rufus.

Nolan looked at Sabrina and smiled, wondering if she was thinking about it as a refuge for them as well. The emperor had been ruthless all week, sending prisoners to their deaths simply to delight the crowds and win more popularity for himself.

"Don't get too comfortable here in Rome, Rufus, because I must send you off to Africa in search of ostriches for the emperor's big birthday celebration," said Nolan.

"That sounds exciting," said Rufus. "When should I leave?"

"Get your team and supplies together as soon as possible, because I told the emperor that I would get right on it, but I have been waiting for you to return. I can't trust just anyone to go get ostriches," said Nolan. "Oh, and can you come by sometime in the morning to see Lavinia and give her the good news?"

"I will do both of those things tomorrow. I must tell you, though, that I would not recommend traveling over land as we did," said Rufus. "We made good time because we were on horseback, but there were some dangerous areas, and we had to cross water a couple of times. It is no trip for a family. I heard that there is a ship that goes there from Rome. It is much slower, but it is safer and could be attempted with young children." He left, and Nolan and Sabrina discussed various ways for Nolan to get away from the presence of the emperor, including moving to the area of Mide, west of Britannia, across a body of water.

The travelers were relieved to find that not only was Julius still alive, but so was the other man, Cyrus. It took several days before the three injured men were well enough to travel. Octavius, Benedict, Flavius, and Maximus were very restless waiting on them to improve.

"I would just like to know how you two were able to escape that big lion by climbing those trees. Certainly you couldn't move very fast and climb those trees with your injuries. That lion could have jumped three-fourths of the way up the tree without even trying," said Flavius.

"It wasn't the lion that scared us up into the trees," said Julius. He smiled at Cyrus.

"You never would guess what it was," said Cyrus.

"Snakes," suggested Maximus.

"No, I bet it was monkeys," said Flavius.

"Monkeys!" said Cyrus. "If it was monkeys, we wouldn't climb a tree to get away from them, would we?"

"I guess not. What was it?" Flavius asked.

"Wild dogs," said Julius.

"How could you get up a tree fast with wild dogs around?" asked Maximus.

"We heard them. Packs of wild dogs make calls to each other, and Cyrus picked up on it," said Julius.

"So we got our spears and started climbing the trees," said Cyrus. "I had lost a lot of blood and I was dizzy, but I have a fear of dogs, so I really struggled to get up that tree. It was the hardest thing I ever did."

"Well, my back hurt so bad that I could hardly walk, let alone climb a tree," said Julius. "But I was pretty scared, too. At first we were mad at ourselves for grabbing spears instead of water. We were up there for a long time, and the dogs howled and yapped and ran around below us. They were trying to wait us out."

"Then the enormous lion came along," said Cyrus. "It scared off the dogs and then it tried to climb up my tree. That's when I was very thankful that I brought the spear up. That lion was smart enough to stay away from the point of my spear."

"Wasn't it strange that the lion jumped on the other lion's cage?" asked Flavius.

"Did you see that?" asked Cyrus. "The cage just couldn't take the weight. If our lion wouldn't have been inside, the cage would have gone flat to the ground."

"Where is that big lion?" asked Julius. "I didn't think he would give up and go away. I mean, he was here two days and two nights. We thought we would die up in those trees before you got back with help."

"Don't ask me," said Francis. "I've been sleeping for a while, right?" He looked at Maximus and Flavius.

"When we came into the area, the big lion charged at us," said Flavius. "Francis was quick with his spear, but the lion jumped on him and squashed him flat. The spear must have gone straight into its heart because it died immediately. We were afraid Francis would suffocate because it took us so long to get it off him."

"We weren't even sure you were under there," said Maximus. "The lion covered you up completely."

"We have been worried about internal injuries," said Flavius. "How do you feel?"

"I'm bruised all over, but I don't think my insides are damaged," said Francis. "I feel like I've had the sense knocked out of me, though."

"When you have the strength to go over and look at that lion, you will understand why you feel that way," said Maximus.

Francis looked over at Octavius and Benedict and said, "I have been wondering why you guys are here."

"Should we tell them?" asked Octavius, looking at Benedict. Benedict shrugged his shoulders, so Octavius decided to go ahead. "Well, after you, Francis, and the others left to rescue Julius and Cyrus, we had some trouble in Cyrene."

Francis frowned and asked, "What kind of trouble?"

"Well, there was a huge group of bad men hanging out together in town, near the dock, and there were intruders near our campsite in the middle of the night. They spooked the animals," said Octavius.

"I hope they are keeping everyone at the campsite, and I hope the soldiers are doubled up and extra vigilant," said Francis.

"Not exactly," said Benedict.

"All right," said Francis, "what's going on? Just spit it out."

"They left us behind," said Octavius.

"No," said Flavius. "My father would never leave me behind in Africa. You must be wrong."

"Well, it wasn't an easy decision for him, but if they would have stayed another day, they probably would have been attacked and killed. They had to get out on the first big ship that came along," explained Octavius.

"How are we going to get away?" asked Maximus. "We will be outnumbered, won't we?"

"They don't know we are still here. I have a ship schedule, and we are supposed to move into town and go straight to the boat dock in the morning or afternoon. I guess the bad men arrive in town in the early evening," said Octavius.

"So Father sent you all the way here to tell us not to go to town in the evening or night time," said Flavius.

"Actually, we were supposed to wait at the edge of the jungle," said Benedict. "It was Octavius who thought we should come and find you."

"So what's the plan?" asked Francis.

Octavius pulled the schedule out of his pack. "What is today, anyway?" he asked.

Maximus went to his pack and pulled a small scroll out. "Today is September 5," he said. "I write in here at least once a day. I also draw pictures when I have time. Here is a drawing of Benedict sitting by the fire last night so the rest of us could sleep."

"If you three are up to traveling, we can leave soon," said Octavius. "We might be able to make it close to town, but not too close, two evenings from now. According to the schedule, a ship will be along the morning of the eighth, heading for Alexandria. If we could get on that ship, we would be out of danger.

Then we could travel to Joppa, where the big group is supposed to be waiting on us. If they aren't there, we are to get back to Rome any way we can."

"I'm not sure I can walk yet," said Cyrus. "I'm very weak."

"That's why we brought two oxcarts," said Maximus. "One is for the lion, and one is for you men who are recovering."

"I guess I'm up to riding," said Julius. "I might even be able to walk some."

The group suddenly wanted to get going more than anything else. They took down their camp and packed all of their belongings in the first cart. Then they backed the other cart up until it was right next to the lion's cage. Using the poles, they tipped the cage way back at an angle. They lowered the back of the cart and tried to slide the cage onto it. The lion growled and slashed out at them, so they had to depend on the poles to maneuver it into the cart. Finally they got it in, hooked the cart up to the ox, and took off with the three injured men in the other cart.

"I have to give you boys a lot of credit," said Benedict. "I didn't think you would take the news this well that the group left us behind. The other night you two were fretting about everything from spiders to jungle noises."

"We were tired and hungry and angry with ourselves that we didn't know how to set up camp and track our way home," said Maximus.

"We haven't been doing our job teaching you young people," said Francis. "Now pay attention this time."

CHAPTER 11

Argus, Felix, and Claudia talked Titus into letting them go to the marketplace in Alexandria while he took the other half of the big group to the lighthouse. They had their soldiers with them, and they were wearing their new clothes. The boys wanted Claudia to choose a piece of jewelry or some flowers, anything to cheer her up. She walked by all those items, and they couldn't interest her in any of them. Finally they came to a section with maps and scrolls like the ones they saw in Oea. They didn't see an expensive piece called *The Word of God* like they saw before, but they did see a smaller scroll titled *In the Beginning*. The man at the market assured them that this was an important book from *The Word of God* that tells about the creation of the world.

"Oh, please buy it, Felix, if we have enough money," Claudia said. "Maximus will be so happy."

Felix counted his money and was surprised that Titus had given him so much. He handed it to the man, who gave them the scroll. The man told Felix to look for a book called *The Departure*, which begins where *In the Beginning* ends. They had enough money left to buy each of them a hard candy on a stick. They even bought one for each of the soldiers with them. They couldn't wait to get back on the ship and begin reading their little scroll.

Once they were on the ship, the three teens went straight down to their sleeping area. The lions were all awake and making noise, and the parrot was saying his favorite phrase about the emperor, so they changed back into their old clothes, called the men down, and spent several hours helping to care for and clean up after the animals. Finally Titus stopped down on the lower deck to make sure everyone was back on the ship, since it would be departing for Joppa very soon. They showed him the scroll that they bought for Maximus. While he was down there, the parrot repeated the phrase, "The emperor is a jerk."

Titus was speechless.

"You have to believe me," said Felix. "I didn't try and teach him that. Cadogan and Kendrick came down here to visit, and I made the statement, trying to make them feel better, and the parrot picked it right up. I keep trying to teach it other things, but it likes to say that."

"Maybe we need to look for another interesting animal to give the emperor for his birthday. I don't want to lose my life over a very bad parrot, do you?" Titus asked. Just before Titus went back up to the higher decks, he told Argus, Felix, and Claudia to come up for dinner, because the captain took on many supplies in Alexandria and they were invited to dine with him each night.

After he left, Claudia said, "We have a little time, so let's check out the scroll." The three of them sat down near the lamp, opened the little scroll, and began reading.

"In the beginning, God created the heavens and the earth. Now the earth was formless and empty, darkness was over the surface of the deep, and the spirit of God was hovering over the waters." They read and read for a long time, taking turns. They read about God creating day and night, the sky, the plants and the trees, the sun and the stars, the creatures of the sea and the birds of the air, and all the animals on the land. Finally they read about God creating man in his own image. They read about God resting on the seventh day.[5] They continued reading for a long time until Cadogan came down and told them to come to dinner.

The three of them, Argus, Felix, and Claudia, changed into their new, clean clothes and went up to dinner. To their surprise, the ship's captain had his wife and daughter with him, and he invited Titus and the five teenagers to join them.

"Well, Captain, where have you been hiding them?" Titus asked.

"They have been in my quarters since we left Rome, and they have been very bored. Only a few members of the crew knew they were aboard," said the captain. "Please meet my wife, Mary, and my daughter, Rebekah, and please call me Riley. I met Mary in Joppa years ago when I first began traveling on the Great Sea. We married and had two boys and Rebekah, but we kept our home in Joppa."

"But we get to go to Rome every summer to visit

my grandparents. They always spoil me terribly," said Rebekah.

"I just found out that one of these teenagers is actually a young lady, and I thought that Rebekah would enjoy socializing with some people her own age," said the captain. "Since we are getting close to home, I thought they could come out."

As the visitors found seats around the large table, Titus said, "So which one of them do you think is the girl?"

Rebekah smiled and looked a long time at each of the teens. Finally she looked at Kendrick and said, "I think it's you. You are the girl."

Everyone burst out laughing, and Kendrick was a good sport. "Guess again," he said.

Rebekah looked again, and this time she focused on Cadogan, who said, "Don't even think about choosing me."

Once again they all laughed, and Claudia said, "I'm the girl. I guess my haircut and clothes are working. My name is Claudia, but around strangers I'm known as Charles."

"Why did your mother let you travel this far away without her?" asked Mary.

"Oh, well, there was a very rich old man who decided he wanted me for his wife, and my parents agreed with me that I was safer hunting lions in Africa," said Claudia.

They had a long, leisurely dinner, and Rebekah asked Claudia if she would like to move to her cabin for the next three or four nights until they reached Joppa. Claudia told her that she was sorry, but they promised their parents that they would stick together, and they were probably already in big trouble for letting Maximus get separated from them. But she invited Rebekah to come down and visit with them, and Captain Riley said that because of the lions, she could only go down there when he was free to go along. They made plans to go down for a visit in the morning. Claudia was excited because she longed for a little girl talk.

⋘⋙

The travelers in the jungle were very eager to pack up and head north. The lion cage was already in the cart and ready to go. They drank a little water and ate some dried meat and started out. Francis was able to walk, and Julius and Cyrus sat up happily in the other cart. Flavius and Maximus were told to follow the trail back to the coast. They walked for hours and came to the place Vernon's body had been. Scavengers had destroyed most of the body, but his shoes and clothes were still there. They stopped and rested, and they told Julius and Cyrus about Vernon's death.

They sat there for a while remembering Vernon, and Maximus asked Francis what Vernon said to him when he was dying.

"Vernon said to tell his mother that he loved her and to give his sister his pack. He said there was some kind of treasure inside," said Francis.

"Where is his pack?" asked Julius. "Did you look in it?"

"No, I forgot all about it," said Francis. "I guess it's still in the cart."

"Do you think we should look in the pack and see

what it is, or just give it to his sister when we get back?" asked Cyrus.

"I don't know. What could he possibly have that could be considered a treasure?" asked Francis.

"Let's find out," said Flavius. "Aren't you curious?"

"I guess it's all right. Go get his pack out of the cart," said Francis.

The boys climbed up into the cart behind Cyrus and Julius and rummaged through the packs and tents and food. All the packs were there except Vernon's.

"It must be in the other cart behind the lion," said Francis. "I guess we'll have to wait to find out what's in there."

The group had a quick snack and a drink and continued on through the jungle. They had not gone very far when a wheel broke on the cart that was carrying the lion. They had no choice but to move the lion into the other cart, and when they did, they were disappointed that Vernon's pack was not behind the lion's cage. They did not dare leave the cart with the broken wheel in the jungle, since they had no way to pay for it when they returned the oxen and carts in town. For that reason, Julius and Cyrus moved to the back of the first cart, so that it balanced on the front two wheels as it moved.

They traveled like that for a couple of hours, until a wheel broke on the other cart. They set to work repairing the cart by taking the third wheel off the bad cart and putting it on the cart that would carry the lion cage. That left no back wheels on the other one. They decided to wait until morning to load the lion back into the cart, since the lion was probably too heavy for it.

"You know," said Francis. "I don't understand this.

We went all the way to the coast with four of the gigantic lions in the carts, and we didn't break one wheel."

"Look at this lion," said Octavius. "It can barely move in the cage that is the same size that the others are comfortable in. This guy is even bigger and heavier."

"Well, also, these are the two carts we used before, so they are getting worn out," said Benedict.

"Well, I've about had enough of it," said Francis.

"If we break another wheel tomorrow, we'll have a very difficult time getting the lion to the coast," said Benedict.

Maximus wrapped up in his blanket and tried to sleep. He prayed to God and asked him to help them get to the coast safely and to keep the wheels from breaking. He also asked God to take care of his parents and especially to keep his father safe from the emperor, and he asked him to keep Argus, Felix, and Claudia safe.

In Rome, Nuncio, the rich man who was interested in Claudia, grew very restless waiting for her return. His two advisors told him to find another girl to marry. They told him that Rome had many young girls who were eager to find a wealthy man to marry. But Nuncio was a man who was used to getting what he wanted. He walked over to the home of Nolan and Sabrina, knowing his advisors would not approve, and stopped to talk to a gardener who was out in front of the property.

"Excuse me. I haven't seen the young woman named Claudia around lately. Have you seen her?"

"No sir. As a matter of fact, I haven't seen any of the young people around," answered the gardener."

"Do you have any idea where they are?" asked Nuncio.

The gardener shook his head, indicating that he did not know, but he had a vacant look on his face.

Nuncio regarded the gardener for a moment and finally said, "I will return to this very spot in two days, at this same time. In that time perhaps you can find out where the young Claudia is. If you can do that, very secretly of course, I will give you more money than you can earn in ten years. Well, what do you say?"

"If I find out for you, how do I know I can trust you to give me the money?" asked the gardener.

"I'll bring it with me and let you have it as soon as you tell me where she is," said Nuncio. "Can you use that kind of money?"

"Of course I can use it. But Nolan has been good to me all these years. What do you have against him, and what are you going to do to his daughter?" asked the gardener.

"I plan to marry her and give her everything she could ever want. But that's not good enough for Nolan," stated Nuncio bitterly.

"Look out," said the gardener. "He's coming around the corner."

Nuncio quickly headed down the street in the other direction, but he looked back and said, "Right in this spot, at this time, in two days."

Nolan didn't see Nuncio on the road, but as he pulled onto his property, he shouted greetings to the gardener. "Good work," he said. "The gardens are very beautiful."

The gardener waved to Nolan and was suddenly overcome with grief. To get the information for the rich man meant that he wouldn't be able to look Nolan in the eye again. And what if the man intended to harm Claudia? A long time ago, when she was a little tot, Claudia helped him plant flowers. She was dirty from head to toe, but she was so proud of herself. She hugged his leg and thanked him for letting her help.

"Nolan, I have something to tell you," said the gardener.

Nolan looked at the gardener and asked, "What's wrong?"

"A man came to see me, just moments ago. He offered me a large sum of money to tell him where Claudia is."

"Do you know where she is?" asked Nolan.

"No, but he thought that I could find out," he answered.

Nolan was very upset, pacing back and forth and mumbling to himself.

"Please forgive me. Forgive me for listening to the man. For a moment, I was tempted to take the money," the gardener said.

Nolan stood there staring at the man for a few moments, and the gardener was afraid that Nolan might be planning to send him running from wild animals at the Coliseum.

"Well, I'm glad you came to me about this. I think we can use it to our advantage. Think about what you would like to do with a lot of money. Is there some-place you want to go? Come back later tonight, and we will come up with a plan," said Nolan.

"Right now, I'm going to go back out and work on

the gardens, in case he goes by. I don't want him to get suspicious," said the gardener.

Nolan went inside and told Sabrina all about Nuncio trying to bribe the gardener. She cried and wouldn't be consoled for a long time. "This is just what I was afraid of. He will stop at nothing to find out where she is," she said.

Nolan assured her that this was actually the break that they need. She settled down and listened quietly.

"Let's make up a convincing story," suggested Nolan. "We can send him on a wild goose chase, and our gardener can go away for a while as a very rich man."

"Where should we send him?" asked Sabrina. "If it's too far away, he will send someone else. We want him to go himself, right?"

The two of them got out the map of the Roman Empire, which was the whole world to them, and spread it all over the dining table.

"Why don't we have the gardener say that he overheard the cooks talking about Claudia, so he listened in?" suggested Sabrina.

"Good idea," said Nolan. "Let's make it good." They studied the map for quite a while. They were interested in an area across the water in Gaul. There was a city there called Marseille that was full of wealthy people.

"What if our gardener tells Nuncio that he overheard the cooks say that Claudia is not caring for a sick relative at all, but instead she is in Marseille, lying on the beach and flirting with rich young merchants?" suggested Sabrina.

"I like it," said Nolan. "He might go there for a while and walk across many beaches, trying to find her."

"Great," said Sabrina. "It could keep him away for

a few weeks, and who knows? Maybe he will find a beautiful young woman lying on the beach who might not mind marrying a not-so-young rich man."

Later that night, the gardener showed up. He was very excited and told Nolan that if he got enough money from Nuncio, he could move to the other side of Rome and run his own landscaping business and garden center. It was his dream.

Nolan suggested that he refuse to give Nuncio the information unless he came through with the amount of money that he needed, even if Nuncio had to come back another day. They went over the story so much that they almost believed that Claudia was actually there, living a rich and pampered life.

CHAPTER 12

Rebekah was just the medicine that Argus, Felix, and Claudia needed. They put away all of their supplies and folded their clothes. The room looked clean and tidy, and all of the animals were quiet.

"Isn't Rebekah nice? I hope I get some time to hang out with her alone," said Claudia.

"Why don't you two girls find a nice place to stand up on the deck?" suggested Felix. "You can watch the seagulls and the dolphins and look at the little fishing villages that we pass. Take one of the soldiers with you and have him stand where he can see you."

The captain and Rebekah arrived and thought their plan was fine, so the soldier went with the two girls up on the deck. Their soldier told them that he would be nearby watching them from the other railing.

The first thing Rebekah asked Claudia was if she had a boyfriend. "Is it Cadogan?" she asked. "I saw the way he looked at you last night at dinner."

"No, it's not Cadogan. I guess he does have a little crush on me," said Claudia. "But there is a guy I like who is so cute, with long red hair and a great build. When I flirt with him, his whole face turns red."

"Is he back in Rome?" asked Rebekah.

"No, he's back in Cyrene, down in the jungle some place with my younger brother, and they might be in trouble. I still have nightmares about the mean, angry men in that city," said Claudia. "We barely escaped with our lives."

"I heard about it," said Rebekah. "We were all lucky to get away from that city. Father came to our cabin very upset and said that he will never take us back to Rome again. He said that traveling around the Great Sea is just too dangerous."

"Do you have a boyfriend, Rebekah?" asked Claudia.

"No, but I really think your brothers are cute," said Rebekah.

"You're kidding," said Claudia.

"They are so handsome, with that black hair and dark eyes," said Rebekah. "You and your two brothers all look alike. Does your little brother have dark hair and dark eyes, too?"

Claudia stood there for a moment looking at the seashore and had a sense about the great distance they were putting between them and Maximus. She thought about Maximus as a little boy. He was so cute and sweet. He was always such a good little boy. "Yes, he looks like us. Now he is as tall as Argus and Felix." Then the tears started running down her cheeks again.

"Oh, I am so sorry I asked about him," said Rebekah.

"No, don't be sorry. Until last night when I met you, I cried all the time about Maximus and Flavius," said

Claudia. "You have been a great distraction. And I do like talking about Flavius. I hope they find their way to us somehow."

The girls visited that way for quite a while, and then after they ate a small meal with the captain's family, they hung out with Argus and Felix. Rebekah thought Argus and Felix were the best-looking boys she had ever met. They explored the ship with their soldier along and came across some of the men from their travel group.

The men were discussing things that might go wrong for Francis and the others on the rescue mission. They hushed each other when they saw the teenagers come into room. The teens went back out to the railing for fresh air, and Felix asked Argus and Claudia if they picked up on the conversation in the room.

"Yes, I heard them. They think the others don't have much of a chance of getting out of there alive," said Argus.

Once again Claudia started crying, and the boys were very upset, too. They walked Rebekah back to her parents' cabin and left her with her mother. Then they went down to the lower level where the lions were. It was hot down there, and the lions were all sleeping. The parrot got excited when it saw them and started saying its favorite phrase about the emperor. They lit the lamps and sat down on the floor and cried. It was just so discouraging hearing the men talk that way that the boys couldn't hold back the tears. They were picturing Maximus being cut up by the knives of the evil men.

Finally Felix suggested they get out the scroll that they purchased in Alexandria. He thought that it might give them some hope, so he began reading again. They read about how God rested on the seventh day from all of his work of creating the world. Then they read the detailed account of when God created man on the earth. He read "the Lord God formed the man from the dust of the ground and breathed into his nostrils the breath of life, and the man became a living being." They read some more, and then they came to the part that told about God making a woman from the rib he took out of the first man. They read all about Adam and Eve and about Cain and Abel. They read to the end of the fourth chapter, where it said, "At that time men began to call on the name of the Lord."[6]

"Do you think we can call on the name of the Lord? Let's ask him to protect Maximus and Flavius," suggested Claudia. So the three of them closed their eyes and poured out their hearts to God about all of their fears, not only for Maximus and Flavius but also for the safety of their father as he worked for the emperor. They were comforted enough that they were able to fall asleep right away.

❧

The trip through the jungle had been slow and difficult, but the group finally arrived safely at a place that was close enough to the town for them to reach the dock the next morning, and yet it was far enough away from town to avoid alerting the townspeople to their presence.

Francis looked at his schedule. "Tomorrow is September 8. We lost one day because of the wheels, but Gaza is an even better choice than Alexandria."

"But if we lose another wheel, the only ship coming the next day is going to the island of Cyprus," said Benedict. "We're never going to get back to our group." The older people fretted like that for a while.

Flavius motioned for Maximus to follow him to an area a little ways from their campsite. "I don't understand what they are so worried about, do you?" asked Flavius. "If the wheel breaks tomorrow, we could go into town and buy another one. I am just so happy that tomorrow we might be on our way to join the others."

"I feel the same way," said Maximus. "Another wheel could have broken way back in the jungle, but it didn't, and here we are."

"When I think that we might get on a ship tomorrow and head east where Claudia is, I get so excited that I just can't stop smiling," said Flavius. "Do you think I am too young to be in love?"

"No," answered Maximus. "It sounds like you are very much in love. Let's get a good night's sleep so we are ready for whatever tomorrow brings."

"I don't think I can sleep because I am so excited," said Flavius.

Maximus led him back to the group and motioned for him to go to bed. Francis joined the group, but he was not smiling. Maximus hoped that when he became an adult, he wouldn't borrow trouble like some people do.

CHAPTER 13

The trip to Joppa seemed to take forever, but finally the big group arrived there with their nineteen lions and their talkative parrot. They were disappointed because much of the city was still in ruins. It had been destroyed in 70 a.d., and now there was construction everywhere.

Titus mentioned that their big group would probably be staying in the city for two or three weeks, so Captain Riley and his wife invited them to set up their camp in the back portion of their own property. Titus asked Riley where they could go to rent wagons to transport their equipment and lions, and he answered that he would take care of that. A half hour later, they were all moving across the city, approaching Captain Riley's place.

Eight-foot-tall gates opened to reveal beautiful benches, Grecian statues, and palm trees. The house and other buildings were elegant. Titus commented to Riley that traveling around The Great Sea in a ship seemed to be paying off for him.

"Well," Riley commented, "I am a very good shopper. I do not have to send off for anything, because I can go directly to the source of the best supplies around the world. And I always feel that Mary, my wife, should enjoy some pleasures to make up for a husband who is gone most of the time. It has been hard on her, I'm afraid."

"If I had a place that looked like this," said Titus, "I don't think I would ever leave home. This is a paradise."

"Twenty years ago this city was destroyed, along with Jerusalem," said Riley. "Mary's father owned all of this land at the edge of town. He gave both of his daughters a portion, which was unheard of around here. The back of our property overlooks the sea, and we can sit there and watch ships approaching."

"If I weren't so worried about my son Flavius and the others we left behind in Cyrene, this would be a true vacation," said Titus.

"Well, I don't blame you for being concerned about them," Riley said. "But I have a week of free time while my ship is being maintained and loaded with supplies, and I thought that perhaps you folks would enjoy a little sight-seeing. You can't do anything for the others right now anyway."

Titus was silent a few minutes. He was thinking about Flavius and remembering him as a little boy. Flavius could walk when he was only nine months old, and he could talk fluently before he was two years old. He was a natural athlete. Then he thought about his wife and how upset she would be right now.

"I don't know about traveling," said Titus. "My wife would be very upset if she knew that I left Africa without Flavius. I probably should stay right here and be at the dock, checking every ship that comes in."

"What is the absolute soonest your group could arrive?" asked Riley.

"It takes three days to go down to the campsite and three days back, so I guess six days from today is the absolute soonest they could get back," said Titus.

"Well, let's make the most of the time," said the captain. "Mary wants to go over to Jerusalem to check out some tapestries she heard about. She's been talking about it for months now, way before our trip to Rome. It won't quite take six days. We might even go down to Gaza, which is a short distance away and said to have some of the most interesting pieces of art."

"Is it all right if I ask the young people if they would like to go along?" Titus asked. "They need the diversion, since they are just as concerned as I am about Flavius and the others."

"I was planning to invite them along to be company for Rebekah," Riley answered.

They moved all nineteen of the lions to an area inside their borders, under a large group of palm trees where the cool ocean breeze would keep them comfortable. The men splashed out the cages, gave food and water to the lions, and made out a schedule so everyone would take turns watching them. They hung the parrot's cage in the tree, and it chattered happily about the emperor. Titus was thinking about giving the parrot to the captain's wife as a thank-you present for housing them.

The teens were all invited to spend the night in the captain's home, and the captain's daughter, Rebekah, shared her room with Claudia. The teens ran around the property looking at all the beautiful pieces of art and interesting animals. Rebekah was very happy to be home with her little dog. It followed her everywhere she went.

That evening at dinner, Titus began the conversation.

"Captain Riley has an idea for a little trip for us to take. We can be away for five or six days, and that is better than staying here, thinking about our missing loved ones. When we get back, we can begin the watch for them."

Titus looked at the teenagers. Cadogan and Kendrick both were sick with runny noses, so they asked if they could just stay there. Argus knew how sad Felix and Claudia had been, so he answered for the three of them. "That sounds wonderful. A trip on land is just what we need to fill the time until we start watching for Maximus, Flavius, and the others. Where are we going, anyway?"

The captain answered, "We will be traveling to Jerusalem, Bethlehem, and finally Gaza before coming back here. With our horses and wagons and tents, it will be as comfortable as being at home."

"We've heard of Bethlehem," said Felix. "That is where the shepherds saw the star." He looked around at the others. Cadogan looked embarrassed, and Claudia looked ill as they remembered the flower that made her sick in the jungle.

Mary, the captain's wife, smiled and answered, "Yes, my grandparents told me all about the star, and we always talked about it in school. The baby was born in Bethlehem, and that's not far from here."

"Well, we will probably visit some interesting sites

like that," said Riley. "Let me know later this evening how many of your people will be joining us."

With the captain's permission, Titus invited a few other men in their group to go along, but only five of them were interested. Most of the men were content to stay around the captain's place and relax and keep an eye on the lions.

Argus and Felix helped Captain Riley load the wagon with tents, cots, water, and other supplies for their trip. Then they joined the others around a large campfire. They talked and laughed as they shared highlights of their journey so far. Claudia didn't even cry when they talked about the first night out on the ship when they celebrated Flavius's birthday and Claudia hit him in the chin and he bit his tongue. Instead she smiled sweetly, thinking that as soon as next week, she might be with him again. Even in the firelight, Cadogan saw Claudia blush. He frowned and felt even sorrier for himself.

❧

Francis, Maximus, Flavius, and the others got up before daylight, packed up, and headed for the coast. They traveled about a half hour, and once again, a wheel broke on the cart with the lion. Francis threw down his weapon, said a few bad words, and stamped off like he did the night before.

"That is not like Francis at all," said Octavius. "I think his frustration is because of his injuries. Come on. Let's get this lion off of here. We have moved these wheels enough now to be really fast at it."

Maximus and Flavius removed a wheel from the

other cart, while the others moved the lion off the cart and then the broken wheel.

"I have an idea," said Maximus. "We might as well remove the last wheel, since the cart is useless with one wheel anyway. That way we will have an extra if we need it. Let's take the ox along and leave the cart here. We can pay for the cart, and if the owner wants to come back for it later, he can."

A half hour later, Francis came back, and they had the job done and were ready to move out.

"What about you two?" Francis asked Julius and Cyrus.

"We think we are up to walking," said Cyrus. "Just don't go too fast."

"That won't be a problem with this giant animal on board." Flavius laughed.

They handed Francis his pack from the abandoned cart. He just couldn't believe that they did so much so fast. He was very relieved, and he liked the idea about taking the extra wheel and leaving the cart behind.

They traveled a while and came to town and went straight to the oxcart place.

"Get inside quickly," said the oxcart man. He seemed very concerned to see them, so they all did as he said.

"We are trying to make the first ship of the day," said Francis, "so we want to settle with you right away."

"I understand, but please listen to me," said the man. "The Renegades will be in the city very soon. They are planning to take over the midmorning ship that is leaving for Alexandria. They are out of supplies, and they think that if they have their own ship, they can go anyplace and take whatever they need."

"Do you think we have time to board the early ship before they start arriving?" asked Octavius.

"It is possible," said the man.

"Well, we need to settle up with you first. We left a broken-down cart about a half hour's walk from here, when we—," started Francis.

"Please," the man said. "That cart is the least of my worries right now. Come on. I'll go with you and help you get on board. I wish I could go with you, because I don't want to be here if these guys get any more powerful."

They went outside and looked at the ox they had tied to a pole. The man undid that one, too, and they moved through town. The oxcart creaked and rumbled, but they kept going. When they reached the dock, there was no ship in sight.

"I have made a decision," said the oxcart man. "Keep the lion on the cart and just walk it right onto the ship. Take this ox, too. The Renegades have already eaten my other two oxen, and I would rather lose these two than see those men get them. Try to send soldiers back here to help our little city."

"I wish we had some way to hide ourselves as we wait for the ship," said Francis.

The marketplace was just coming alive for the day, so the oxcart man left them and went out to talk to some of the people. Right in front of their eyes, some of the townspeople moved their displays in front of the dock and blocked the view. The boys noticed their ship off in the distance and poked Francis to get him to look at it.

"I won't celebrate until we are safe on board," said Francis.

The oxcart man came back to the dock and said, "Well, it's going to be close. I see the ship coming, but I also saw two Renegades go into that eatery over there."

They all stood there, holding their breath, watching the ship move slowly in their direction. Octavius suggested that they keep their weapons ready, just in case there was trouble. Peeking between a fruit stand and a fish vender, Cyrus saw four men dressed in black walking toward the eatery. One of them glanced in their direction but kept going.

Finally the ship arrived, and as soon as the plank came down, they led that oxcart with the lion onto the ship. The oxcart man came on board with them. "Please raise the plank and take off immediately," he said to a sailor. "We are all in grave danger."

The sailor looked at him blankly and didn't move.

Francis stepped forward and told him to raise the plank now and talk to the ship's captain after they were all safe. This time, the sailor obeyed them and raised the plank. Then he turned and ran off through the ship. The group kept looking anxiously over at the market area, but so far no one was paying any attention to them. Finally the ship's captain arrived.

It was the oxcart man who talked to the captain. "Please, Captain. Our city has been captured by some very bad men who have killed off all of the soldiers who were stationed here and many private citizens as well. Please move your ship away from the dock, and we can discuss this matter safely."

The captain looked at all of those standing there, and then he looked out toward the market area. He turned and walked away, and a few minutes later, the ship moved away from the dock. The group all laughed and hugged each other with relief. The captain came back to talk to them.

"Captain, the evil men in our city are planning to take over the ship that is coming along this morning, heading for Alexandria," said the oxcart man. "Do you have any way to warn them of the danger? I think they are going to kill most of the crew."

"We will move away from the coast and wait for them right here," said the captain of the ship.

"Here is our letter of passage in the way of a payment," said Octavius as he handed the note to the captain.

The captain stared at the letter and finally said, "This passage is for eight men, am I right?"

"Well actually, one of our men died in the jungle," said Octavius. "Perhaps this kind man would like to take his place."

The oxcart man looked very astonished.

"Well, you said you would like to go along," said Octavius, "and we have payment for one more. You have helped us a lot, and we owe you for the broken cart."

"I was planning to swim ashore once they were told about the danger, but I do want to get away from here," said the man. "I think I will accept your offer. Thank you."

"Once we warn the other ship," said the captain, "we will head straight for Gaza." He left them then, and they figured he was going to a place where he could watch for the other ship. The ship made a wide turn, and it was soon facing west and anchored a safe distance from the shore.

The group was given a room to sleep in with hammocks. It reminded them of the first ship they were on, when the teenagers had their own room. Maximus and Flavius jumped in their hammock and took a little nap. They remembered that they had not slept much the night before due to the excitement about going to the others and the anxiety about the bad men in town. They woke up to the sound of the ship's horn. It was blasting very loudly to catch the attention of the other ship. The boys went up on the deck to watch the action.

At first the approaching ship continued its path to the shore. Finally it stopped. The captain on the first ship yelled at them, "Don't go ashore." He yelled that phrase several times. The ship turned and slowly moved toward the awaiting ship. When they were side by side, the two captains of the ships talked for a while. They decided that the first ship, with Francis and the others, would travel east, making a quick stop in Alexandria to spread the word about the takeover of Cyrene. They would continue to their scheduled stop in Gaza. The other ship was going to return to Oea and warn others about the danger.

The other captain thanked them for saving their lives, waved goodbye, and then turned and headed west. As their group headed east, they looked over at the shore and counted twenty-four men dressed in dark colors, and the men looked very angry.

Francis asked his group to go off with him so they could talk. He began, "I never thought things would work out this well. Thank you for making it happen. I was ready to give up back there in the wilderness."

"We figured that you were just burned out or some-thing," said Octavius.

Francis pulled his robe back and revealed a very badly bruised chest and shoulder. "I think this will heal, but the pain has had its effect on me."

"That is definitely where the spear came down on you with the force of a very heavy lion," said Maximus.

"Well, I think I will heal," said Francis. "But let's not worry about that now. Tonight we celebrate, because we are on our way to join the group."

❧

Nolan and Sabrina's gardener followed Nolan's direc-tions and met Nuncio at the arranged time. He asked Nuncio for a huge amount of money in exchange for the exact location of Claudia. Nuncio didn't even blink but told the gardener that he would need two days to get that kind of money together. Just as the gardener turned to go back toward the villa, Nuncio attacked him by hitting him over the head, and then he motioned for his wagon driver, who came quickly. They lifted the gardener into the wagon and took off as Nolan watched helplessly from inside. He didn't know whether to stay out of sight and trust the gardener to take care of him-self or follow the wagon and risk exposing their plan.

Sabrina came into the dark room. "What's going on?" she asked.

Nolan turned to his wife. "I should have known that Nuncio wouldn't pay him any money for the informa-tion," he said. "He put our gardener in a wagon, and they took him away. He's probably going to beat him until he tells him where Claudia is."

"You don't think he will tell him, do you?" asked Sabrina.

"He doesn't know where she is. Hopefully he will tell him our made-up location," answered Nolan. He grabbed a spear and headed for the door.

Sabrina yelled to him, "Whatever you do, don't let Nuncio see you. Hang way back!"

"I promise," Nolan yelled back as he disappeared into the darkness.

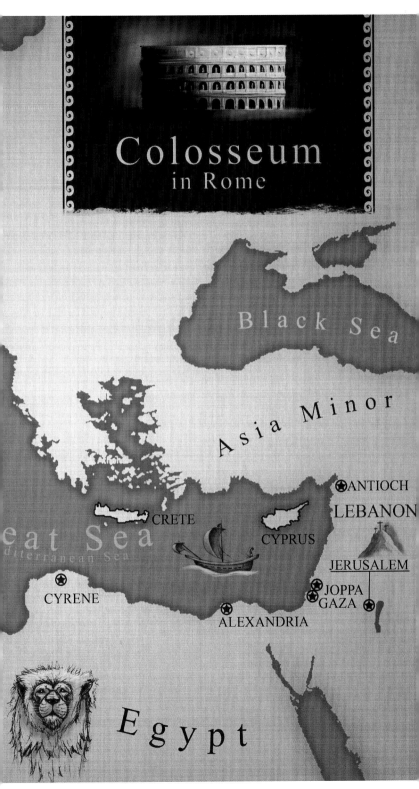

Colosseum
in Rome

Black Sea

Asia Minor

CRETE

CYPRUS

⊕ANTIOCH
LEBANON

⊕JERUSALEM

JOPPA
GAZA ⊕

⊕ CYRENE

⊕ ALEXANDRIA

Great Sea
Mediterranean Sea

Egypt

CHAPTER 14

The captain and his wife assigned all of the travelers a place in a wagon. The horses were hitched to the wagon, and they took off at an incredible speed. Felix was very excited about this trip, but he wished that Maximus could go along, especially to Bethlehem.

Maximus was such a good little brother. Felix knew that all of his life, Maximus looked up to him more than anybody. If Felix was running a race, Maximus was always there to watch, cheering him on. And Maximus valued his opinion above everyone else's. It was a huge responsibility, and Felix never wanted to lead him astray in any way. Hopefully Maximus would be back with them in a few days and Felix would be able to stop feeling so guilty.

As they traveled along, Argus noticed the sober look on Felix's face and asked him what was wrong. Felix told him that since the day that Maximus took off through the jungle without them, his stomach burned and he felt really guilty.

"We shouldn't have let him go," said Felix.

"No," said Argus, "you are wrong this time. Maximus wanted to make the trip. Hopefully it will be good for him. He loves us, but he doesn't always want to be thought of as the helpless little brother. I have a good feeling when I think about Maximus and the rescue mission. I'm proud of him."

Felix rode along for a long time, thinking about what Argus said. *Maybe I have been too protective. Maybe I don't give Maximus enough credit for being able to survive without us there to protect him.* Felix decided not to worry about Maximus. *After all*, he thought, *Maximus depends on God for everything, so why should I worry?*

The captain had directions to the best little marketplace in Jerusalem that sold the tapestries they were interested in. When Mary saw the tapestries displayed around the market stand, she gasped and sat down on a chair. They were the most beautiful pieces of art she had ever seen, and she knew that it would kill her if they had to leave without purchasing some of them.

A few of the tapestries depicted the war between Rome and Jerusalem that had taken place twenty years earlier. There were also two tapestries featuring the star of Bethlehem with shepherds on the hillside. Argus and Felix saw a small tapestry showing the three men on a road, entitled *The Walk to Emmaus*.

"What is this one about?" asked Argus.

"Oh, that particular piece of art is very special to me, because one of the men in the picture is a relative of mine," said the woman working there.

"Did he tell you about it?" asked Felix.

"Yes, he told me the story, and a few years later I designed this tapestry, based on what he told me," she answered.

"Can you tell us the story?" asked Felix.

"Of course I can," said the lady. "Just after the crucifixion, these two men were very sad as they walked to the town of Emmaus. You actually just came through there."

She pointed to the road, and the boys looked that way.

"Anyway, a man joined them and asked why they were so sad," she said. "They were surprised, because they thought everyone in the area had heard about Jesus being crucified on the cross. So they explained to the man that Jesus had been crucified and buried, but now the tomb was empty. Some of the women said they saw a vision of angels who told them that Jesus was alive."

"What did the man say?" asked Argus.

"The man called them foolish for not believing. He explained the Scriptures to them, concerning Jesus, and how the prophets had foretold that he would die on the cross for our sins, be buried, and rise again. The man said they should have expected the tomb to be empty," she said.

"Was that the end?" asked Felix.

"Not quite," explained the lady. "They talked the man into staying with them, since it was getting late. They sat down to have a meal, and the man broke the bread and gave thanks for it, and just as he handed it to them, they recognized him. It was Jesus himself!"

"The one they were talking about?" asked Argus. "Why didn't they recognize him?"

"No one knows," said the lady. "But when they recognized him, he just disappeared."[7]

"Please can you answer a question for me?" asked Felix.

"Yes, I would be glad to," she replied.

"Is this Jesus the baby who was born in Bethlehem, which the shepherds went to see?" Felix asked.

"Yes," answered the lady. "And most of these tapestries depict stories about Jesus."

Argus and Felix bought the tapestry to remember the day and to share the story with Maximus and the family.

They all stared for a long time at a large tapestry with a bunch of men looking over the side of a boat at a man who was walking across the water.

"What is that about?" asked Titus.

The lady selling the tapestries was very happy to tell the story about Jesus walking on the water out to the boat to join the disciples.[8] The piece was very expensive, but Mary had to have it, and the captain was very happy to buy it for her. There was also a tapestry showing a beautiful temple. When they asked the woman about it, she said that she was sorry to tell them that the temple was completely destroyed twenty years ago, along with most of the city. She said that her own mother sketched the drawings of the temple for her.

The group moved on down the street, passing fish markets, flower stands, and trinkets for children. They came to a place that was selling a few wild animals in cages. There was a beautiful baby white tiger. Titus stared at it for quite some time and decided that it was exactly what they needed to replace the parrot as a birthday present for the emperor. He paid the man, rented a small wagon and horse, and left to take it back to the captain's house. He explained that he was happy to go back and begin watching for his son and the others.

Claudia and Rebekah were giggling and walking by the fruit stands. Argus and Felix were alarmed when they noticed a bunch of young men following the girls. They got Captain Riley's attention, so he ran across the road, grabbed each girl by the arm, and escorted them back to the group. Claudia was embarrassed that she was so careless, but Rebekah just laughed and told her father that the young men were harmless.

Argus said, "Claudia, remember, you are supposed to stay close to us."

"I know, but it was really fun being a carefree girl for a while," she answered.

The three of them crossed the road and looked through many scrolls that were arranged in a large basket.

"Can I help you?" asked the man who was selling the scrolls.

"Well, we were hoping to get a copy of scripture," said Felix. "Do you have any?"

The man began pulling out scroll after scroll, trying to find the one he was looking for. "I have a copy of Matthew's letter and several of Mark's letters, but I seem to be out of Luke's letters."

"What's the difference?" asked Felix.

"Well, they all agree about the life of Christ. It's just that they are told by different people," said the man.

The teens asked about the price of Matthew's letter, because it was longer, and Felix didn't quite have enough money, but the man sold it to him anyway, saying it was close enough.

Captain Riley and his wife, Mary, came over and

showed the kids the beautiful tapestries that they bought, and then they looked at the tapestry and the letter that Felix purchased. Riley asked a man at a little stand what they should see on their way to Gaza.

"As you can see, our city is still under construction and it will be for a long time. I suggest that you visit Bethany and Bethlehem. The landscape is beautiful, and there are people there who can show you where Jesus brought Lazarus back to life and where Jesus was born," said the sales man.

When the travelers visited Bethany, Riley purchased beautiful pieces of jewelry for Mary from a local merchant. They heard the story about Jesus visiting his friends Mary, Martha, and Lazarus in Bethany and how he brought Lazarus back to life.[9] Then they went to Bethlehem and purchased beautiful pieces of pottery. The people there were more than happy to tell the story about Jesus's birth and the shepherds and the angels. The story was even more special when they heard it in the land that it happened.

Argus, Felix, and Claudia wanted to leave Bethlehem and return to Joppa and begin the watch for Maximus and Flavius, but Riley and Mary had other ideas. They were planning a visit to Gaza on the Great Sea, down the coast from Joppa.

☙❧

The gardener was inside with a rope tied around his arms and legs. Nuncio questioned him repeatedly about the whereabouts of Claudia. Nolan couldn't hear their conversation very well, but he could tell that Nuncio was very angry. After hours of questioning, Nuncio let the gardener go. Nolan hid in the bushes and quietly watched his gardener leave the area. He waited there a long time, just in case Nuncio was watching. Finally he slipped out and ran home. When he reached his villa, the gardener was waiting in the shadows, shaking from head to toe.

"Oh, Nolan," said the gardener. "I'm afraid our plan has failed."

"I am so sorry we put you in danger," said Nolan. "Did he hurt you?"

"Just my wrists, where the ropes were too tight," said the gardener. "I told him our story about how I overheard the cooks talking and that they said that Claudia was not caring for a sick aunt at all, but that she was actually lying on the beaches in Marseille trying to catch a rich, young merchant as a husband."

"Oh, I guess he didn't believe it," said Nolan.

"No," said the gardener. "He believed the story, and it made him very angry."

"Then how did our plan fail?" asked Nolan.

"Well, he's not going to give me any money, and he said if I tell anyone about this, he will kill me. And you know what? I think he will," said the gardener.

"How much money did you ask him for?" asked Nolan.

"Fifty thousand denary," answered the gardener. "That was the amount I needed to buy a bunch of plants and start a nursery on the other side of Rome."

"Are you planning to just come back to work for me, like nothing happened?" asked Nolan.

"No, because Nuncio told me to go far away and just disappear. He said that he will kill me if he ever sees me again," said the gardener.

"I can give you ten thousand denary," said Nolan. "Can you do anything with that?"

"I'll make it work," said the gardener. "You have been very good to me. I'm going to miss you and this beautiful villa."

"It's beautiful because you made it beautiful," said Nolan. They went inside together, and Nolan gave him the money. The gardener ran away, and Nolan figured he would never see him again.

CHAPTER 15

Early in the morning when the group was getting ready to leave for Gaza, Riley approached Argus and Felix.

"I believe you might be interested in these," he said. "Mary and I did a little shopping in Bethlehem while you young people were listening to the storyteller."

Felix looked at them and said, "Wow! The book of Luke and the book of John. How can we ever pay you for these?"

"That's not necessary. I have other good news for you, too," said Captain Riley. "We are still going to Gaza, but we looked at the map, and it is easier to travel south over land and then take a ship back to Joppa."

"Come over here, girls," said Mary to Rebekah and Claudia. "Look what I bought for us." She pulled out three beautiful robes and gave one to Rebekah and one to Claudia. "I can't wait to try them on."

Argus was very thoughtful, because in the night he had a dream, and it was very strange. In the dream, he was in an old chariot. There was a man sitting next to him with very dark skin, like the people from Africa, and he was reading from a scroll. The man was very frustrated, and Argus had tossed and turned and woke up very early.

The group sat around visiting as they ate their breakfast. Argus told about the dream he had in the night, and he was very unsettled because of the frustration of the man in the dream. They took down their camp and traveled on the desert road to Gaza. The captain and his wife sat together in the wagon, admiring some of the pottery they purchased in Bethlehem. Most of the pieces they pulled out had paintings of the birth of Jesus with a baby in a manger or shepherds on a hillside. But they pulled the wrapping off a bowl with a painting that confused them. There were many horses and men tearing little children away from their mothers. As they looked around the bowl, they saw people crying and soldiers killing the little children.

"How horrible," said Mary. "What do you think these paintings are about?"

Claudia was sitting a ways off in the wagon, and as she looked at the paintings on the pottery, she could see the terror on the faces of the parents as the little ones were ripped from their arms. She threw her hand to the side of her face as she remembered the plant that had poisoned her.

"I know about that," she said. "King Herod had all of the boys two years old and under killed because he was determined to kill the baby Jesus."[10]

"Oh, yes. I heard about that when I was a girl. How could I forget?" said Mary.

They traveled all day and finally stopped and listened as some people told a story.

"Many years ago, it was at this very spot that Philip,

one of Jesus's disciples, was traveling down this road and an angel of the Lord spoke to him."

"What did the angel say?" asked the captain.

"Well, the angel told Philip to go on this road, and when he did, he came across an Ethiopian eunuch," the woman explained. "The man was a very important person in charge of all the treasury of Candace, the queen of all the people of Ethiopia. The Ethiopian man was sitting in a chariot, reading scripture from the book of Isaiah the prophet. He was very frustrated because he had no idea what the prophet was talking about. The Holy Spirit told Philip to go up to the chariot. Philip did, and he asked the Ethiopian if he understood what he was reading, and the man answered that he needed someone to explain it to him. So he invited Philip to come up into the chariot and join him. Philip told the man all the good news about Jesus."

"When they came to this spot," said the man in the family, "the Ethiopian noticed this water and asked him why he shouldn't be baptized. So they went down into the water together, and Philip baptized him. And when they came up out of the water, the Spirit of the Lord took Philip away, and the Ethiopian eunuch did not see him again. The Ethiopian went on his way rejoicing, and Philip showed up in another area where he preached the Gospel."[11]

Then they went to their camp to sleep for the night. Mary, Rebekah, and Claudia tried on their new robes, and they looked lovely. Rebekah twirled around in front of Argus and Felix, but they were busy reading one of the scrolls that Captain Riley had given them.

Rebekah put her hands on her hips and said, "Aren't you guys interested in anything but reading?" The boys looked up to see Rebekah and Claudia in their new robes, so they stood up and told them that they looked very pretty. The boys tried to visit with the girls for a while, but they really didn't have much to say. They made up an excuse to go get ready for bed.

"You don't think Claudia is turning into a silly girl who needs a lot of compliments, do you?" asked Felix.

"No," answered Argus. "She's just going along with Rebekah. What do you think of Rebekah? Do you like her?"

"She's all right, I guess," said Felix, "but I am planning to marry Miranda someday."

"Miranda from back in Rome?" asked Argus. "I always thought that she was just a friend."

"She's a very good friend," said Felix. "When we are together, I am never lonely. She can talk about any subject. Even though lots of boys like her, I know she likes me more than any of them."

"Does she know where you are now?" asked Argus.

"Well, I sent a message to her the night we left that I would be gone for the rest of the summer but that I would be thinking about her," said Felix. "I hope that is good enough. Of course, I know some rich man like Nuncio could take an interest in her, and she might not have a choice."

"I think Rebekah would be very sad to know about all of that," said Argus.

"Oh, I don't know," said Felix. "I think you are the one she is really interested in."

"Does it really matter?" asked Argus. "Besides, I'm just not sure she's right for me."

"Well, do you think it's safe to go back?" asked Felix. "I just can't take all of that flirting."

"Let's stay here a little longer and make sure the girls have gone to bed," said Argus. "I'm not up to it, either." So the boys sat beside the small lake where the Ethiopian eunuch was baptized years ago.

"There is something special about this area we've been visiting," said Felix. "I heard someone call it the Holy Land."

"I have felt it, too," said Argus. "Remember that I told you that I had a dream last night? I dreamed about something that we hadn't even heard about yet. It was the Ethiopian eunuch. He had the darkest skin I have ever seen, and he was so frustrated trying to figure out what he was reading. I tossed and turned all night because of that dream."

"You dreamed about it before you ever even heard about it, right?" asked Felix.

"Yes," answered Argus, "and it was so real. As I was listening to the story, I knew he was going to tell about Philip climbing up in the chariot and explaining the Scripture before they even told that part. The word of God is very real to us, don't you think?"

"Yes, and I hope we can remember everything to tell Maximus," said Felix.

❧

Nolan had to go to work at the Coliseum very early, after being up most of the night with the gardener. The emperor was very agitated because his advisors told him that his horoscope looked very bad for the day and he should be very careful not to trust anyone. When the emperor saw Nolan with his red eyes, puffy face, and bad hair, he was certain that he was up to no good.

To make matters worse, a ship loaded with sixty-two angry, crazed elephants was stuck on the shore. It seemed that so many workers and slaves were killed just getting them from Carthage to the dock near Rome that they didn't have the manpower or the know-how to get them across the land to the Coliseum. Nolan knew that it would not be smart to tell the emperor about the problem, so he excused himself and went searching for supplies and people to help him solve the elephant dilemma. His best men, unfortunately, were away filling other hunting assignments. He had to put together an inexperienced team and somehow pull off a miracle. The thought struck Nolan that there could be something to the emperor's dire horoscope, but he realized that his lack of sleep was clouding his judgment.

Nolan spent hours calling in men and interviewing them about how they would solve the problem of getting the elephants to the Coliseum. If they had any clever or original ideas, he put them on the team. He told them to eat a hearty meal, gather any supplies they thought might be useful, and meet him at the seventh hour at gate 35 on the west side of the Coliseum. Nolan ran home to tell Sabrina about his plans and found Lavinia and the twins there.

"Look, Nolan," said Sabrina. "The babies are walking all over the place."

"Good for them," said Nolan. "I'm going to have to go over to the coast this afternoon and somehow transport sixty-two mean elephants to the Coliseum."

"But you look terrible," said Sabrina.

"I could really use a nap. Could you wake me up in an hour and have some food ready for me?" asked Nolan.

"No problem," said Sabrina. Nolan went off and had a good sleep while Sabrina and Lavinia prepared a feast and set it on the table outside. Nolan cleaned up after his nap and joined them.

"Well, you look a hundred times better," said Lavinia.

"Thanks," said Nolan. "I'm afraid I about gave the emperor a heart attack today when he saw me."

Nolan had a quick meal with the ladies, kissed Sabrina goodbye, and hurried back to meet his travel team. The young men that he chose to go along were very excited and looking forward to the challenge of moving the animals. They traveled in a wagon led by four horses, so they reached the coast in record time.

CHAPTER 16

Early the next morning, Captain Riley, Mary, and the entire group loaded into the wagon and headed down the road toward Gaza. Felix and Claudia thought that Maximus and Flavius and the group could arrive in Joppa any day now, so they wanted to skip Gaza and head straight back to the captain's house. Mary had other ideas. She heard that they could purchase a beautiful flower that grew on a vine and an archway to display the flowers on. Mary planned to buy both items and have them installed as soon as they got home.

Rebekah chattered happily about jewelry and perfume and knick-knacks and all kinds of things that Claudia didn't want or need. She tried to act interested, but she kept thinking about Flavius and wondering if he was approaching Joppa. She was worried that the little group would arrive there and not even know that they were in the area. Argus and Felix managed to sit on the other side of the wagon so they could talk to each other and not have to listen as Rebekah and Mary planned their purchases. The boys were tired of traveling and were eager to talk to Maximus.

They arrived in Gaza in no time at all, and the entire group happily walked around the marketplace. Mary immediately found three items that she just had to have. The flowering vines and the archway were as beautiful as they expected, and they purchased those first. Then they saw a pond to put in the ground, made out of burlap lined with clay. There was a waterfall that could be attached to the pond. During parties, a servant could sit behind a shrub and pump the water, making it flow over a bunch of rocks into the pond, just like a natural waterfall. Mary also found a large fertility god to put in the garden.

Felix was about to object, but Argus elbowed him. Rebekah spoke up and said, "Mother, how can you buy a false god like that after hearing all those stories about the one true God who gave his only Son for us?"

"Oh, well, dear, I thought we could use a little help. Your father and I haven't been able to have another baby since you were born. Your brothers are gone all the time now, out on one ship or another. I just thought the fertility god could help us with that," said Mary.

"Well, why don't you ask God and his son Jesus for another baby?" asked Rebekah. "If you are supposed to have one, you will. But don't waste your time asking some statue."

Argus had a new respect for Rebekah for the way she spoke up to her mother about the idol. Mary must have been convinced, because she and the captain purchased the other items and left the fertility god standing in the marketplace. Argus, Felix, and Claudia were in very good spirits, thinking that soon they would hop on a ship and sail up the coast to Joppa, join the others in their party, and wait for Maximus, Flavius, and the others to arrive from Africa. As they walked, the teens skipped and twirled and sang silly songs. Rebekah's long, curly brown hair flew through the air, and Argus had to admit to himself that there was more to that girl than he first thought.

The group traveled and stopped at an eatery that featured very rich and fancy meals. The travelers walked through the line, piling their plates high with all kinds of food, and then found a seat at the outdoor picnic area to eat. Argus, Felix, and Claudia were raised on simple food such as fruits, vegetables, bread, and meat, so they ate very lightly. After the meal, they stopped and watched a bunch of young people running races.

Felix watched the event and wished he could be running races. He promised himself that when he got home, he would start training again. He looked over at the captain and his wife, and they did not seem to be enjoying the races.

Argus nudged Felix. "Look at Rebekah. She looks miserable." Suddenly, Rebekah started vomiting. Before long, it was obvious that most of their travel party was sick, and they were thinking that it was probably food poisoning. Argus and Felix had to help most of them into the wagon, and the boys drove the wagon while Claudia tried to comfort and care for everyone. The boys set up a camp area just outside of town.

Argus, Felix, and Claudia sneaked away from the group and sat on a hillside near their wagons, watching the sun set over the Great Sea.

"Just think," said Argus. "Maximus and the group

could be out there in a ship somewhere, heading this way."

"If we all get back together again," said Felix, "let's not separate for any reason until we get home."

"We promised Father and Mother that we would look after each other," said Claudia. "I imagine they are resting right now, sipping a cool drink, confident that we are together."

The elephants sensed that something was going on, and they began to pace back and forth and make trumpeting sounds. The men moved the woodpile, creating an opening wide enough for an elephant to exit. The first three elephants to notice the opening charged up the ramp and headed for the walkway to exit the ship. Some of the men closed the opening while others followed close behind, trying to think of a way to get the rope around the mammoth legs. The three elephants charged out on the dock and ran in circles looking for the opening so they could escape.

Nolan was about to shout for someone to block the exit when he saw a familiar form heading into the ship. It was the evil Nuncio. Nolan gasped, put his hand to his mouth, and watched as the elephants found the opening and trampled the man down. Some of Nolan's men chased the elephants, but Nolan knelt down beside the injured man.

"What were you doing here?" asked Nolan.

"I was going to board this ship to Marseille to find your daughter," said Nuncio. "I would have been good to her." The man died in Nolan's arms. Nolan just sat there, stunned. A part of him wanted to jump up and dance in celebration, but he actually felt sorry for the man. All of his money and fancy clothes never bought him happiness. Nolan looked across the dock and saw Nuncio's two lawyers in a wagon. They turned and went away.

"Did you know that rich man?" asked one of Nolan's team members.

"I did," said Nolan. "Get those elephants under control. We don't want anyone else to die."

CHAPTER 17

After a short trip into the woods and a drink of water, the captain, Mary, Rebekah, and most of the travelers went back to sleep. Argus, Felix, and Claudia decided to walk into Gaza and look around. They passed the marketplaces where they had shopped yesterday, and they passed the eatery where their friends got sick. They certainly didn't want to stop there. They walked through town and finally came to the seaside. There were many ships docked there as well as some quaint little shops nearby. A place serving fish smelled so good that they had to investigate it.

"I have some money," said Felix. "Titus gave it to me before he left with the baby white tiger. I hid it away and forgot all about it until today. He told me to share it with you two for helping me look after the lions on the ship. Anyway, let's eat."

The three of them walked up to the little fish stand on the dock. They each got an order of fish, freshly baked bread, and fruit. They went out to the tables on the dock and ate and ate until they were full. Then they had fun feeding the sea gulls that kept squawking at them. Soon they could toss pieces of fish or bread up high, and the gulls caught them in the air. They had so much fun that they lost track of time.

Finally Argus said, "I suppose we should get back to the group now, but I seriously doubt if they will be up to traveling back to Joppa today. I'll bet we will be stuck in Gaza all day."

"Oh, no," said Claudia. "Maximus and Flavius and the others might arrive there today, and they won't know that we are staying at the captain's house, or even know that we are still in the area."

"I'm sure Titus will be checking every ship that arrives," said Felix. "We don't need to worry."

"I guess you're right," said Claudia. The three of them were out of food to feed the seagulls, but they sat there, staring out on the water, not wanting to return to all of their sick friends. A bunch of teenage boys went speeding by on a small sailboat. A father was chasing his two little boys along the beach.

As the three of them watched, a large ship approached the dock. "Let's go over and watch them unload," suggested Argus. They watched as all kinds of people walked down the ramp.

"Oh, my," shouted Claudia. "It's Flavius! I see his red hair."

"You're right," said Felix. "I see Maximus, too."

They started running toward them, shouting their names. When the boys saw Claudia, Argus, and Felix, they ran and grabbed them.

Flavius put his arm around Claudia and told her that he hoped they would never be apart again. Argus and Felix walked arm in arm with their little brother in the middle.

"You look great," said Argus. "What did you do to yourself?"

"I guess it was just all of that good food and exercise and moving that gigantic lion," said Maximus. They took time to help Francis, Julius, Octavius, Benedict, and Cyrus unload their colossal lion and all of their gear.

"What are you doing here in Gaza?" asked Maximus. "I didn't think we would see you until we arrived in Joppa."

"We have been traveling around the area with the captain of our ship and his family," said Felix. "We can't wait to tell you all we've learned."

They decided to park the lion and gear near the dock and take turns guarding them. Francis and the other men waited there and had a meal, while the teenagers went to the campsite to see how Captain Riley and the others were recovering. When they arrived, Rebekah was angry that they were gone so long and that they didn't even tell her where they were going. They introduced Captain Riley to Maximus and Flavius and told him that the rest of the group had to wait near the dock because of the weight of the lion. The captain pulled a schedule out of his pack and discovered that a ship to Joppa was arriving in the morning.

"Do you suppose that we could take Maximus and Flavius back on this road to the place where they told us the story about Philip?" asked Felix. Captain Riley and Mary were still very weak and were glad for an excuse to stay right where they were. They thought it would be fine for the young people to travel back on the road, but they sent some of their travel party along for protection, and they sent someone to the dock to tell Francis that they would all be arriving early in the morning to travel with them up the coast to Joppa. Rebekah was not up to traveling yet, and she was very disappointed.

As they walked along the road, Maximus asked, "What's wrong with that girl? Why did she cry just because she is still too weak to travel with us?"

"We have become very close to Rebekah," said Claudia. "We were together on the ship all the way from Cyrene, and then we have been together ever since. And I think she kind of likes Argus."

They ran and skipped and laughed all the way to the historical place on the Gaza road. The people were very happy to come out and greet them and tell them the story of the Ethiopian eunuch who could not understand the Scripture he was reading, and how Philip baptized the Ethiopian, and then the Spirit took Philip away.

Maximus looked down at the water. "Why shouldn't we be baptized? I really want to be baptized." The teens all looked at one another for a moment.

Finally one of the people who told the story smiled and said that he would be very happy to baptize him and that, if he wouldn't mind, he would like to go and get a few of his friends.

After he left, Felix turned to the others. "I think I would like to be baptized, too," he said.

The others spoke at the same time, saying they wanted to join him. On their rescue mission, Maximus had told Flavius so much about God and his Son that he believed and wanted to be baptized too.

The man returned to baptize them, and along with him came about twenty-five people who lived nearby. They were all laughing and praising God. The teens went down into the water together, along with the man who told the story. They let Maximus go first. The man turned to him and asked him to repeat the confession after him, "I believe that Jesus is the Christ, the Son of the Living God, and I accept him as my personal savior." Maximus repeated it, and then the man said, "I now baptize you in the name of the Father, and of the Son, and of the Holy Spirit, for the remission of sins and the gift of the Holy Spirit." He lowered Maximus under the water and then lifted him back up. Everyone watching them cheered and clapped. Then he baptized Argus, then Felix, then Claudia, and finally Flavius.

As they came out of the water, the people threw towels around them to dry them off. They all sat down near the water's edge and the people sang hymn after hymn for nearly an hour. It was the most beautiful music they ever heard, and Felix remarked about it.

"Don't you have a church near you?" asked one of the women. "Where do you live?"

"We live in Rome, and I am sure there is no church around," said Maximus. "I would have found it."

"I believe you are wrong," said one of the men. "The church in Rome is healthy and active. But they are under a great deal of persecution from the emperor and many others, so if you are associated with the emperor in any way, you would not know about it. We can give you a name to contact, but you must be very quiet about it. We wouldn't want people to lose their lives because we gave you their name."

"We will keep it hidden away," promised Maximus.

"And we will go see them when we get back in Rome. I want to have what you people have."

The teens hugged their new friends and said their farewells. They sang one of the hymns all the way back to the campsite. It went, "Oh, how blessed I am, that he would die for me; that I may one day go to him, and live eternally." As they approached their travel group, they all came out of their tents to welcome them. Captain Riley, Mary, Rebekah, and the others were feeling much better.

❦

Nolan was away on the elephant mission for three days. He and the men were more exhausted than they had ever been in their lives. It took them a whole day to get the elephants moved out of the cargo hold of the ship, rinsed off with sea water, and fed and watered. It took even longer for them to gain the confidence of the animals and get them under control. They decided to head toward Rome in the morning, because it could take an entire day to move them.

CHAPTER 18

The captain and the group of travelers arrived at the dock early. Everyone had to help load all of Mary's purchases onto the ship. Those things required as much effort as loading the gigantic lion, but eventually the group was heading north to Joppa.

The teenagers sat out on the deck of the ship, chatting happily. "I can't wait to see my father," said Flavius. "He must be so worried about me."

"We tried not to worry," said Felix. "We had to believe that you would be all right."

"Well, we did miss you," said Claudia.

Flavius and Maximus spent some time telling them all about rescuing the three injured men and how Benedict and Octavius came along and helped them just as they were getting discouraged. Then they told about their exciting escape from the city and their attempts to spread the word about the takeover. Argus, Felix, and Claudia shivered as they realized how close the boys came to leaving on the later ship—the one that the bad men were planning to take over and kill everyone on board.

"Maximus, was that the most scared you ever were?" asked Claudia.

"Yes, but it could have been worse," Maximus said. "The oxcart man had some of the people move their market stands right in front of the dock, blocking their view. If those men would have seen us waiting to get on the ship, they would have attacked us."

"Listen. We are safe now. Let's talk about something happier," said Flavius.

"I just remembered watching you two and Francis and Vernon walking off into the jungle and feeling so helpless. You know, I don't remember seeing Vernon get off the ship yesterday," said Felix.

"I was really hoping we could talk about something happier," said Flavius.

"They have to know sometime," said Maximus. "Vernon was attacked by a snake in the jungle and died almost immediately. He didn't suffer much."

Everyone was silent for a while. Finally Flavius said, "We searched everywhere for his pack, and we never found it."

"That's because he didn't take it with him," said Felix. "Remember. Your father was going to go with you on the rescue mission, and everyone reminded him that he needed to stay with the big group, so Vernon volunteered to take his place at the last minute. He literally turned and walked away with you guys. He didn't take anything with him but his weapon. I saw his pack and kept it with us down with the lions."

"Do you still have it?" asked Maximus and Flavius together.

"I left it at Captain Riley's place," said Felix. "I'm sure it's fine. Why?"

Maximus and Flavius were silent and looked around at their group. No one was near their little circle of teens. Finally Maximus asked Felix, "Did you ever look in his pack?"

"No. I just kept it for him," said Felix.

"When Vernon was dying, we thought he said something about giving his pack to his sister. He said there was a treasure in it," said Maximus.

"How will we find out who his sister is?" asked Felix.

"Let's not tell anyone about the treasure," suggested Maximus. "But when we tell the group about how Vernon died, we can ask if anyone knows how to get in touch with his family. Probably some of the soldiers will know."

"You know," said Flavius, "I'm really surprised that old Cadogan isn't hanging around. He usually stays pretty close to Claudia."

"Cadogan and Kendrick were sick, so they didn't join us on our little trip," said Claudia.

"So he didn't steal you away from me?" asked Flavius. He smiled at Claudia.

"No, he did not," she said.

Rebekah was very quiet during all of the discussion, and Argus noticed. "You're looking sad, Rebekah. Is something wrong?" he asked.

Rebekah didn't want to tell them that she felt left out now that Claudia was focused on Flavius and Argus and Felix were hovering around Maximus. "Oh, that was just so sad about that man Vernon," she said.

"You know," said Argus, "we haven't heard much

from you, and Flavius wanted to talk about something happy now. Tell us the best thing that ever happened to you."

Rebekah smiled and thought for a moment. Then she said, "I guess last year when I got my little dog was the happiest I've ever been. It was really hard to leave her to go to Rome to see my grandparents."

Felix answered, "I believe that. I always wanted a pet."

"Oh, I wouldn't want to be your pet," said Claudia. "You would tease it to death."

"Not if I had you around to torment," Felix answered.

"Flavius, what was the best thing that ever happened in your life?" asked Claudia.

"When I was about ten years old, my mother had a baby. She was a little girl with hair as red as mine and big blue eyes. She loved me more than anything," said Flavius. "She died of a fever. My father never talks about her. I think it's too painful."

"I'm so sorry," said Claudia.

"Well, that's why I hope to have lots of children," said Flavius. "Do you want a big family, Claudia?"

"Yes, that's what I want to do. I want to raise a big family and have them as close as we are," she answered.

"That's what I want, too," said Rebekah. "I've been like an only child with my brothers and my dad out on a ship all the time."

The group arrived in Joppa in the evening, and Titus was waiting for them at the dock. He grabbed Flavius and held him tightly. "If anything would have happened to you, I don't know what I would have done."

"I know, Father," said Flavius. "I'm fine."

"Well, I think we've been gone long enough. Let's get these lions and tigers and head for Rome," said Titus.

That evening, Titus and Riley looked over the ship schedules very carefully.

"I have to be honest with you," said Captain Riley. "Travel on the Great Sea is not recommended this late in September. You would be welcome to stay here and wait until spring. Mary would be thrilled to have the company. We have many rooms for many people."

"Well, you are going out, aren't you?" asked Titus.

"Yes, it is my job. But I always find a safe harbor, sometimes for many months," answered Riley. "I have a perfect record so far."

"When are you leaving and how far are you going?" asked Titus.

"I am leaving tomorrow," said Riley, "and I am traveling up the coast to Lebanon and then to Antioch, and then I will sail west, going north of the islands of Cyprus and Crete. Weather permitting, we will arrive in Syracuse on the island of Sicily in two or three weeks. Then we hope to head up to Rome."

"That sounds perfect," said Titus. "Do you have room for all of us and twenty lions?"

"Yes, I believe I do," said the captain. "If the weather is cooperating, we will make it to Rome, and I will stay with my parents over the winter."

"Then we will hope for good weather. I'm afraid that we don't have much choice," said Titus. "If we don't get those lions to the Coliseum before the big birthday celebration, people will lose their lives."

The captain's family entertained Titus and the teenagers with a wonderful farewell dinner. Titus presented Mary with the parrot and told her to teach it some new sayings. Rebekah cried through the entire meal, knowing they would all leave the next day. That night she went to her mother.

"Mother, I know this is the last thing you want to hear right now, but I want to go with Father and the others on the trip to Rome. I can't bear to stay here all year while my new friends go off without me," Rebekah said.

"Your father will never let you go," said Mary. "Travel on the sea this time of year can be very tricky. He's had some close calls."

"I could stow away," said Rebekah.

"Please, darling. You are all I have," said Mary. "All of these tapestries and flowers and beautiful things have no meaning at all if I don't have you to enjoy them with me."

"Mother, eventually I will get married," said Rebekah. "Then what will you do?"

"I will probably go to see you every day," said Mary. "I promise you this. We will talk your father into taking us to Rome next summer, just like every other year. And we will go and stay with your friends for a long visit. How does that sound?"

"It sounds like an eternity to wait," said Rebekah.

"I will keep you busy. You will learn all kinds of skills to make you into a wonderful wife someday," said Mary. "Besides, how could you go away and leave your precious little fluff ball?"

Rebekah picked up her little dog and buried her face in its fur. She couldn't help but cry. "I just feel like my heart is breaking."

The parade of sixty-two elephants going through the countryside was quite a sight. The elephants were probably happy just to be on dry land. The men were concerned about taking them through the city, but they marched along without any trouble and entered the large holding area on the ground floor of the Coliseum.

Nolan told the emperor that the elephants were settled and waiting for the big celebration. Nolan looked even worse than the last time the emperor saw him, and he had a foul odor that smelled like a combination of wet elephant and dung pile, and that made the emperor draw away in disgust. Nolan's nose was running and he was sneezing. Nolan wondered if the emperor would look down on him for his raggedy appearance and somehow connect it with his own impending bad fortune related to the latest horoscope. Nolan excused himself and hurried home.

Normally Sabrina did not worry about Nolan when he was away, but this time she was a nervous wreck, thinking about him with the wild elephants. When he entered their villa, she put her hand over her heart.

"I'm fine, Sabrina, but I need to clean up, eat a little something, and get hours and hours of sleep. But first, sit down, because I have big news for you," Nolan said.

"I don't think I can take much," said Sabrina.

"You can take this news. Nuncio is dead, and Claudia can come home and be free. I would give you a big hug, but let me clean up first," said Nolan. Sabrina sat right there, speechless, until he returned. After he was clean,

Nolan told Sabrina about the three elephants trampling Nuncio to death.

"You don't look as relieved as I thought you would," said Nolan.

"That's because you said the two lawyers were there to witness it. I'm just afraid that you will be blamed. You did have a reason to want him dead," said Sabrina.

"Nuncio's lawyer friends didn't even come over and say 'good-bye' to him or have him buried. I had to pay to have his body moved back to Rome," said Nolan.

"They might cause us trouble just the same," said Sabrina.

"Well, I'm not going to let it get me down," said Nolan. "Nuncio is dead, and our little girl doesn't have to marry a middle-aged man."

CHAPTER 19

Titus, Francis, and all the men led the way through Joppa to the dock. Moving the entire hunting group and all of the lions made an impressive parade through town. It took several hours to get everything loaded onto wagons, moved through town, and then unloaded onto the ship. Rebekah and Mary were there to see them off, and Rebekah cried so much that her face was red and blotchy.

"Argus, aren't you going to give Rebekah a hug and say something nice to her?" asked Claudia. "The rest of us said our goodbyes, even Maximus, and he barely knows her."

"Just give me a minute. I'm thinking about it," Argus said. Then he walked down the ship's walkway and stood in front of her, talking for several minutes. He looked back at his brothers and sister, and they didn't think he was going to do anything. He wrote down her address and promised to write. Then he gave her a quick hug and walked away. Rebekah smiled, and then she started crying again as he got back on the ship. Her mother put her arms around her, and they waved as the ship pulled away.

"That wasn't much of a hug," said Claudia as she waved.

"I may never see her again, and I think it's best to keep things simple," said Argus. "Besides, Rebekah lives right here in the Holy Land, and she never even told us about Jesus."

"Good point," said Felix. "I have something interesting to tell you all. I picked up Vernon's pack when we were moving our stuff to the wagons. It's below with our things and the lion supplies."

"Do you mind if we wait until Flavius is with us before we look in the pack?" asked Maximus. "Where is he, by the way?"

"He's spending some time with his father," said Claudia. "I think he's telling him about his baptism."

"I wonder what Father will think about our baptism," said Maximus. "I'm just a little worried that it will put him in danger with the emperor."

"How could he be in any more danger?" asked Felix. "The emperor could take his life at any time."

Just then Cadogan and Kendrick walked up to the four siblings, and they stopped talking. They were all thinking the same thing: that they did not want the boys to know about the treasure in Vernon's pack, and the boys weren't even sure they could trust them with the fact that they were Christians now.

Cadogan was happy to see that Flavius wasn't around Claudia, because yesterday he was not at all happy when they arrived together.

"How was your shopping trip?" Cadogan asked Claudia.

"Good," said Claudia. "It took our minds off Maximus and Flavius for a while and gave us some other things to think about."

"Like what?" asked Cadogan.

Claudia was about to answer him, but she saw Argus shake his head and give her a look that told her not to say anything. She was very puzzled, but she only said that they had fun watching Mary spend all of the captain's money.

The rest of that day, the two brothers followed them everywhere they went on the ship. Captain Riley told them that for the next two days, they could go wherever they wanted because the crew on his ship was the best. They thought Cadogan and Kendrick would get tired of chasing after them, but they stuck like glue. Titus informed them that they did not need to keep an eye on the lions anymore, because his men did the job quite well while they were traveling around the countryside with the captain and his family. That was not great news, because now they had no time to themselves, and they had no way to earn any more money.

That evening, Felix talked to Cadogan. "Did you have a good time at the captain's house?"

"Your group hadn't been gone an hour when we regretted staying behind," said Cadogan.

"Why?" asked Felix.

"At first we were bored out of our minds," said Cadogan. "Then the older men started giving us jobs to do, such as carrying disgusting lion meat, splashing out the dirty cages, and even cleaning up the dining area after we ate our meals."

"Were the men working, too, or were they just ordering you two around?" asked Felix.

"I guess they were working, too," said Cadogan. "All that work just made us wish we would have gone with you."

"It looks like you guys got over your runny noses," said Felix.

"Yes, we weren't that sick," said Cadogan. "We should have gone with you. What did you all do?"

Felix was quiet a few minutes, and Cadogan thought he fell asleep. Felix was trying to decide whether to tell him about becoming a Christian. After all, how can Cadogan become a Christian if no one shares it with him? *What's gotten into me keeping that a secret?* thought Felix. *It's not like he's going to go run and tell the emperor. He's terrified of the emperor.*

"Actually, we have a lot to tell you about our trip. We will probably begin by reading you some of the letters we bought," said Felix. "But it's kind of late tonight. Do you want to wait until tomorrow?"

"I am getting sleepy," said Cadogan. "I just wanted to ask you if Claudia ever mentioned me on your trip. Do you think she missed me at all?"

"I think you need to face the fact that she is in love with Flavius, and he loves her, too," said Felix. Cadogan did not say anything else, but Felix felt very sorry for him and wondered if he did the right thing, just killing all of his hopes like that.

❧

Nolan got up early and went to the Coliseum, which was bursting with animals in almost every lower room and even some of the second-floor rooms. He went around the place, making sure the animals looked healthy and that someone was responsible for each of them. Many more ships were scheduled to arrive with giraffes, gorillas, monkeys, ostriches, hippos, tigers, and many others. He was thinking that Titus and the group should be arriving soon with the lions. He couldn't wait to see his children and to tell them that Claudia no longer had to worry about Nuncio.

Nolan went to the emperor's room to give him a report on the elephants, and he was greeted with an icy reception. Nolan bowed briefly and asked, "Is there a problem, Your Excellence?"

"My advisors told me that, according to my horoscope, I will be betrayed by someone that I work very closely with, and that the person would have red eyes and wild hair," said the Emperor. "That is what you looked like the other day."

"I had gone without sleep for many hours, Your Excellence," said Nolan. "And I was getting sick."

"Well, I also heard that Nuncio was trampled by elephants and that you were there at the time. I remember that you had something against the man," said the emperor.

"Nuncio was in the wrong place at the wrong time," said Nolan. "There was nothing I could do."

"Well, I am going to keep my eye on you from now on," said the emperor. "Certainly you know that everyone who enters my Coliseum must be properly dressed and impeccably groomed. It that is true for the general public, just imagine how much more imperative it is for the manager of this place."

The emperor turned his back, letting Nolan know that he had been dismissed. Nolan left the room and headed straight out the exit toward his own safe villa.

One of the members of the senate caught up with him and pulled him aside, out of sight of the Coliseum.

"If I were you, I would avoid him altogether for a while," said the man.

"What do you know?" asked Nolan cautiously.

"I know that you caught the attention of his advisors last week when you scoffed at the idea of turning to the goddess Minerva for help. The emperor and his aides hold the goddess in the highest esteem," stated the senate member.

"I have never had the slightest regard for gods and goddesses, and idols are banned from my private property," said Nolan.

"Members of the emperor's own family have lost their lives for less than that," said the senator.

"I understand, and I will try to be more careful," said Nolan. "I have some ideas that will get him excited about his birthday celebration, and hopefully they will get his mind off all these superstitions and suspicions."

"I certainly hope so," said the senator, "because he is a very paranoid man. All of us in the senate know that our lives can be taken at any moment."

"Then I will pray for you, but it will not be to any god or goddess," promised Nolan.

"Thank you," said the member of the senate, "but let's keep that between the two of us. Haven't you heard that the emperor is on the warpath against the new group called the Christians?"

"No, but I heard that he killed a group of people just for sympathizing with the Jews," said Nolan.

"Yes," said the senator, "that story is definitely

true. Be very careful and keep your religious beliefs to yourself."

Nolan thanked the man for all of his advice and promised to keep a low profile from now on. He ran home to talk to the only person he truly trusted these days, and that was his beloved wife, Sabrina. He told her about the disturbing conversation with the emperor and about the warnings of the senator. It was always very comforting to share his problems with Sabrina, but the terrified look on her face almost made him regret telling her.

"Please don't worry," Nolan said. "One thing about the emperor is that he has a very short memory, and he is very easily distracted by anything that he thinks will make him popular. I will just have to think of something bigger and better than all of the wild animals he hopes to watch trample helpless victims or be brutally sliced and speared by gladiators."

"I just don't want you to be the one trampled by the wild animals," said Sabrina.

CHAPTER 20

The travelers arrived on the shores of Lebanon. The emperor had ordered a load of fine cedar for the construction of a summer palace, which was to be located on the sea, away from the heat and noise of the city. The captain said that it would be fine for the teens to go ashore, as long as they were back before dark and as long as they went with some of the men.

Once on shore, their group walked around the marketplace. People at little stands sold olives and bananas, as well as some handcrafted items. Francis purchased a bowl made out of cedar to replace the necklace he gave to a couple in Africa who gave them water. The group walked back to the dock and watched as huge cedar logs were loaded onto the ship. They could see that it was going to be an all-day job, so they asked around for something to do. A person at one of the marketplaces pointed to some horses and wagons and suggested that they might be interested in a tour. A very loud, jolly man and his wife greeted them and asked if they would like a tour into the mountainous forests of the cedars of Lebanon.

Titus had the money for their group to take the tour, and Octavius and Francis were along, as well as all of the teenagers. They hopped onto the wagon seats and took off. The horses knew the trail well and seemed to scamper around and around as they went higher and higher toward the mountains. They rode along that way for a long time and finally stopped at a beautiful lookout.

"What you see before you," said the guide, "is the famous Forest of Lebanon. It was from this forest that King Solomon got the lumber to complete the Temple of God and then his own home, which was called the Palace of the Forest of Lebanon. In the palace, there were four rows of cedar columns, thirty cubits high, supporting forty-five cedar beams, which gave the impression of a majestic forest, and that is where it got its name."[12]

"We've heard of Solomon," said Maximus. "Remember, Felix, we read about him in the Book of Matthew that you got on your trip. Jesus said that we don't need to worry about the clothes we wear, because the lilies of the field don't labor or spin, and yet not even Solomon, in all his splendor, was dressed like one of them."[13]

"You are correct," said the guide. "Solomon was greater in riches and wisdom than all the other kings on the earth."

The guides had them all jump back in the wagon and took them farther up the mountain. Soon they came to other majestic trees. The teens all got out of the wagon and threw snowballs at each other. Maximus made a sketch of Felix hitting Claudia and Flavius and then one of them catching Felix and putting snow down his robe. Cadogan lost his footing and slid down a little hill on his backside. Everyone laughed at the sight, but soon they were finding pieces of bark and sliding down the hill, too.

Titus said that they really needed to be on their way, so once again they climbed in the wagon and traveled back, winding their way downward. Around and around they went down the path, when suddenly the wagon swerved in the mud and hit a tree. No one was injured, but the wheel was broken. Titus asked if they were close enough to walk back. The man and woman looked concerned but said they probably could do it.

So the group hiked on the trail. They saw beautiful birds and small woodland creatures and pinecones and interesting rocks. Titus was very worried about the time, but the teenagers said that the captain surely wouldn't leave without them. Titus was afraid that the captain wouldn't notice their absence. It was beginning to get dark. And still they continued to walk down the trail. Finally they reached the marketplace. All of the little stands were covered, and the sellers had gone home. They began to run toward the dock. Francis was out of breath and could not keep up. Titus asked Felix to run ahead and let the captain know that they were all on the way.

After a while, Felix came back and met them and said that the ship had left, but there was a ship heading toward the shore, and he hoped it was theirs coming back for them. They all reached the dock just as the ship arrived. Captain Riley was there as the plank was lowered, and they all ran on board. The captain said that Cyrus and Benedict noticed that they were missing and ran and told him. After they had the ship searched, they turned around and headed back. Titus apologized for setting them back, but the captain assured them that many things come up in their travels to delay them and not to worry about it.

⬥

"I have a brilliant plan that I hope will get the emperor's mind off all his problems," Nolan said to Sabrina. "We will build two full-size battleships somewhere near the Coliseum, and when the celebration is almost over, we will flood the entire place and perform a sea battle that he will brag about for years to come. We will send announcements all over the world that the grand finale will be the biggest and most exciting of all performances and will be something that has never been done in any show before. It will make the emperor forget all about us."

"Could you really do that?" asked Sabrina.

"I think we will do it, and when the sea battle is going on, and important people come from all over the world to witness the event, we will secretly move far away and not leave a trace of our whereabouts," said Nolan. "The emperor will have to find someone else to run his Coliseum. Just think. In a little more than a month, we can be free of him."

Nolan went off to work, prepared to hire shipbuilders to build the battleships and the smartest men he could find to plan the flooding of the Coliseum.

CHAPTER 21

Titus was very happy that he made the decision to sail with Riley on his ship called the *Four Winds* and that the captain was not angry with them for returning late. They arrived in Antioch in the evening and took on a great deal of cargo that was to be delivered to Rome. They also took aboard an entire hunting party along with fifty captured ostriches.

The teenagers stood at the railing and watched as the ostriches were loaded onto the ship. The hunters used one huge, flexible, portable fence that surrounded the fifty ostriches. The men narrowed the fence into a long enclosure and moved the ostriches right onto the ship. They were directed down below to the cargo area. As they began the decline, the ostriches went wild, refused to move forward, and began kicking the fence. The hunters had to stop movement and figure out what was wrong. Finally they realized that the ostriches sensed the presence of lions and weren't going anywhere near them. It was decided that the ostriches had to remain on the upper, open deck of the ship.

Just as the ship was about to depart, Captain Riley spotted his brother's ship at another dock. He got off the ship and ran to see his brother, his son, and his nephews. When he returned, it was dark outside. He came on board and brought the family with him. The captain informed his crew that they would not be departing until morning and that they would be traveling alongside his brother's ship, the *Waverider*.

The captain invited his family, Titus, and all of the teenagers into the common room, and they all sat around the tables for a time of socializing.

"Everyone, I would like you to meet my brother, Joseph, and my son, James. These two young men are my nephews, Elijah and Edward. Their ship will sail tomorrow after taking on rhinos, monkeys, and gorillas, all headed for the Coliseum. Joseph and I have decided that our ships will sail together and hope we make it to Rome."

"Are we in some kind of danger?" asked Titus.

The captain looked very sober and he said, "As you know, it is late in the season. We could experience some violent weather."

"What are we going to do?" asked Titus.

"We have no choice but to try and make it. Any time we are carrying cargo destined for Rome, we have to ignore the dangers and hope for the best," said Riley. He looked at his brother and said, "Tell everyone about your experience."

"About thirty years ago, I was an apprentice on a ship very similar to this one," said Joseph. "We were leaving for Rome from a city not far from here, carrying a large cargo of grain and many prisoners and soldiers. We were warned by one of the prisoners not to attempt to go, but the captain listened to the owner of the ship and was assured that we would be fine. At first, it seemed that we were blessed with good weather, for we enjoyed a gentle southerly breeze. But as we sailed on, the breeze turned into hurricane-strength winds. We went for many days, throwing cargo and grain and tackle overboard. We lost all hope, and we couldn't eat anything at all."

"You can see that I came close to losing my only brother," said Riley.

"It certainly looked like we were all going to die," said Joseph, "but a prisoner on board named Paul, the same one who warned us not to go at all, said that an angel of God told him that none of us would die. He encouraged us and got us to eat, and we all made it safely to the shore of an island. Of course, the ship was destroyed."

"That happened thirty years ago, and you still remember the details," Felix marveled.

"Oh, I remember it like it was yesterday," said Joseph, "and there is more to the story. The islanders were very kind to us when we arrived. We were all very cold, so they built a fire to warm and comfort us. The prisoner named Paul was putting wood on the fire, and a viper fastened itself onto his hand. All of us gasped and were certain he would soon be dead, but he shook it off into the fire, and he never even got sick. We were certain he was a man of God."[14]

"Wow," said Maximus. "What did you find out about his God?"

"Oh, I went on another ship and never saw him again after that time on the island," said Joseph.

"I just don't understand that," said Flavius. "Why

would anyone meet a man who knows the one true God and just walk away and not pursue learning more?"

"Son," said Titus, "That was not very nice to say."

"Oh, I am sorry," said Flavius. "I am happy that you survived the storm."

"Yes, I am, too," said Joseph, "and I hope we survive our trip to Rome. It has been many years since I have ventured out on the sea this late in the year. But the emperor's birthday celebration seems to be more important than our safety."

"James, we enjoyed spending time with your father, mother, and your sister Rebekah," said Felix. "They took us on a trip through the Holy Land, and it was very enlightening."

"You know Rebekah?" asked James. "What did you think of my baby sister?"

"I am so thankful for the time with her," said Claudia. "I was longing for some girl talk. I miss her so much already."

"Yes, we all do," said Argus. Felix and Claudia looked at each other and smiled.

"Father," asked James, "could I move to your ship? I would like to get to know these passengers of yours."

Captain Riley looked at his brother Joseph and asked, "Can you spare him? And maybe Elijah and Edward would also like to be around young people for a change."

"I think that could be arranged. Would you boys like to ride on your uncle's ship for a while? I plan to be close by at all times," said Joseph.

"That's nice of you, Uncle, but I think I will stay with Father. We kind of promised Mother that we would stay close to him. Maybe later on, when we get close to Rome, we will ride on your ship," said Elijah.

Argus, Felix, and Maximus went with James to the other ship to get his belongings, and Flavius managed to pull Claudia aside before Cadogan noticed they were missing. They ran up to the deck of the ship to a place that was hidden by the ostrich fences and stood by the railing.

"I promised you that the ride back to Rome would be romantic," said Flavius, "and yet this is the first time we've been alone together. It has been frustrating."

"I have just been so happy that you and Maximus are alive and with us again," said Claudia. "We can put up with a little irritation."

"Claudia, I had a lot of time to think while we were apart," said Flavius. "I realize that my feelings for you are very strong. I guess I'm trying to tell you that I love you. When we get back to Rome, the rich man might insist that you marry him. That would just destroy me."

"It would destroy me, too," said Claudia. "I don't want to marry an old man."

"You and I could get married on the ship," said Flavius. "Captain Riley could marry us. What do you think?"

Claudia was speechless. Many girls did get married at fourteen, but she never thought that she would be one of them. Finally she asked, "Could I have some time to think about it?"

"Of course you can think about it. Let's keep it a secret until you make up your mind," suggested Flavius.

"I want you to know how much this means to me,

though," said Claudia. "That is probably the nicest thing anyone ever did for me."

"Well, I'm not just doing it to save you from that man," said Flavius. "I want you to be my wife, and I think I could take care of you. I could work for my father." Flavius turned a bright shade of red, and Claudia could see it because of the lamp nearby.

Claudia put her hands on his shoulders and said, "Normally, I wouldn't even consider making a decision like this without discussing it with my mother, but this is kind of an emergency. I will think about it. I promise."

Flavius kissed her on the cheek and put his arm around her, and the two of them stood and enjoyed the warm breeze and the beautiful view of the harbor. They watched as her brothers came laughing and running back to the ship with James, obviously already good friends.

James looked a lot like Rebekah, with brown hair and brown eyes. He smiled and laughed all the time. He especially thought it was funny to have a girl sleeping in their room. He said the hammocks were bigger and nicer than the ones on his uncle's ship, and he hoped the food was better, too. The teenagers laughed and laughed as James told them silly jokes about girls and parrots and naked sailors. They were all certain that the trip back to Rome would be loads of fun.

⌒⟡⌒

Sabrina was spending the morning with Lavinia and the twins. The two women were getting to be very good friends. They did all kinds of activities together—

everything from shopping to visiting and caring for the poor and the elderly.

"Do you have any idea when our children are coming home?" asked Lavinia. "I miss them so much. I try not to worry about them, but I know there is some danger in lion hunting. Do you think we did the right thing, letting them go?"

"I hope we did the right thing. I have no idea when to expect them," said Sabrina, "but Titus knows that he needs to have the lions here by the middle of October. I think the emperor wants to begin the celebration about a week before his birthday, which is getting close."

The two women took the twins outside to walk around the grounds. It was only about a week since the gardener left, but the place was going downhill fast. There were weeds popping up all around, and the flowers were drying out and wilting.

"It looks like I'm going to have to start doing some gardening," said Sabrina.

"It's too bad you can't get in touch with your gardener and let him know that it is safe for him to come back now," said Lavinia.

"Well, for his own safety, we did not get his new location," said Sabrina.

The women were startled when they heard a door open near them. The gardener came out of the little storage building.

"Please don't be scared. I left some of my favorite tools here, and I thought maybe I could sneak in here and get them," said the gardener. "Did I hear you say that it is safe for me to come back?"

"Yes," said Sabrina. "Nuncio was trampled by elephants, and Nolan was there to witness it. It was really a freak accident, but the emperor heard about it and suspects that Nolan somehow arranged it. Now he doesn't trust Nolan as much as before. Of course, the emperor doesn't trust anyone very much."

Just then, Nolan came running around the corner and was surprised to see Sabrina outside, talking to the gardener. Sabrina could tell by the look on his face that there was trouble, but Nolan took time to greet his gardener and welcome him back to work.

Then Nolan said to them, "You are not going to believe what is happening in the emperor's household. Some fortune teller told him that someone at the palace was going to poison him, and he had all of his cooks killed. Members of his own family are terrified that they will be next."

"That's horrible," said Sabrina and the others.

"I'm really swamped," said Nolan. "I just wanted to let you know what's going on. I may get back very late tonight."

"Does this mean that the emperor trusts you more now?" asked Sabrina.

"I doubt that. But it is nice when his attention is on others so I can just do my job. His advisors and fortune tellers enjoy getting him very excited," said Nolan. "I don't think they realize that it could backfire on them sometime."

"Well, I hope it does," said Sabrina. "Please be careful, dear. We can't leave until our children return." Nolan gave her a sympathetic smile and returned to his job. The gardener was already watering the flowers.

CHAPTER 22

Early in the morning, the teenagers were allowed to go over to Joseph's ship and watch them load the animals on board. The rhinos were moved onto the ship in huge cages on wheels. The sight of them reminded Argus and Felix of the day they watched the rhinos charging through the Coliseum, breaking all the scenery and running down the hunters. Their decision to save Ravi's life resulted in this entire trip around the Great Sea. They looked at Cadogan and Kendrick and hoped the rhinos didn't make them think about their father's death.

Then the monkeys were loaded onto the ship. There must have been one hundred monkeys, and they all seemed to be screeching at once. The young people covered their ears and laughed at the amusing animals. The gorillas were moved up the walkway next in their large cages. Their faces and chests were huge, and they looked them in the eye as they went by.

"I am so glad the gorillas are on that ship and not ours," said Claudia. "They give me the creeps."

"Oh, don't you worry about those gorillas," said James. "If they come around, I will save you." Argus and Felix looked at each other and rolled their eyes. They certainly hoped that James would not begin flirting with Claudia. The competition between Cadogan and Flavius for her heart had provided more than enough drama on the trip.

Once the animals were loaded, they all ran back to their own ship and went aboard. The ships took off at once with a safe distance between them. The weather was perfect for traveling, and it seemed that they were in a race. Captain Riley's ship took the lead, and everyone, including Francis, the hunters, and all of the soldiers, enjoyed standing at the railing around the deck. The men were all in good spirits since they were finally heading for home.

Several of the men began playing a game similar to arm wrestling, only the goal was to knock the other off his feet. When two of the larger men played the game, they lost their balance and fell into the ostrich pen, breaking one of the portable walls. The ostriches got loose and were soon running wild all over the ship. Some of them stumbled onto the ramp area leading to the lower level. They seemed unable to handle the decline and toppled awkwardly with their long necks and legs tangling up.

Other ostriches were running back and forth across the ship, grunting at people who got in their way. Flavius was immediately at Claudia's side, shielding her. The teens managed to get between the pen and the railing and were somewhat protected. The hunters responsible for capturing the animals soon began using shepherds' hooks to catch the birds and steer them back into the pen. Many of the ostriches resisted capture, flapping their large wings and kicking with their powerful legs. By time for the midday meal, the ostriches were back in their repaired pen, and the people, although exhausted, were not injured.

After the meal, Argus, Felix, Maximus, and James settled on cushions on the deck and began reading the Book of Luke. They read all about the birth of John the Baptist and the birth of Jesus. They continued reading about Jesus being tempted, Jesus healing many people, and Jesus calling his disciples. Then they quit reading for a while.[15]

"I'm just amazed that you know Rebekah," said James.

"She's a nice girl," said Felix. "We liked her a lot. And your parents were very good to us. It was your father who bought us this book."

"I feel bad leaving Mother and Rebekah all the time, but I need to learn as much about sailing as I can," said James. "I plan to have my own ship someday."

"Did someone say that you have a brother?" asked Argus.

"Yes, I do. His name is Benjamin," said James. "We don't know where he is. He took off on a ship over a year ago, and we haven't heard from him since. I'm not sure that Mother and Rebekah know that last part. If you see them, please don't mention that to them. Father and I think he will show up one of these days."

❦

Nolan looked at the calendar, and he was worried that there were still ships out on the Great Sea with supplies, animals, and all kinds of equipment for the big celebration. It was getting late, and he was concerned that they might not make it at all before winter. Of course, he was the most worried about his own children. He decided not to tell Sabrina and Lavinia about the danger of traveling on the Great Sea this late in the year, and he just hoped that they arrived soon.

The project of flooding the Coliseum was going very well. Nolan hired two ship construction teams to build the battleships and another team to prepare to flood the entire floor. Bringing water to the place was going to be difficult, but it was not his problem. The only good thing about working for the emperor was that money was never an issue. If he had to, he could even order people to do the things that needed to be done. In this case, people needed the work and were glad to take on the project.

Sabrina and Lavinia decided to prepare for their escape to another country. Lavinia was getting rid of many clothes that her children had outgrown as well as many items that would not be needed in her future. Sabrina was sad to be leaving their beautiful villa. She was getting rid of nonessentials and making gift boxes to give to each and every person who worked at the villa.

"You know," said Sabrina. "I would be very sad right now if I weren't so excited that the children should be arriving any day now."

"I feel the same way. I just hope the boys are feeling better," said Lavinia. "When they left, they were in shock after seeing their father killed, and they were really scared of the emperor."

"I'm sure the trip has been good for them," said Sabrina. "I just can't wait to tell Claudia that she doesn't have to hide anymore."

CHAPTER 23

The two brothers' ships arrived at a harbor called Fair Havens on the island of Crete. Both ships took on fresh supplies, and Joseph's ship dropped off some cargo. After just an hour, they were on the way again. They took off at a fast pace, just like when they left Antioch. The warm breeze was out of the south, and the sun was shining.

Although they were quite a distance from home, Claudia was getting very nervous about the rich man in purple who wanted to make her his wife. The last two nights, she woke up having nightmares about him. In last night's dream, she was running happily with her girlfriends when suddenly the man grabbed her and threw her in a wagon. She woke up screaming. The boys lit a lamp and some soldiers came running, and Claudia cried and told them all how sorry she was for waking them up.

Flavius was very concerned, because in the daylight, she looked very pale and worn out. He decided to approach her again about marriage.

"Claudia, I can see that you are really worrying about the rich man in Rome. Have you thought any more about my idea?" he asked.

"I have been thinking about it. In fact, I was thinking about asking my brothers what they think about the idea," Claudia said.

"Would you mind if I asked my father what he thinks?" Flavius asked.

"No, I think that's a good idea," she answered. "I know we are still far from home, but the nightmares started when our ship turned and headed west. I need something else to think about."

"Think about me," said Flavius. "I wonder if they have any cabins on this ship for married people."

Claudia had such an alarmed look on her face that Flavius realized that she was just not ready for all of that.

"Would it be all right if we wait a little longer before we ask our families for advice?" asked Claudia. "I don't know how my brothers will take it."

Just then a strong breeze got Claudia's scarf, and Flavius charged across the ship to get it. He ran into James, Cadogan, Kendrick, and all three of Claudia's brothers.

"You two missed breakfast," said Argus. "It's too late now, because they are locking down all the food and equipment."

"What's going on?" asked Flavius.

"Haven't you noticed the black clouds rolling in?" asked Maximus.

"The two of them are oblivious," said James. "He just chased her scarf across the ship and didn't even notice that the wind is picking up."

Claudia looked up in the sky and said, "Look at those dark clouds and their strange shape. I never saw anything like that."

"The wind is frightening," said Flavius.

The waves were picking up, and they had to grab the handrails to steady themselves.

Just then Captain Riley approached them and said, "You young people are to go to your sleeping quarters immediately. Don't leave the room for anything until we tell you to come out. We are going to have our hands full for a while, and we can't worry about anyone washing off the ship. Oh, and don't light any lamps. If they fall, a fire could start."

The teenagers ran down to their room immediately. They could barely find their way to their hammocks in the dark.

"At least with all this excitement," commented Felix, "we don't have to worry about Claudia waking up screaming, because she probably won't sleep at all."

"That's right. What are your nightmares about?" asked Argus.

"I don't want to tell you," said Claudia. "I guess I don't want you worrying, too."

"Does it have something to do with the man in purple?" asked Felix.

"The man in purple?" questioned James. "That sounds like an interesting story."

"Didn't you wonder why our sister is on the hunting trip with us?" asked Argus.

"I did wonder, but I got the idea that all of you are here to be away from the emperor, and I just figured that included her," said James.

"Not exactly," said Felix. "A very rich man who

always wore purple, and who was at least forty years old, wanted Claudia for his wife. He was a man accustomed to getting whatever he wanted. He didn't take no for an answer."

"I couldn't leave our villa because he was always around, leering at me," said Claudia. "And, yes, he is in my nightmares."

"So you sneaked away to hunt lions?" asked James.

"Exactly," said Argus. "We promised our parents that we wouldn't let her out of our sight."

"I see," said James. "That is odd, because it seems to me that you three have been hanging out with me, but Claudia has not been around."

"Well, she's been with Flavius," said Maximus.

"And you think he's harmless," said James. "Do you think your parents will be happy if she returns to Rome involved with some fifteen-year-old boy who has no way to support her?"

"I'm seventeen years old," said Flavius, "and I can go to work for my father any time I want."

"I'm sorry," said James. "I forgot you were here in the dark with us."

Claudia was furious. "You might be interested to know that Flavius just returned from a very dangerous rescue mission into the jungle. His father is very proud of him, and so am I."

"Flavius," asked Felix, "were you actually considering supporting Claudia?"

Except for the sound of the storm and the slapping of the waves against the ship, it was silent. Everyone was uncomfortable, and Flavius was glad they were in the dark so that his red face was not obvious. He didn't know what to do, because he kind of promised Claudia that he wouldn't say anything until she was ready. "I think I'm getting sea sick," said Flavius.

Finally Claudia spoke up. "Actually, Flavius and I have considered asking the captain to marry us. Then when we return, the rich old man will have to leave me alone."

"There are easier ways to solve the problem than marriage," suggested Argus. "We can take you to the Coliseum with us every day."

"Oh, that's a great suggestion," said Flavius. "I'm sure she will be safe there."

"Ouch," said James. "I guess I broke open a hornet's nest. Have any of you noticed the storm outside? You all heard my uncle's story about the storm he was in when he was young. Our ship may not even survive. His didn't."

"Yes, but all of the people on the ship survived," said Maximus.

"Well, we might not be lucky enough to stumble across an island with nice sandbars for us to run into or to have a man of God along with us," said James. "We need to prepare for the worst and stop arguing about what will happen in Rome. Rome is still a long way away."

"You are right about being prepared," said Felix, "but I don't think luck had anything to do with that island. God steered them to that island to save their lives. We may not have a man of God with us, but I think he will take care of us, too."

"I'm sure you're right," said Argus. "Claudia, please don't do anything permanent without asking Father and Mother. You know they will hold us boys responsible, and they will make us feel guilty for years."

"I know you're right," said Claudia. "They do know how to make us feel guilty."

"Speaking of feeling guilty," said Kendrick, "I'm going to feel very guilty if I don't go to the bathroom. I'm really feeling sea sick too. What are we going to do about that?"

They all had to go, too, so they decided to crawl on hands and knees down the hall to the bathroom, four at a time. Once they were out of the hammocks, they were amazed at the rocking of the ship. They were right to crawl because they couldn't walk if they tried, and since it was pitch dark down below, they had to go slowly so they didn't miss the bathroom door.

Cadogan, Kendrick, Flavius, and James went first, since the four siblings were going to go together next. They returned and were shocked at how bad the storm was. The ship was tipping at one point during their trip down the hall.

Claudia, Argus, Felix, and Maximus went next. They managed to get there and take care of their needs, but when they came out of the bathroom, they heard a strange sound in the hall.

"Maybe we should check it out," said Argus. "Someone could be hurt. They might need help."

"I think we should just obey orders and stay in our room," said Felix. Then they heard the noise again. It was very strange, and it did sound like a cry for help.

"Stay right there and wait for me," said Argus. "I'm just going to see what it is."

"I'm going with you," said Maximus. "You'll stay here and take care of Claudia, won't you, Felix?"

"You know I will, but what if it's a lion?" asked Felix.

"Anyone there?" yelled Argus. They could hear a strange sound. The two of them crawled toward the noise. Argus stuck out his hand and felt something like a furry leg. He ran his hand farther along it, and came to a huge feathery body.

"It's an ostrich," he called back. "It must be injured."

"Be careful," yelled Felix and Claudia.

Argus knew that it could bite him, but he followed the long neck up to the head, and realized that it was probably dying. They backed away, joined the other two, and then the four of them returned to the room. It took them a long time to find an empty hammock and get into it safely.

"There's a dying ostrich in the hallway," said Felix.

"That's not good," said Flavius. "That probably means they are all out of the pen. What a mess."

"You don't think the lions could get out, do you?" asked Claudia. "Let's close the door."

"I'll get it," said Cadogan. He toppled out of the hammock and banged to the floor. He kept quiet about his pain and closed the door.

"Thank you, Cadogan," said Claudia. "I feel safer with the door closed."

"I have the feeling that we are moving very fast, driven along by the storm. Do any of you think I'm right?" asked Felix.

"I think that is exactly what is happening," said Flavius. "As long as they steer it with the wind, we go fast, but when they fight it, that's when we tip on our side."

Sabrina and Lavinia were restless, thinking that the children should be back by now. Nolan decided that they needed to get out of the house, so he took them to a nearby arena where the two battleships were being constructed. The ships were as large as real ones, but only the top decks were real. They were just a shell made to look realistic, but they had to be capable of sailing short distances. All of the weapons had to be real, because two hundred slaves and prisoners were going to man each ship and fight to the death. The emperor would demand a performance with huge quantities of blood and suffering.

Next, Nolan took the women to another building where a model of the Coliseum was being filled with water. The emperor had visited both sites earlier and was very excited. Invitations to the event had been sent to every impressive, famous, or powerful person in the world. Nolan was hoping that the emperor would be so involved with all of the guests that he would not notice the absence of his family when they left Rome.

Nolan wanted to take Sabrina and Lavinia to enjoy a nice meal in the city, so he took them on a scenic route to a well-known place. They were seated near a large group of people who were laughing and having some kind of party. After a few moments, the people quit talking and were so quiet that all they could hear was the clinking of knives and forks. Nolan was very puzzled at such behavior. When they were outside, getting in the wagon, Nolan brought up the incident.

"I just do not understand why all of those people quit laughing and talking when we arrived. You would think we were dangerous criminals or something," Nolan said.

"I happened to overhear someone whisper that you work closely with the emperor," Lavinia said. "Then the man motioned for everyone to be quiet."

"Are you telling me that people are afraid of me because I work for the emperor?" Nolan asked. "Don't they know that I am in far more danger than any of them? I certainly wouldn't hurt them." He sat there for a moment, and then he got down from the wagon, said he would be right back, and went inside.

Nolan walked right up to the man at the head of the table and asked, "Excuse me, sir, is it true that you folks are afraid of me? The woman who was dining with my wife and I thought she heard something like that."

"We have heard that it is not a good idea to attract the attention of the emperor or those who work closely with him," answered the man.

"Certainly you can tell that I am not the kind of man who would hurt innocent people," said Nolan. The people just looked at him, obviously afraid to talk. Nolan walked out, feeling frustrated and rejected.

Later, Nolan and Sabrina were lying in bed.

"You seem so sad and thoughtful tonight," said Sabrina. "Is something wrong?"

Nolan was quiet a moment and then said, "It really bothered me today when those people were afraid of me. The thing is this: I don't care at all what the emperor thinks of me. I don't care what any of the people who work for him think of me. I don't even care what my own parents think of me. But those people looked special. They were just the kind of people I would like to know. I mean, they loved each other. You could tell."

"I thought the same thing when we first sat down," said Sabrina. "To have a group of friends like that would be so wonderful. You know what I mean? Everyone we know works for you in one way or another. They have to respect you."

"Maybe when we get to Mide, we will have friends," said Nolan. "Maybe everything will be better there."

"I hope so, dear," said Sabrina. "Friends are what I want more than anything. Well, friends and safety, too. Do you think the children will get back tomorrow?"

"I have someone watching at the dock every day now," said Nolan. "I just hope it's soon."

CHAPTER 24

Titus went to the door of the teenagers' room with a lamp and told them that the storm was over and they could come out. It was just beginning to get light outside, and they could not believe their eyes when they saw the deck of the ship. There were dead ostriches all over the place, but the pen had been repaired, and there were many ostriches in there.

"Father, were you up here for the entire storm?" asked Flavius.

"Oh, no," Titus answered. "We were all sent to our quarters as well. Only the ship's crew was dealing with the storm. I want you young people to help clean up this mess."

For the next hour, they picked up and straightened things all over the ship. Captain Riley addressed them.

"Well, the good news is that we survived the storm. We were very fortunate. The bad news is that we have lost contact with my brother's ship, and we don't know exactly where we are," the captain said.

Argus, Felix, Maximus, and Claudia went up and walked around the deck of the ship. They were standing along the railing, talking happily when a member of the crew spied a ship in the distance. He ran and notified the captain, who quickly identified it as his brother's ship. Soon they were easing their way alongside the Waverider, and the captain was asked to go onboard the other ship.

Soon the captain returned. "My brother Joseph's ship has been damaged beyond repair and many aboard lost their lives," he said. "The survivors will be joining us for the trip back to Rome."

A ramp was set up between the two ships, and the surviving animals and people came on board. They also brought on all of the cargo. Everyone, including the teenagers, helped with the move. It was soon obvious that the passengers had been through a terrible ordeal. The captain's two boys, Elijah and Edward, moved their belongings to the teenagers' sleeping quarters, and then they joined them up on deck. They were weak and weary and looked like they had been crying.

"So cousins, what have you been up to?" asked James.

"You wouldn't believe it," said Elijah.

"Try me," said James.

"We should have gotten on your ship when we had the chance," said Edward. "We have had a miserable experience. Do you know that Father is missing?"

"What? Are you sure?" asked James.

"Yes," answered Elijah. "He must have been washed overboard. There are two others missing as well."

"I don't believe it," said James. "Uncle Joseph would be very careful."

"We can't believe it, either," said Edward. "Father always said safety was the most important thing."

"When the storm first began, we were given the job of securing the monkey cages with ropes so they wouldn't be thrown overboard. Monkeys can be nasty animals when they are scared," said Elijah.

"Later, the storm got really bad, and the ship was rolling back and forth. That's when one of the gorillas got loose," said Edward.

"I have never been so scared in my whole life," said Elijah. "When we saw the gorilla, we hid in a built-in storage container up on the deck. We raised the lid a little and saw the beast break monkey cages apart and squash the monkeys. We saw it grab and kill two men, but there were many others who were probably killed and injured by the gorilla. I hope it didn't kill Father and throw him overboard."

"The worst thing was when the gorilla came over and sat near our hiding place," said Edward. "The ship was rocking so hard that the gorilla actually grabbed the box we were in to steady itself."

"We were afraid to breathe, and we didn't raise the lid and peek out for a long time," said Elijah, "but finally we did. A giant wave swept over the deck and washed the gorilla overboard. "We saw him go."

"Unbelievable!" said James.

"Well, it's all true. This morning we stood at the rail and looked for Father for a long time once the storm settled down," said Elijah. "I guess they gave up when they saw your ship."

Argus, Felix, and Maximus overheard their conversation, but they stepped away as James cried and clung to his cousins.

"I know the chances are slim that their father is still alive, but let's pray for him anyway," said Felix. The three brothers went to the other side of the ship and prayed earnestly to God that if Captain Joseph was alive, they would find him soon. They stood at the railing for a long time.

"You know, I think I see someone in the water," said Maximus. "Look over there."

"I'll run and tell Father," said James.

Two minutes later, the ship came to a stop and they lowered a lifeboat. Maximus yelled and pointed to the floating object in the water. They went in the direction that he was pointing, stopped, and yelled back to the ship.

"It's not a person," the man yelled. "It's a gorilla floating on a piece of wood. It's alive."

The men waited a safe distance away. Finally Titus shouted for them to leave it there, because there was no way to capture it without endangering their lives.

"Hold on," said Francis. "We can think of something." The hunters put their heads together and came up with a plan that involved a huge net. The two men in the boat came back to the ship, and two of the hunters went out in their place. They threw the net over the gorilla, and it roared at them loudly and fought the net. Using the net, it managed to pull itself to the boat and push down on the side, throwing the two men in the water.

"Swim to the ship," yelled the people on board. The men realized that the gorilla would drown them if they let it, so they swam rapidly to the ship. The crew threw down ropes and pulled them up. They all watched as the gorilla struggled with the net and went under the water. Everyone stood helplessly at the rail, wishing they could think of a way to save the animal, but the gorilla did not reappear. Finally Captain Riley said they couldn't afford to leave the lifeboat there, so two members of the crew swam out to the boat. They climbed in the boat, retrieved the oars, and were about to row back when someone yelled that they could see something else floating in the water. The men rowed far away in the direction of the floating object. They were too far away for the people on the ship to make out what was going on, so everyone waited patiently. As the lifeboat approached the ship, they could see that there were two more men on board.

"It's Father!" shouted Edward. James, Elijah, and Edward threw their arms around each other in joy and thankfulness.

The crew pulled the four men aboard and secured the lifeboat. Joseph was saved, along with a member of his crew.

Argus, Felix, and Maximus decided to give their new friends time alone with Joseph and Riley. They came across Claudia and Flavius and told them all about praying for Joseph just before he was rescued. They realized that they were all finally alone with Flavius.

"We were thinking about grabbing Vernon's pack to see if there really is a treasure inside," said Maximus. "Do you think we should?"

"Well, if there is nothing special inside, there is no hurry to find his mother and sister," said Flavius.

"We should go tell them that Vernon was thinking of them as he was dying," said Maximus. They decided to go to their sleeping quarters and check out Vernon's pack.

They went charging into the room, and there were Cadogan and Kendrick lounging in their hammocks.

"What are you two doing down here?" asked Felix. "After spending hours and hours in here, I would think you would be enjoying some fresh air."

"Well," said Cadogan. "You're here. Why aren't you enjoying the fresh air?"

"We have been up there," said Claudia, "and now we're going back up. Right, boys?"

"Right," the boys answered, and they left the room and ran upstairs.

"Well, that was a waste of time," said Flavius. "I have been wondering what's in that pack."

"It wasn't a waste of time at all," said Felix. He pulled Vernon's pack from behind his back. They found a quiet place behind the ostrich pen where no one could see them, and they all sat down on the floor in a little circle. Felix began taking items out of the pack. He had a blanket, some tools, and a few changes of clothes. Down on the bottom was a piece of cloth. Felix carelessly pulled it out, and a round object fell on the floor and started to roll away. Maximus was able to catch it. He held it up for everyone to see, and it was a beautiful pearl.

"Wow, a pearl," said Flavius. "Where do you think he got that?"

"He certainly didn't have time to tell us," said Maximus, "and we can't ask anyone, because it has to be a secret."

"Well, he was right about it being a treasure," said Flavius. "That's the biggest pearl I have ever seen. How are we going to find his sister?"

"Well, we can ask the other soldiers about that," said Argus

The teenagers carefully put the pearl back in the pack, just as Vernon had it, with the other things over it. They couldn't help but notice that the wind was really picking up.

"We couldn't have another storm so soon, could we?" asked Claudia. The boys all thought that it was certainly possible. They went to the common room and had some food. Then Captain Riley stood up to speak to the group.

"I understand that another storm is bearing down on us. You all have witnessed what happens to people up on the deck when the waves are washing overboard. I am going to ask you all to help lock down any and all objects."

Then Titus stood up and announced, "Please, men, find a way to secure the monkeys and the ostriches. We can't afford to lose any more animals."

After that Captain Riley said, "You have very little time to do all of that, and then please go to your sleeping quarters down below and remain there until the storm is over. And remember, no lamps."

The teenagers barely did any work at all, because the older men told them to get to their room. They went in and closed the door. After a while, James, Elijah, and Edward joined them. They fumbled around in the dark for a long time, trying to find the empty hammocks and get into them. The room was hot and stuffy, and when they complained about it, Elijah and Edward reminded them of the dangers of being up on deck. That reminded them of the gorilla, and they all hoped that the lions, monkeys, rhinos, and gorillas were all secure. They were thankful that none of those animals could open a door.

"I just wish we could have some light," said Maximus. "I could be happy even in this hot room if we could read one of our letters."

The next ten days, the ship was tossed about on the sea. The storm was not as severe as the first one, but it seemed to last forever. The two brothers took turns serving as captain, and their crews took turns as well, keeping everyone as fresh as possible. The hunting teams only came out of their quarters occasionally, taking care of the animals. Everyone was served a little food and water each day by the cooking staff.

At first, the teenagers spent the time in the dark talking, laughing, and playing silly mind games. After a while, they just wanted fresh air and sunshine. They promised themselves that if they survived this time at sea, they wouldn't complain about anything again.

Everyone knew that time was passing by, but they lost track of the days. Claudia was happy that it was taking a long time to get back home. She could put up with a little hunger, motion sickness, stuffiness, and boredom to stay away from the rich old man who dressed in purple. Elijah and Edward were very happy because they had thought their father was dead and he was alive, and they always had the most fun with their cousin James. It had been two months since the big group left on the trip, so Cadogan and Kendrick were recovering from their grief and fears. They were all becoming such good friends.

Nolan decided to take some time away from the Coliseum one day and spend it with Sabrina. He certainly deserved some time away from the place. Both battleships were almost finished and were resting on wheeled structures, prepared to transport them to the Coliseum just before the emperor's birthday. The linings that were to hold the water were prepared and stored in a room next to one of the gates, and men were assigned to put them in place following the final gory performance featuring wild animals and helpless victims. The best engineers in the empire would be standing by to run the water into the Coliseum the moment the battleships were in place. Nolan had been notified that one hundred eighty out of the two hundred slaves and prisoners were confined nearby, each fitted with either a red battle costume to represent Athens or a blue one to represent Sparta. Weapons for each combatant were being stored on the decks of the ships. Nolan was assured that the last twenty men for the battle were to be captured today by a group of soldiers who were acting under the orders of the emperor himself.

Sabrina noticed that Nolan was very quiet as they sat at the back of the property, enjoying their beautiful gardens and colorful birds and butterflies.

"What's wrong, dear?" asked Sabrina.

"I don't know where to begin. The last two days I have been searching the schedules for anything going to Mide. Remember the man we sent told us not to travel across land like he did with a family because it is too difficult. So to get to Mide, a ship must leave our dock and travel west around Spain, out into the

Atlantic Ocean, and then north. It must travel between the islands of Britannia and Ireland and land in Ireland near Mide. The entire voyage takes at least a month, and not many ships go there. In the next three weeks, there is only one ship scheduled for there, and it is leaving just five days from today, and there is only room for five individuals."

"Oh, Nolan, there are six of us," said Sabrina. "You have influence, don't you? You could get all six of us on that ship."

"Do you want to go without me?" Nolan asked. "I have to stay and make sure that everything is perfect for the emperor's big celebration, or I will be hunted down and killed. But I could send you and the children ahead and join you later."

"I would never leave without you. We will find a way to escape, and we will escape together," she answered.

"What would you think about sending Lavinia and her four children on that ship?" asked Nolan. "They could find their way to her relatives without our help."

"Yes," said Sabrina, "that is exactly what we should do, if the children get back in time."

"I'll make reservations for them this afternoon," said Nolan.

"You still don't seem like yourself," said Sabrina. "What's wrong?"

"I feel so dirty," said Nolan. "I'm not proud of what I do. The slaughter of all those beautiful, wild animals for the amusement of the emperor and his crowds is bad enough. But now I am responsible for two hundred people being killed. The ship battles were my idea, and the emperor reacted to it just as I hoped he would. Will God ever forgive me? What choice do we have now?"

"Just get through it, and then we will put it behind us forever," said Sabrina.

Nolan broke into tears. "How can I ever put it behind me when innocent people will lose their lives?" She had never seen him cry before, and she hoped he would be able to hide these feelings of remorse when he was around other people, especially the emperor.

CHAPTER 25

Just about the time the teenagers thought they were never going to see the light of day, Titus showed up at their door with a lamp and told them that they could come out. The lamps in the hallways were finally lit. They made their way up to the deck, and although it was a very cloudy day, they were happy to see it and to feel a fresh breeze on their faces.

Captain Riley came out to welcome them and to give his son and nephews a big hug. He explained that they missed the harbor at Syracuse but luckily found their way to the Straits of Messina, the narrow passageway between the island of Sicily and the boot-shaped peninsula of Italy. He explained that the seas often get dangerously rough going through there, and if that should happen, they were to return to their room. But he said that once they got through the straits, the rest of the journey to Rome should be safe sailing. He predicted that they could reach Rome in about three days.

The teenagers wanted to stand at the railing and watch the beautiful land pass by, but they were weak and filthy. First they went and cleaned up, and then they went and had the first solid food in days. When they finally arrived up on the deck, many members of the hunting teams, the soldiers, and even the off-duty crew were standing at the rails, watching the ship move through the straits. The teens had to stand behind them and peek through at the land. They listened to some of Joseph's crewmembers as they discussed the straits.

"There is a tale that a Roman ship carrying elephants was swept away and destroyed going through this very strait," said one of the crewmembers.

"Yes, I heard of that," said another. "But for that story, there are a thousand others. Our lives are in danger, and that's a fact."

As the men talked, the ship was beginning to go up and down as the waves grew higher and higher and the current grew swifter. The teenagers moved away from the others and sat down on the floor.

Elijah and Edward joined them and sat there on the floor as well. The waves were very high, but the sun was shining and the wind was blowing, and it was very exciting. The teens all joined arms and formed a circle, and they laughed and cheered each time they rode a very tall wave. All of the men standing at the railing enjoyed watching the teens as much as the coastline they were passing by.

Joseph, Captain Riley's brother, who was not on duty now, came over and sat down near his sons. Two other crewmembers sat down as well.

"I'm glad you young people are enjoying the ride," said Joseph. "You can be thankful that my brother and his crew are so skillful. Some ships don't survive going through here. Look over there."

There were two ships wrecked and stuck on the rocks. One was small, but the other looked as large as the one they were on.

"Uncle Joseph," asked James. "How are you going to get another ship?"

"Oh," he answered, "I will probably be the captain for someone else's ship and save my money for a while. Eventually I will have my own boat again. I'm not going to name it the *Waverider*, though. I think I will name it *Tranquility* and hope for calm water. Of course, I will try to avoid the sea this late in the season. That will help."

"It looks like the excitement is almost over," said one of the men who had joined them. "That is, if we steer to the right." He winked at Joseph.

"Well," said Joseph, "I certainly hope my brother does go to the right up ahead. We wouldn't want to get drawn in."

"I thought the danger would be over once we passed through the straits," said Elijah.

"Oh, no," said the crewmember with an ornery smile. "Nothing is more dangerous than beautiful women."

The teenagers all looked horrified, and Joseph laughed and said, "Don't you worry about it. Up ahead, there are three little islands that are said to have sirens, mythological female creatures who can sing so magically that sailors are tempted to go there and lose their lives on the sharp rocks or the jagged cliffs."

"I hope we won't be going near there," said Kendrick.

Joseph laughed and said, "If you hear any exotic music, just cover your ears."

Argus, Felix, and Maximus noticed a group of

young soldiers standing near a railing. They decided to see if they knew anything about Vernon. The soldiers pointed to an older soldier standing off to the side and said that he knew Vernon very well.

"Excuse me, but we were told that you were a friend of Vernon, and we wondered if you could help us get in touch with his family to tell them about his death," said Argus.

"Yes," said the soldier. "I know his family."

"Where do they live?" asked Felix.

"They live in Rome, near my own family," he answered. "Shall I write down their name and directions to their house?"

"That would be very helpful," answered Argus. "What can you tell me about his family?"

"He was very close to his mother and his sister," said the soldier. "His sister is crippled. I guess their father is very abusive and hurt her. Vernon said that his father spends all of his time at the Coliseum, watching the shows. I guess it is their dream to move away and hide from the man."

The three of them took the directions to Vernon's house from the soldier and thanked him. When they found Flavius and Claudia, they had plenty to share.

"Flavius," said Maximus, "we can carry out Vernon's wishes. We know where his sister and mother live." They told them about the crippled sister and the abusive father. They also told him that Vernon's family wanted to move away from the man.

"When we get home, that's the first thing we should take care of," said Felix. "They can sell the pearl and take the money to move someplace where the man will never find them."

The ship full of hunters, animals, cargo, and crew enjoyed three days of smooth sailing and finally reached the harbor near Rome.

❧

Nolan was about to walk from his villa to the Coliseum to check on the progress of every aspect of the big celebration when he was approached by a man near his gate.

"Excuse me, sir," said the man. "I wonder if I could talk to you."

Nolan looked at the man for a long time, trying to figure out where he had seen him before.

Finally the man spoke. "We met a few weeks ago at the eatery north of town."

"Yes, I remember now," said Nolan. He remembered that he was with the group of people who were afraid of him, and from the look on the man's face, nothing had changed.

"I realize that by coming to see you, I may never return to my beloved family," said the man. Nolan could see that sweat was running down his forehead, and his hands were shaking at his sides.

"Please, relax. I'm not in a hurry. Would you like to come in? Or we could go to the back of my yard by the gardens," said Nolan. "We could talk there."

The man merely nodded, so Nolan led him back to the place where he always went when he was upset or puzzled. The gardens were like a paradise. The two men sat down, and Nolan waited for him to begin.

"The night we met, you insisted that you were not a

dangerous man, and yet I know that you work side by side with the emperor," he began. "How can that be?"

"I have done a lot of soul searching since that night," Nolan said. "I guess that I should have told you that I never intentionally hurt anyone, but the things that go on there are evil, and I know that many people are brutally killed. I hate it and wish I could stop it, but as it is, my life is on the line every day."

The man broke down and cried. "You are my only hope. My dear wife and our teenage sons and even my parents were arrested two days ago, along with some others in their group. They have been taken away to some prison, and the rumor is that the emperor plans to have them tortured and killed to amuse people at the Coliseum. Could this be true?"

Two days ago, one of the men at the Coliseum told Nolan that he could relax now, because they had all two hundred people for the grand finale of the celebration. Nolan could hardly breathe as he realized that these innocent people were probably the same ones. *How could such a thing happen? Weren't they finding criminals—bad men who needed to be eliminated from society?*

"Why would they choose your family to arrest?" asked Nolan.

"Don't you know? It's because we are Christians. The emperor doesn't trust us. He thinks we are some kind of threat to him," said the man.

Nolan had heard from the senator that the emperor's advisors were pushing him to arrest Christians and Jews. He knew that it could be true. Nolan's head was swimming, and he felt like he was going to be sick.

Finally Nolan said, "I don't know anything about

Christians or Jews. I guess they don't share their religion with me because of my ties to the emperor."

"I have a wagon parked down the street," the man said. "The children are having special Bible training this week. That's why I wasn't with my wife and teenage sons. They went to a leaders' conference in Rome, and I stayed home with our four younger children so that they wouldn't miss the fun."

Nolan went in and got Sabrina, and the two of them walked down the street with the man and joined him in his wagon. As they traveled along, Nolan told Sabrina about the man's missing family and confided to both of them his greatest fears—that they were among the last twenty people scheduled to be armed warriors on the battleships for the grand finale on the emperor's birthday, just nineteen days away.

"My name is David," said the man. "Something tells me that I can trust you not to hurt us or tell the emperor or his men about our church."

"I will do whatever I can to help," said Nolan.

They arrived at David's church, and they went in and sat at the back of a large room with a stage at the front and three sections of seats in front and to the sides of the stage, forming a circle. There must have been three hundred children there, from about two years old to about fourteen. Nolan and Sabrina were fascinated. They noticed that the little toddlers were in the front with lots of adults and teenagers holding them. The children in each row got older and older toward the back of the room.

A very dynamic leader went up on stage and led the singing.

Nolan and Sabrina listened as the children sang and

sang, listened to a story about Jesus, and then prayed at the end.

David led Nolan and Sabrina outside. Children were running around everywhere, and his children came running by several times, letting him know they were around but certainly not ready to go home.

"The children do not know about their missing mother and brothers and grandparents," said David. "I just can't tell them yet. Please, can you help us? I don't know who else to ask. You are the only one in a position of power who could help us."

Nolan decided to confide in the man about his need to run away, far away from the emperor and to start a new life. He needed to be very careful and not ask careless questions about David's missing family. If he did find a way to rescue them, Nolan didn't want to endanger the lives of his own dear family. David said that if they needed to hide out, he would be glad to help. So far, the emperor and his men had not noticed their little church out in the country.

"There is not time now," said Nolan. "But I want to learn about your belief. I think that I have been searching for this my whole life."

"I just remembered that I drove you here in my wagon. Shall I gather up my children and take you home?" asked David.

"That would be great," said Nolan.

Four children, ages four, seven, ten, and twelve, climbed in the wagon and asked Nolan and Sabrina all kinds of questions. Sabrina thought they were adorable, and they made her miss her own four children. Nolan told David to drop them off a block away, just to be safe, and he and Sabrina walked home.

CHAPTER 26

Nolan didn't know how to search for David's family without asking any questions. He decided to have everyone involved come to his office and give a report on the progress. He took notes and was determined not to show the slightest interest if he learned something.

One of the workers, a man named Ulric, bragged that he now had all two hundred prisoners ready for the battleships with costumes of the correct size lying outside each prison cell. Nolan wanted to ask where they were keeping the last twenty prisoners, but he didn't know how to do it in such a way that the man would not remember telling him. He decided to just let the man go on bragging. He gave him a drink and a piece of cake. The man laughed about snatching the last group at a convention in Rome. Nolan tried to look bored as he poured the man another drink. The man drank it, stood up, and began to excuse himself. Nolan was frustrated and knew that he didn't dare ask the man anything.

As he was leaving the room, the man turned and

bragged, "You should have seen that last group when we put them into the fourth-floor cages. They were so scared climbing those stairs that we had to use whips to keep them moving."

Nolan said, "I am expecting twenty lions, fifteen rhinos, fifty monkeys, not to mention gorillas, ostriches, and giraffes. I hope you haven't taken rooms that we are going to need for the animals."

"Oh, do you need me to move them?" asked the man.

"Yes," said Nolan. "Let me think a moment." His heart was racing as he tried to think of a place. "Move them all to Room 135. We never keep animals in there. How many are there?"

"Twenty. You know, they were the last twenty that we needed," said the man.

"Well, they will be crowded, but it's not our job to make them comfortable, is it?" said Nolan. "Don't forget to put this lock on the door." Nolan tossed him a lock, knowing that he had the extra key. It was still going to be tricky, but at least he had hope.

Just then one of Nolan's friends ran in and told him that Titus and his group had arrived, and in fact, they were not far behind him. Relief flooded Nolan. Now he could take his own children home to Sabrina, and he had just the distraction he needed to help the twenty people escape.

Nolan's children never looked so good to him. He thought they all grew about two inches. They hugged him, and then they all tried to talk at once. They asked him if it would be all right if Flavius and their three new sailor friends came to stay at the villa for a while.

They explained that the ship was damaged and was going to spend the winter being repaired.

"Flavius, don't you think your mother will want to see you?" Nolan asked.

"Oh, yes," he answered. "I'll just be kind of a day guest whenever my parents don't need me."

Nolan led the bunch to his home minus Flavius, who realized that he should spend some time with his mother but said he would be over later. Sabrina was overjoyed and said that her children weren't to leave the property for anything and they were never allowed to go to the Coliseum again. They looked at Nolan, and he agreed with her. He said that the danger was greater than ever.

Cadogan and Kendrick said goodbye and went around back to their little home. Sabrina was going to visit later and tell Lavinia about their reservations on the ship that was leaving in just two days. They had kept it from her in case the boys didn't get back in time.

Argus got his father aside. "Father," he said, "you don't seem very happy that we brought friends home to stay. They won't be any trouble, I promise."

"Oh, Son, I'm just surprised. That's all," said Nolan. "There is a lot going on now."

"We have a lot to tell you, too," said Argus, "but not now."

"Where do you want your friends to sleep?" asked Nolan.

"If it's all right with you, Elijah will stay in my room, because he's the oldest, James will stay with Felix, and Edward can stay with Maximus," said Argus.

"That sounds fine, Son. Go ahead and move them

in. I need to go back to the Coliseum for a while." Nolan grabbed Argus and held him close for a long time. Argus thought they must have been really worried about them.

Nolan returned to the Coliseum and entered a gate that would place him right by Room 135. Sure enough, the people were crowded in there, barely with room to sit down. Nolan looked inside, and he was filled with compassion at the sight of them. He went to his own room, closed the door, and prayed to God for wisdom. He barely got the words out when Titus burst into the room with two smiling men.

"Nolan, I would like you to meet two brothers who are captains of ships and very good friends. This one is Joseph, and this is his brother, Riley, who we affectionately call Captain." They all talked for a while, and then the brothers told Nolan about their problem.

"Even though we delivered all the required animals and the coveted load of cedar, we aren't allowed to repair our ship in Rome's main harbor," said Riley. "We have to move ten miles up the coast to a little unknown harbor."

Instead of sympathizing with them, Nolan was overjoyed. He closed his door.

"Do you think some people could hide on your ship and go up the coast to the other harbor?"

Joseph said, "I have a wagon waiting outside that could probably transport ten people." Riley said that he would be happy to fit ten in his wagon, but it was very dirty since he had just arrived with six filthy monkey cages.

Nolan grabbed his key, and they headed for Room 135. "Wait right here. I'll be right back." The Coliseum was in total chaos, as many animals were still being unloaded and taken to various rooms.

Nolan unlocked the door and told the people to follow him quietly. He was amazed that no one was around. It was dark out now, so no one could see much of anything as they climbed in the wagons and went down the road to the harbor. Titus and Nolan got in a wagon of their own and followed along. When they arrived at the dock, Nolan went on the ship with them. Once on board, he asked for David's family. A woman and her sons and an older couple all stepped forward. Nolan told them that David came to him for help and that he would go to their church tomorrow morning, find him, and let him know that they were safe and could be found at the harbor up the coast. At that moment, all of the people realized that they were being rescued, and they cried and thanked them and praised God.

Both captains said that they had to wait until their crews returned to the ship, so they might not sail until midnight. They decided to hide the people down below in the sleeping rooms until they reached the other harbor.

Even though he didn't want to, Nolan knew that it was very important for him to return to the Coliseum. As he was going in, some of the hunters asked him where to put ten ostriches. He took them to Room 135, attached the lock, and gave them the key. Then he returned to his room to think. After a while, Ulric, the man who had captured the twenty prisoners came by, his face white. He told Nolan that the prisoners were all gone and that the room was full of ostriches.

"Oh," said Nolan. "Please don't be alarmed. I guess

they had to move the prisoners to another room. It seems that ostriches can't handle inclines of any kind."

The man looked very relieved. Nolan patted him on the back and said that he looked terrible and needed to go home.

CHAPTER 27

Nolan and Sabrina's home was alive with all kinds of rough housing as the six boys cleaned up and prepared for breakfast. Once they gathered around the table, Nolan thanked God for their food and their safe return.

"There is something we need to tell you, Claudia," said Sabrina. The teenagers all looked at her. "Tell them, Nolan."

"Nuncio, the man in purple, is dead. I was there to witness it. He was trampled by elephants. It's a long story, but that will have to wait."

Claudia laughed and said that she would never cut her hair again.

"We have news for you too, Father and Mother," said Maximus. "We are Christians now. We accepted the Lord and were baptized in the Holy Land."

"All of you?" asked Sabrina.

"Well, the four of us and Flavius," said Felix.

"I'm very happy for you, children," Nolan said, "but you need to know that the emperor has begun arresting people just for being Christians. I rescued twenty Christians last night who were scheduled to die at the Coliseum during the big birthday celebration. I am leaving for their church in a few moments to let them know they are safe."

"Can we go along?" asked Felix. "We have never been to a church."

"Of course you can go," said Nolan, "but what you will see is just a program for children that they have each year just before school begins."

"I want to go again," said Sabrina. "I can't get enough of it." Nolan and Sabrina rode in one wagon, and the teens were in another. Flavius arrived and got in with the teens.

"Were you surprised at Claudia's reaction to the news about Nuncio?" asked Nolan. "She just laughed it off. I know she was scared of him, but he did lose his life."

"Nolan, she's still a child," said Sabrina. "I am so thankful that she can stay that way a little longer."

"Did you tell Lavinia about their opportunity yet?" Nolan asked.

"Yes," she answered. "I figured you would get in late last night, so I went to their place and told them."

"How did they take the news? Are they going to go?" asked Nolan.

"I think they will go," answered Sabrina. "Lavinia is scared, of course, to make such a trip without us. I was more concerned about Cadogan. It was obvious that he did not want to go."

They arrived at the church in time for the singing again, so Sabrina took all of the teenagers and sat down in the back where they were yesterday. Nolan knew he needed to find David as quickly as possible, so he wandered around looking for him. He found him sitting alone outside with his head in his hands. Nolan approached him and cleared his throat.

David was startled and looked up and said, "I didn't expect to see you again so soon."

Nolan told him all about the rescue and that his family and the others would be on a ship in a small harbor north of the main Roman harbor. David was so emotional that he couldn't talk at first, but he grabbed Nolan, expressed his gratitude, and said that he thought he knew where it was and that the church people would help him go get everyone.

In the very back row of the church, Nolan saw his family. His wife, his four teenagers, the two captains' teens, and Flavius all sat clapping and singing along with the children. Nolan felt a yearning that he never experienced before. He wanted to be a part of something good like a church. He wanted to have special friends like the people here.

He walked over and sat down next to Sabrina.

When the singing was over and the awards were given, the man asked if anyone there wanted to accept Jesus and be baptized. Two of the older children raised their hands and walked down the aisle to the front. Felix leaned in close to his parents and said, "That is what we did. We all accepted Jesus, and then we were baptized." Nolan and Sabrina never heard about any of this before, and they watched intently.

When they were all in the wagon on the way back to town, Argus told his parents that they should read some of the letters they brought home with them from their trip. Then they would learn the truth about God.

Once they were back at the villa, the boys asked if they could visit Vernon's mother and sister, and Nolan grudgingly allowed them to go. It was a long walk to the other side of Rome, so they ate their noontime meal and started off. Everyone wanted to go: Argus, Felix, Maximus, Claudia, Flavius, James, Elijah, and Edward. They walked through the city streets, and as they walked, they talked about what they were going to do this year. Argus, Felix, Claudia, and Maximus knew that they would probably move far away and start a new life, not knowing anyone, and probably not telling anyone their hiding place. Flavius had just learned about the death of Nuncio, so he figured that Claudia wouldn't be in any hurry to marry him now. James, Elijah, and Edward thought they would probably go and stay with their grandparents while the ship was being repaired, since that is where they usually went when they were in Rome. It was all very depressing, being separated now that they were all so close.

After walking about forty minutes, they came to the address of Vernon's mother and sister. From across the street, they could see that someone was coming out of the house. They watched as a big, boisterous man came out, yelling for someone inside to go shopping and have his favorite food and drink there when he returned. The teens waited until he was out of sight, and then they walked up to the house and knocked on the door.

A woman came to the door and peeked out at them. She had a black eye, and she looked very fragile and scared.

Maximus asked, "Are you Vernon's mother?" She

nodded that she was, and she opened the door and let them all in.

"I know about Vernon's death," she said. "Francis was here yesterday and told me all about the snake and all."

"Did Francis mention anything about a treasure?" Maximus asked.

A girl came out of a room walking with a cane and said, "I'm Vernon's sister Victoria. Francis told us that as he was dying, Vernon said to tell our mother he loved her and to give me a treasure. Francis said that he never found Vernon's pack."

"We forgot to tell Francis," said Flavius, hitting himself on the forehead.

"Yes, we should have told him," said Maximus. "Our brother Felix found Vernon's pack after he left, and he took care of it for him." Felix went forward and gave the pack to his sister.

Victoria sat down with the pack, and her mother sat down next to her. Together they pulled the various items out. When they came to the cloth, Felix said, "Be careful. The treasure is in that cloth." She unwrapped it very carefully and held up the pearl. It was big and flawless.

"Where did he get this?" his mother asked.

"We'll probably never know," said Maximus. "If we ask about it, someone could get interested in it. We wanted to keep it a secret for you."

"Somehow we can use this to escape from my father," said Victoria. "We have wanted to leave for years. He beats us if we don't have everything perfect for him when he gets home."

"Why don't you just leave?" asked Claudia.

"Where would we go?" her mother asked. "What would we use for money?"

"Mother, if we can find a place to sell this pearl, we could leave," said Victoria.

"Are you thinking what I'm thinking?" asked Argus, looking at Felix.

"Yes," said Felix. "Grab your most important things. We can all help carry them. Come and stay with us until you sell the pearl."

"I'm sure Mother and Father would approve," said Argus. "You can stay in our tree house if nothing else."

The mother and daughter looked at each other. Suddenly they took each other's hands and smiled.

Then Victoria looked sad and said, "I can't go. I can barely walk across the room. My father has beaten me so many times that I can barely walk with a cane."

"I'll carry you," said James. "The others can carry your stuff."

Victoria smiled broadly, and they set to work gathering their things together. It didn't take long. The mother said that her husband just gave them enough money to buy their food. He didn't work very much, since he spent all of his days at the Coliseum watching the shows. They made a pile at the door of things to take.

"That's it?" asked Flavius. "I have more stuff in my travel pack."

"Oh, don't forget to grab Vernon's pack," said Felix.

Victoria picked up his pack and handed it to Claudia with a smile. Claudia also took her cane as James picked up Victoria and headed for the door.

When they were all outside and walking away, Elijah asked, "Don't you want to lock the doors or anything?"

Victoria's mother laughed and said, "We don't care what happens to the place."

❧

While the teens were making their way across town with Victoria and her mother, Lavinia and her boys were packing up their belongings to leave Rome in the morning. Sabrina was sitting in their house, playing with the twins, and the wagon driver was carrying things to the wagon as fast as they could pack them. Lavinia had been getting rid of nonessentials for weeks, but she didn't expect to have just one day's notice to leave.

"I guess the thing I'm most worried about is our safety on the ship," said Lavinia.

Sabrina tried to comfort her. "Tomorrow when we arrive at the dock, we will be there with you. Nolan will go aboard ahead of you and talk to the captain of the ship. If he has any doubts at all about your safety, he won't let you go."

"Well, I do have another concern," said Lavinia. "I don't have any money. We might need something before we reach my parents."

"Nolan is taking care of that today. He will send some money with you," said Sabrina, running after little Harmony.

"Oh, we're going to miss you so much," said Lavinia. "You have been like a sister to me."

Nolan returned, and the servants had prepared a picnic for all of them at the back of the yard. They went outside just in time to see the large group of teenagers entering the place. Argus and Felix went straight to Nolan and Sabrina and told them about Vernon's family and how they invited them to come there to hide out until they could get some money to support themselves.

"I said they could stay in the tree house if nothing else," confided Argus.

"Father," said Claudia. "The boys all have guests. Couldn't I have Victoria stay with me in my room for a while?"

"Yes," said Nolan, "that's fine."

Sabrina went to Victoria's mother and welcomed her. "You can stay in a room that I use to sew and do crafts. This is an uncertain time for all of us." Then she told the boys to take all of their belongings inside and then join them in the back of the yard for the picnic.

Everyone sat around the tables near the beautiful gardens and ate their meal. Then Nolan stood up.

"This certainly reminds me of a picnic we had two months ago," he said. "Do you all remember?" Many of them nodded their heads. "First of all, I would like to welcome our new friends, Enrica and her daughter, Victoria." The women smiled shyly and still looked very nervous.

Nolan continued, "I would also like to say farewell to Lavinia and her children. We will pray for your safety, and maybe someday we will join you." Lavinia and Sabrina cried. They were each holding one of the twins, but they reached out and took each other's hand. Kendrick reached for one of the girls and took her from his mother's arms. He looked very happy. Cadogan, however, looked angry. Claudia and Flavius sat on each side of Victoria, obviously trying to make her at home.

Cadogan knew that his leaving was the last thing on Claudia's mind.

Then Nolan said, "Today, when we returned from the church, Argus gave me a copy of the Book of John to read. Sabrina and I read the first three chapters, and we made a decision. We are going back to that church to see if we can find anyone around who could take our confession of faith and baptize us in that lake." Sabrina smiled at him. "Well, we need to go back anyway and see if our rescue was a success."

"Father," said Maximus. "If no one is around, we can go down into the lake and baptize you and Mother. Any Christian can do it."

"Thanks, Son. Would anyone else like to go and watch?" Nolan asked. Everyone wanted to go. There were seventeen of them altogether, so he had to get three wagons so the women would all be comfortable.

They had a wonderful ride out to the church. It was a sunny day with a breeze blowing and wildflowers blooming everywhere. The teenagers talked and laughed the entire time. Lavinia was getting very excited about her journey, thinking that she might get to see her parents again and present her four dear children to them. She even thought of a certain man, not so young now, who she once loved and wondered if he ever married.

Victoria and her mother sat together, looking very timid. Enrica's black eye looked dreadful in the sunlight, and bruises could be seen on Victoria's arms as well.

When they reached the church, several people were walking in with scrolls in their hands. The people recognized Nolan and greeted him warmly. They told Nolan that David and his family were spending the evening in their home, recovering from their scare. The other fifteen rescued people were hiding with various church families, trying to decide whether it was safe to return to Rome.

When Nolan told the man about their plans to be baptized, he was very happy. He went inside and got the people who were already in there, and they all went down to the lake.

After the baptisms, they were about to walk back to the church when James said, "Hold on a minute."

Everyone looked at James, and he said, "Do you think I could get baptized, too? I mean, I don't know the whole story, and I should have learned it before now. When I was a child back in Joppa, we used to learn about Jesus in school. But now I know that Jesus died for all of us, right?"

The preacher laughed and said that was the most important thing to know and he would be glad to baptize him. He asked if there was anyone else.

Elijah said, "I believe that God saved our father's life in the storm, not once, but also that time many years ago, when he was with the man of God. Yes. I will get baptized too." Edward went forward too. So all three of the boys became Christians, and once again, everyone cheered. They walked back to the church and dried off, and the three boys were given scrolls of their own, telling the story.

Nolan and the preacher went off together and had a long talk. Nolan told him all about the life he had been leading as manager of the Coliseum and how he hated the things he did, and how his life could end at

any time at the whim of the emperor. The preacher
told Nolan that he would pray for his safety around the
emperor and the safety of the others, and he invited
them to attend the worship service on Sunday.

CHAPTER 28

Nolan and Sabrina went to the harbor with Lavinia and the children the next morning. Felix and Maximus and James went along, too, to send them off. Cadogan was upset that Claudia didn't come along, but when he asked about her, Felix said that Claudia didn't think she should leave Victoria alone.

They reached the dock, and Nolan told them all to stay put until he talked to the captain about the trip schedule and about the safety of the family. After a while, he came off the ship, smiling, and waved to them as he ran to the wagon.

"Lavinia, I think your family will be just fine," said Nolan. "The captain tells me that his crew is the best anywhere. He is putting your family in a cabin right next to his own. And he said not to worry about the safety of the ship, either. He said that they follow the coast all along northern Italy, across Gaul, and go all the way around Spain. He said that they are never very far from land, and they stop many times along the way for fresh supplies. He said he has led this trip this time of year for the last five years, and it is his most enjoyable route."

They moved the family and all of their belongings onto the ship. One of the crewmembers kept staring at James as he went in and out carrying things. Finally Nolan asked the man why he was staring at James.

"He looks like someone I know," said the man.

James heard a little of the discussion and approached the man. "Who do you know that looks like me?"

"A member of the crew," he said. "He will be back soon. I think he had to go purchase some items for the captain."

"What is his name?" asked James.

"We call him Ben," said the man.

Just then James looked up, and coming toward him was his brother. "Benjamin," he shouted.

"James," he said. The two brothers stood there and hugged for a long time. James was crying, and Benjamin couldn't believe how much he had grown.

The two brothers went off to the side and talked a long time while Nolan, Sabrina, and the boys said goodbye to Lavinia and the children.

Nolan and Felix and Maximus approached James and his brother, and James was happy to introduce him to them. Nolan said it was almost time to leave.

"You know you need to come with me," said James. "Father misses you so much, and Mother is trying to have another baby, so you know how much she misses you. And it's not fair that I don't have a brother around."

"But I'm needed on this trip," said Benjamin. "I am learning so much."

"You can learn it all from Father," said James. "Please come with me."

"Let me just take this last trip, and when we get back to Rome, I'll come home," Benjamin said.

"I think it's wrong," said James. "I am convinced more than ever that family is important. If you don't come with me now, you could meet a girl who lives far away and always be torn like Father is. And I just want you around."

Benjamin was very thoughtful, and James's tears were affecting him. Finally he said, "Wait out on the dock, and I'll see what the captain says."

Nolan and the boys went off the ship after they pulled Sabrina away from the twins and Lavinia. They waited there quite a while and noticed that the crew was preparing to pull away. Suddenly Benjamin came running out, shouting farewells to the crewmembers as he left. He was carrying a bag with all of his possessions.

"I wouldn't do this for anyone in the world but you, little brother," said Benjamin.

They stood there a long time, waving to Lavinia and the children. Cadogan looked sad, but the rest of them were happy. Kendrick was holding Heather, and she was smiling and waving "bye-bye." Lavinia was laughing as Harmony bounced up and down in her arms. Sabrina had the feeling that she would never see them again.

Since they were near the place where Titus and Flavius lived, they decided to stop by and see them. Titus came to the door and welcomed them in. He introduced them to his beautiful wife, Sonya, who had big blue eyes and gorgeous red hair about the same color as her son's. They said that Flavius was not around because he was spending most of his time these days near a certain young lady. His mother said that she was dying to meet Claudia.

Titus surprised them by saying, "I'm afraid that I won't be able to work for you anymore, Nolan. I just can't live with myself, knowing how they treat the animals that we capture. And I don't want to have anything to do with the Coliseum. I'm glad I was able to help rescue those twenty prisoners, but there are so many more that we can't help. I guess you are fed up with it too."

"You could definitely say that," said Nolan. "I can't do it any more either."

Nolan explained that on the emperor's birthday, during the grand finale of the celebration, he and his whole family planned to drop out of sight.

"What about Flavius and Claudia?" Titus asked.

"I don't know," said Nolan. "We will just have to find a way to let you know where we are."

"Well, I'm sure you'll think of something," laughed Titus. "You have, what, several days to decide what you are going to do and where you are going to live for the rest of your life."

"Well, what are you going to do to earn your living?" asked Nolan.

"I haven't figured that out yet," said Titus. "But it will be good honest work."

Titus and his wife served them all a noontime meal and some tea. They had a nice visit, trying to solve their problems, and then they left.

"I know I should check in at the Coliseum," said Nolan. "But first, let's find our way to that little harbor so that a certain captain can see his sons."

They got in the wagon and traveled rapidly through town and were soon on a country road. Nolan followed the directions given him as they went round and round on a very curvy road. Finally they arrived at the harbor. There was only one ship docked at the harbor. The crewmembers were standing around on the deck or lying around the beach. Captain Riley was on the deck and saw the wagon coming. He ran down the walkway to join them and stopped suddenly as he saw his two sons together.

"Run and get Joseph," he called to a crewmember. And then he quietly said, "My boys are together again at last."

Captain Riley and his brother Joseph stood and visited for a long time. He couldn't stop smiling about having his son back again. But they were very frustrated about the harbor they were in. It just didn't have accommodations for all of their men, and it was too far away for him and Joseph to stay at their parents' house. The hardest thing to deal with was the lack of a marketplace to buy all of the supplies needed to repair their ship.

"Father," said Benjamin. "I think you should take the ship to the harbor at Naples. It has even more marketplaces than the harbor at Rome, and I'm sure no one will care if you spend the winter there to repair your ship."

"That sounds like an excellent idea, Son," said Captain Riley. "We could actually travel on the roads every now and then to see your grandparents."

"Oh, the housing is very reasonable there, so your crew would be happy," said Benjamin. "There is another wonderful thing about Naples, but I'm not sure I should tell you."

"You have me worried," said his father. "What could be so bad that you can't tell me?"

"Well, it's not bad at all," said Benjamin. "There is a Christian church there that I love. The people there are wonderful. Many of them knew the apostles Peter and Paul, and they love to tell stories about them and share the wisdom about Christ that they learned from them."

"Are you a Christian?" asked James. He looked very excited.

"Yes, I am," Benjamin answered. "I became a Christian in Naples last year. Our ship stayed there for two months, and most of us became Christians."

"I'm a Christian, too," said James. "So are Nolan and Sabrina and all of their kids." Then he looked at his Uncle Joseph and said, "Elijah and Edward are Christians too."

"Well, I promise that I will check out that church if we go to Naples," said Captain Riley.

"Well, what are we waiting for?" asked Joseph. "We aren't doing anything here but sitting around. I might even find a ship there that needs a captain and a crew."

"Are you coming on the ship with us?" Captain Riley asked James.

"Well, not if you are going right now," James answered. "I wanted Benjamin to meet the rest of Nolan's family." He looked at Nolan and Sabrina and said, "Of course, maybe you don't have room for Benjamin to stay."

"Oh, he can stay with us," said Sabrina. "It's just that we don't know how long we'll be there."

"We are leaving Rome," said Nolan. "We don't know where to go. I just have to get away from the emperor, and I was hoping to leave during the celebration when the emperor will be too drunk on power, popularity, and fine wine to notice I'm gone."

"Why don't you come with us to Naples?" suggested Joseph.

"Why don't we all go to Naples?" said Riley. "Nolan, all of your children could come with us in the ship down the coast. We could even take your furniture and all of your belongings in the cargo hold."

Felix and Maximus had been quiet until now, but Felix finally said, "You could go too, Mother. We could go now. If we get everything moved out, it will be easier for Father to slip away during the celebration. And right now, we have lots of boys around with strong arms to carry things to wagons and then to the ship."

"I love the idea of getting the family away safely," said Nolan. "But is it far enough away? People will recognize me."

"You could just consider it a temporary move," said Joseph. "Just put some distance between you and the emperor."

"Who knows?" said Captain Riley. "Maybe the emperor will die. He probably has some enemies."

"More than he could count, I'm sure," said Nolan.

"I think you will be safer in Naples," said Benjamin.

"Nolan, can you get away today?" asked Riley. "You could come along with us and check out Naples. You could get a feel for the place. We will all sleep on the ship, of course."

"What do you think, dear?" Nolan asked Sabrina. "Are you ready to leave?"

"I think we need to move now, while we can," Sabrina answered. "We might not get another chance."

"I can't decide whether to move out of our home today and have everyone stay on the ship, or just have the family go on a temporary journey to Naples to see if it would work for us," Nolan said.

"When does the birthday celebration take place?" Sabrina asked Nolan.

"It begins just a few days from today, and it will last an entire week, with the grand finale on the emperor's birthday," said Nolan.

"That is so close," said Sabrina. "Let's just go ahead and get our furniture and everything on the ship now, while it's available. That way the children and I will be one less thing for you to worry about, because once the festivities begin, you won't have time to think about us."

"That will be a huge relief to me," said Nolan. "I will be able to focus on my job. Let's do it."

Nolan and Sabrina squeezed onto the wagon along with the ones who came with them, and also Joseph and four of his strongest crewmembers. They dropped Sabrina off at the villa, and Nolan warned her not to tell the servants that she was moving until they think of a good story to tell them.

Next, all the rest of them went to the market area to get wagons. Each wagon took a different route to the villa to avoid attention. Nolan went to everyone and told them the plan.

Sabrina saw the shocked look on Enrica and Victoria's faces, so she went to them immediately. "You two are not the only ones fleeing for your safety," she said. "If you are willing, we will take you along with us to see if Naples is a good place to settle."

"I think some of my husband's family lives in Naples," said Enrica.

"Well, we will leave you on the ship while we visit the city," said Sabrina. The two refugees looked satisfied, so Sabrina turned her attention to Claudia, who was standing next to her.

"What about Flavius?" Claudia asked with her hands on her hips.

Flavius was watching off to the side. Sabrina motioned for him to come over. "Flavius, I met your mother this morning. Do you want to ask if you can go along to Naples with us? Nolan will be returning to Rome in a few days," Sabrina said. "You could travel back and forth with him." Flavius looked very relieved and said he would be back later.

The teens and men all went to work moving everything out of the house and into the wagons. All of the servants looked completely devastated, and Sabrina didn't know how much she could tell them. She went to Nolan, who gathered all of the servants together and assured them that even though Sabrina and the children were leaving, he was not, and he would be back at the villa in a few days, and for now they were to maintain the property and not to worry. Then he took off for the Coliseum to make sure that everything was on schedule for the big show.

Sabrina had been packing all week, so this part of the move was quite simple. They moved everything from the outer buildings in the back to the hanging flower baskets in the front. By nightfall the wagons were loaded and ready to go, and Nolan was back. He instructed each driver to go a different path through town, and then go together once they reached the country road.

Flavius arrived just in time and said that his parents were happy that Nolan's family had a plan and that for now he could go along and help. But he was reminded to keep in touch.

Sabrina and Enrica rode in Nolan's wagon, but Victoria was in a wagon that James was driving with Flavius and Claudia. When Enrica saw Victoria laughing and joking with the teens, she got tears in her eyes.

"I have been afraid that Victoria was damaged emotionally beyond repair," she said. "But look at her laughing. I think we did the right thing when we ran away."

"I know you did the right thing," said Sabrina. "And I think we are doing the right thing, too, but it is hard leaving our homes, isn't it?"

"Well, it's not that hard for me to leave our home, but I can see why you feel that way," said Enrica.

They traveled to the little harbor without any interference, and when they got there, the rest of the crew helped move everything to the cargo hold below. The teens were right at home on the ship and went straight to their room. Claudia was thrilled to have a girl along for a change, and Enrica did not object when they took Victoria off to the teen room with them. It took two people to get Victoria into her hammock, but she seemed to enjoy the attention.

After a while, they could feel movement, and they knew the ship was on its way to Naples.

Benjamin was twenty years old and quite a world traveler, but he had not been around anyone his own age for a long time. He was fascinated with the group and how well they got along. He had to ask, "How do you four feel about leaving your home?"

"Well, we've only been home for two days," Argus answered. "That was not enough time to settle in."

"We've known for a couple of months that this day would come," said Felix. "I'm just disappointed that I didn't get to run any races, and I didn't get to see my best friend, Miranda. I hope she's not getting involved with anyone else."

"I'm going back to Rome with your father," said Flavius. "Why don't you come, too, and go see her?"

"I don't think they will let any of us go back," said Felix. "But I might send a letter, and you could give it to her. Of course, I don't want her falling for that red hair of yours."

"Don't worry," said Flavius. "I only have eyes for one girl." He sat up in his hammock and smiled at Claudia.

"Victoria," James asked. "What have the doctors told you about your legs?"

"I've never been to a doctor," she answered. The others couldn't believe it, but they didn't want to embarrass her, so they didn't ask anything else.

The teenagers continued to talk into the night, and the ship traveled all night and most of the next day, entering the harbor in the early evening.

CHAPTER 29

The travelers stood at the railing.

"Look over there," said Benjamin. "If you look way up there on the hillside, you can see our church."

Captain Riley said, "Shall we go over to that church and see if they can offer any suggestions for you?" Everyone thought that was the best place to begin.

A huge party of family members and crew alike left the ship and headed for the church. Enrica and Victoria stayed behind because of the walk. As the group got close, they could tell that something was going on, because there were horses and wagons all over the parking area. All at once, a bride and groom burst out the doors, followed by many happy, laughing people.

"Oh, dear," said Benjamin. "We came at a bad time. No one will be available to talk to us."

But the bride and groom saw Benjamin and shouted for him to come over. He was self-conscious because he wasn't dressed up, but they ran to him and welcomed him anyway. Then the wedding couple kissed their families and left to begin their new life together.

Many people went over to welcome Benjamin and meet his father and brother. Then Benjamin introduced them to Nolan and Sabrina and others. Riley told the people that Nolan had a problem and needed help. They took him and Sabrina over to a seating area and listened as they explained their need to relocate and hide their identity from anyone with ties to the emperor. The people explained that they, too, were planning to take attention away from themselves. In the past, they wanted people to see them from far away, and now they wanted to plant trees and shrubs to hide their building.

One of the men listening said that he had an idea that possibly could help them. He explained that recently he built a nice villa for his family to live in, and now they had to move to a nearby town to care for his parents. His family was very disappointed, but they had no choice but to move. He asked Nolan if he would like to see the place. They could actually walk there from the church.

The family got very excited when they saw the villa. It had more bedrooms than their place in Rome and more buildings as well. It had a lovely view of the harbor with a path that went right down to the beach. The only drawback was that it didn't have any flowers or shrubs. It didn't have the beautiful garden area they were used to. But the place was available, and it was close to the harbor, the marketplace, and best of all, the church. They decided to purchase the place immediately. Since it was so late in the evening, they were going to sleep on the ship and move their belongings the next morning.

Nolan and Sabrina tried to comfort Enrica and Victoria. They told them about the new villa and invited them to stay in one of their buildings until something else came along for them. They also invited the two captains and their boys to stay as well while they repaired the ship and any time they passed through Naples.

Argus, Felix, Maximus, and Claudia talked about which rooms they were going to get in the new house.

"Which room do you want, Maximus?" asked Claudia. "Do you want a view of the harbor?"

"You know, I think I want a room with windows on the church side of the house. I think it would be nice to look out and see people arriving at church," said Maximus.

"You don't seem very happy, Felix," commented Argus. "What's wrong?"

"I'm so mad at myself for not going to see Miranda when we were in Rome," said Felix. "We were there two whole days. When will I ever get a chance to see her again?"

"I told you," said Flavius. "Go back with your father and me. You could stay at my house."

"I don't think Father will let me," said Felix, "but I would like that."

"Please don't blame yourself for not going to see her," said Claudia. "We were very busy rescuing Victoria and her mother. And you went along to see Cadogan and Kendrick sail away. You were gone all day."

"That's right," said Felix. "I shouldn't have gone along to see them off to Mide. Father kept us busy the rest of the day."

"What are you going to tell her, anyway?" asked Claudia.

"I'll take it slow," said Felix. "We need to get to know each other again."

"Well, I think Father will let you go with him and stay at Flavius's house," said Claudia. "Just promise him that you won't go near the Coliseum or our villa."

For the next two days, they were all very busy moving into the villa. It took longer because they had to do everything for themselves without the help of any servants.

CHAPTER 30

Felix and Flavius made the trip back to Rome with Nolan after helping with the big move into the villa. The next morning, Nolan went to the Coliseum and Felix went to see Miranda. Flavius had a long talk with his parents.

"You wouldn't believe their new villa," said Flavius. "It is beautiful, and it has a view of the harbor that is breathtaking at night. There is even a path that leads directly from their villa right down to the docks."

"It sounds lovely," said his mother. "We should go for a visit very soon."

"Mother," said Flavius, "I won't be happy going for a visit. I want to move there with them. There is a big church right next door to their place. Argus, Felix, and Maximus are all going to get involved there. The two captains and their boys are spending the whole winter there repairing their ship. It's where I want to be."

"How will you support yourself?" asked Titus. "I don't want you to be a burden on Nolan's family."

"Well, how are you going to support yourself?" asked Flavius. "You quit your job working for Nolan."

"We're all right for a while," said Titus. "I always set money aside for a rainy day."

"Father, I think you know how I feel about Claudia," said Flavius. "I want to marry her someday. I have been thinking about becoming a physician. Rescuing those hunters in the jungle was very fulfilling to me. I think I could learn how to take care of people and their injuries and diseases."

"Oh, son, I would be so proud if you became a doctor," said Sonya, his mother.

"Let's go with Flavius down to Naples and find a physician with a good reputation and see if he will teach him everything he knows," suggested Titus.

"Oh, yes, let's do that," said Sonya. "When is Nolan going back to Naples?"

"I think he's going back in a few days," said Flavius, "on the emperor's birthday."

"Good," said Sonya. "That gives me time to pack and prepare to be away for a few weeks."

"Well, Son," said Titus. "You've given your mother something to look forward to. Now get busy and pack up your own things. You probably won't be coming back for a while."

❦

Felix finally got to go see Miranda. Two months without a word from him had been hard on her, and it was obvious by the look on her face and the tears in her eyes.

"I'm so sorry, Miranda, that I didn't tell you I was leaving," Felix said. "Argus and I saved a man's life at the Coliseum. That should have been a good thing, but since the emperor and his crowds wanted to see him trampled and killed, it put our own lives in danger. Father thought we needed to get away from Rome for a while, so he sent us off with his hunters to Africa. We had quite an adventure."

"Well, I'm very happy for you," said Miranda. "It must seem pretty dull being back here in Rome with me."

"I have a lot to tell you," said Felix. "I'm a Christian now."

Miranda stood up and looked at him. She was silent for a moment, and then she said, "My sister and her husband are Christians. My mother and father are so worried about them because the emperor wants to kill Christians. Did you hear about that?"

"Yes, I did," said Felix. "My father helped twenty Christians escape who were scheduled to perform at the Coliseum. They were going to wear costumes and fight until they were killed."

"How horrible," said Miranda. "Could that happen to you?"

"Our family is moving to Naples to get away from the danger," said Felix. "Would you like to read about my new faith? I brought one of my scrolls to give you."

Miranda said that she would like to read it. Then Felix and Miranda went to see their other friends, and some of the boys told Felix all about the big race that he missed. They told him they would have won had he been on their team. After he and Miranda hung out with their friends for a while, he told them that he was a Christian now. One of his friends had heard about the big arrest and told him to be careful. Felix told them to get a copy of the Book of Matthew, Mark, Luke, or John, or the *Word of God*.

It was getting late when Felix took Miranda back to her home.

"So did you miss me while I was gone?" Felix asked.

"I did miss you," said Miranda. "You and I have had some really good times together since we were little, but for all I know, you are going to move to Naples, and I will never see you again."

"I know this is all new to you, but how do you feel about Jesus?" asked Felix. "Do you understand yet who he is and what he did for us?"

"I thought we were talking about us," said Miranda, "about you and me."

"Without Jesus there is no us," said Felix.

Miranda really didn't know what to say. She thought, *What am I going to do? If I don't accept his religion right now, I will lose Felix. And if I do accept it, I will be committed to a religion that I barely know anything about.*

"I'm really rushing you, aren't I?" asked Felix.

"I'm sorry," said Miranda. "It's just all so new to me."

"If we are supposed to be together, we'll find a way," said Felix. "Maybe I'll wear a disguise when I come to Rome to see you, so anyone related to the emperor won't recognize me." They said good-bye, and Felix left.

❦

Nolan's first day back in Rome was not as relaxing as it was for Flavius and Felix. Even though everything was set for the big celebration before he went to Naples, the plans were falling apart now. The emperor invited so many people from around the world to his birthday celebration that many of the regular fifty thousand fans could not get tickets. They were furious and were damaging property all over the city. Some of the food served at the Coliseum was contaminated, and people were throwing up and getting rowdy and cranky. The object of having monkeys in the show was to have hunters catch them and kill them, but instead the animals could climb the walls and were terrifying the audience.

The emperor was on the warpath, because he thought that these problems might come up next week at the real celebration. His advisors told him that someone was trying to sabotage his birthday celebration. Nolan spent a long time convincing him that sometimes things just go wrong. He presented the emperor with the baby tiger that Titus brought back for him, and that seemed to please him. Nolan suggested that he go back to his seat and try not to worry about a thing.

Nolan breathed a sigh of relief and returned to his office, but the moment he got there, Ulric walked in.

"Nolan," he began, "I have looked in every room in the Coliseum, and I have not located the twenty prisoners."

"Really?" Nolan began. "They could have been moved to one of the thirty-five prisons we have around the city. You can get that list of prisons from the main prison guard and go check out each one of them."

"What if I don't find them?" he asked.

"Who will know the difference?" Nolan said. "We will just have one hundred ninety people on each ship, instead of two hundred. I wouldn't even bother looking for them if I were you."

Nolan had the feeling that the man was not going to give up that easily. Someone told Nolan that Ulric was after his job. Nolan would be very happy to let him have it, but he didn't want to lose his life in the process.

"There are people who think you let the prisoners go, and I must say I have suspected it, too," said Ulric. Nolan studied the man. His little eyes were squinted, and his forehead was covered with sweat. Nolan realized that Ulric was a very ambitious man who thought that getting close to the emperor would bring him wealth and power.

Nolan started to leave, but Ulric stuck out his arm and said, "I am going back to the place where we arrested the twenty Christians, and if I see even one of them there, I will know they were released. I might even torture some poor soul to find out who let them go."

"I think a better use of your time would be getting those monkeys away from the audience and back in the cages," said Nolan. "They weren't even supposed to be used until next week. We need to put something on the walls so they can't climb up where the people are."

"How would that be my job?" asked Ulric.

"Who hired you to track down and arrest Christians?" asked Nolan.

"The advisors to the emperor personally chose me to see that certain loose ends were tied up," said Ulric.

"I see," said Nolan. "Well, monkeys terrorizing the audience and visitors vomiting contaminated food have the emperor in a panic. Now those are loose ends that need to be tied up."

Ulric turned and stamped away, screaming that he would follow through with the job he was asked to do.

Nolan decided to visit a man he knew who bought and sold properties. He told the man that he already moved his family out and asked him if he knew of anyone who would be interested in buying his villa. The man looked through his notes and said he could think of two men who might be interested.

The other thing Nolan hoped to do before leaving the city was visit the church where he was baptized. He took a wagon to the place, but there was nothing going on there. He sat there a long time. He looked out at the lake where he was baptized, and he thought that it was so peaceful here at the church. Then he wondered how he ever got involved with the emperor and the work at the Coliseum. Was it ambition? He enjoyed having so many people working under him. He loved having Roman soldiers for his personal use. He wondered if he would be able to use his skills in Naples to support his family. And he worried about all of the good people who worked for him. Would they be punished in his absence? He prayed that they would not. Just as he was about to leave, the preacher came by.

Nolan stood up and said, "I was afraid my trip out here was in vain. I really wanted to talk to you."

"I heard they were trying to round up Christians again," said the preacher.

Nolan looked shocked. He had only been away from the Coliseum a couple of hours. Could Ulric act that fast? "What are you talking about?" he asked.

"Today the same group of soldiers came by the conference center where they arrested the twenty people," said the preacher. "We think they are trying to find them."

"Did they take anyone?" Nolan asked.

"Not yet," said the preacher, "but I guess one man was so frustrated that he was ready to start arresting anyone, Christian or not."

"Was the man short and stocky with squinty eyes and graying hair?" asked Nolan.

"That's what they told me. Why?" asked the preacher.

"Apparently, he doesn't believe the story I gave him about them being moved somewhere. I think he is going to keep digging until he finds out what actually happened to them," said Nolan.

Then Nolan told him all about moving his family and about the Christian community there in Naples.

"Oh, I know the leader there and many of the people. I'm so happy you will be with them, and perhaps I will get to see you now and then."

"If I live long enough," said Nolan.

"I don't know if you will ever realize what you did for those people," said the preacher. "You saved their lives, yes, but so much more. Their families need them and we need them."

Nolan said goodbye, and the preacher promised to pray for his safety. Nolan didn't know where to go next. He didn't want to make extra work for Titus and his wife, so he went to his villa and slept on the floor.

CHAPTER 31

On the first day of the big celebration, Nolan arrived at the Coliseum and wandered around the place, checking on the animals and the landscaping props. One of the animal controllers ran up to him and asked for help.

"I did what you told me. I put monkey guards just below the stands, and it worked for the monkeys," he said.

"Good," Nolan said. "What's the problem?"

"Come and see," the controller said. Nolan followed him to the first level observation area. The monkeys were swinging and jumping all over the fake trees. The man pointed straight across the Coliseum to a gorilla that was grabbing the monkey guard and using it to pull himself up into the stands.

"Get a net and go catch that thing," yelled Nolan

"It's out of control. Look around the place," yelled the man. "They are everywhere."

Nolan watched a gorilla grab a man and throw him to the floor below. Then it turned and growled loudly at the people nearby. It seized people by their hair or their clothes and tossed them around. People were screaming and trying to get away from it.

The controller got Nolan's attention back and said, "What should we do?"

Nolan scanned the audience and could see that gorillas were causing havoc everywhere. "How many did they release?"

"All fifteen of them," he said. "The emperor was hoping they would chase the monkeys and kill them, but they were more interested in the crowds."

"Get fifteen nets out of storage, and I'll get some men to go after them," said Nolan. Before he left the observation area, he looked over at the emperor's seat. His advisors were trying to persuade him to leave, but he stared in horror as a gorilla dragged a man by his head and used him as a club to knock people out of their seats and onto the floor of the arena.

Most of the audience fled the Coliseum and did not return for the evening shows. It took hours to capture the gorillas, and one managed to get away. Not only was there a gorilla loose in the city of Rome, but there were two hundred spectators dead and probably just as many injured.

The emperor's advisors came to Nolan's room and escorted him to the emperor. "What were you thinking when you put those monkey guards up?" the emperor asked.

"Who could predict that the gorillas would use the monkey guards to climb up to the audience?" asked Nolan.

"You should have thought of that," shouted the emperor. "I should just get rid of you right now. I could, you know. One word from me, and you'll be running from the lions tomorrow."

"Then who would bring in the battleships and fill the place with water for the big finale, Your Excellency?" asked Nolan. Nolan walked away with his heart pounding and his skin tingling. *Don't look back*, he said to himself.

Over the next several days, the shows went better, and the audience saw large quantities of violence and blood. Performances that featured rhinos, giraffes, and ostriches delighted the crowds. The emperor was happy that he was getting the praise and attention he deserved.

Nolan had been sleeping at the home of Titus and his wife ever since the day the emperor threatened his life. On the evening before the last day of performances, Nolan sat visiting with Titus and Francis.

"So is tomorrow the last performance of the big birthday celebration?" asked Francis.

"Yes," answered Nolan, "except for the grand finale, with the battleships."

"Do you feel that your life is still in danger?" asked Titus.

"Anyone who works near the emperor is in danger of losing his life," said Nolan.

"Are you all set for tomorrow's performance?" asked Francis. "You don't want anything to go wrong at the last minute."

"I am a little nervous about tomorrow, because it features the oversized lions. I have worked with the regular lions before, but we don't know how these giants are going to work out," said Nolan. "If something goes wrong, the emperor might throw me in the arena. I still tremble when I think about his threats the other day."

"I know I said I couldn't work there anymore," said Titus, "but I will be there for you tomorrow, if you want."

"I'll be there too," said Francis. "I want to see you escape from Rome in one piece."

"Thank you so much, my friends," said Nolan.

Felix and Flavius had walked in just in time to hear the conversation. "Father, we have some experience with the lions. Do you want us to help too?"

"No," said Nolan. "I don't want you any where near the Coliseum."

Titus said the same thing—that the boys should stay far away from the place. "We will be leaving the city in a couple of days," he said. "Aren't there people you want to say good-bye to?"

Flavius was eager to leave the city and go see Claudia. Felix had not seen Miranda since the day he told her that they could only be together if she became a Christian.

"I will try to find Miranda tomorrow," said Felix. "I'm afraid if I don't see her tomorrow, we'll never get together."

"Well, you boys finish your business tomorrow, because the day after that, we will attempt to sneak away from the city," said Nolan.

❦

Felix went to see Miranda, and her mother told him that she was at her sister's house on the other side of the city. "Her sister has been telling her about Jesus," she said. "She will be back here tomorrow. Is it true that you are leaving Rome soon?"

"Yes, but I will come and say good-bye to her just before we leave," said Felix.

⟨੭ⱽ੭⟩

Nolan, Titus, and Francis supervised the release of the twenty lions, some regular and some enormous, into the arena of the Coliseum. They went up to the observation area to watch the action. They looked over at the emperor and were surprised to see Ulric sitting next to him, chatting happily and feeding him grapes. Ulric looked over at the three of them with a haughty look that made Nolan think he was up to something.

They watched the floor of the arena. Twenty-four men dressed in black were released, and the door was slammed behind them. Each man wore protective armor and carried a very sharp sword.

"Twenty-four men fighting against twenty lions," said Nolan. "I wonder where they got those rugged characters."

Francis looked at Titus and asked, "Do you recognize those men?"

"I saw men just like that when we left the dock at Cyrene," said Titus.

"That's who I thought they were, the Renegades" said Francis.

The men looked very small compared to the lions, but they fought bravely. The men yelled orders to each other as they divided into groups of four. When a lion pounced on one of the fighters, the other three dug their swords deep into the animal, killing it swiftly.

Although they were slaughtering many of the lions, the men were losing their own members at a faster rate. After hours of action, Nolan counted six fighters to five lions. Three Renegades took on a lion at one end of the floor and were able to kill it without losing one of their own. The crowd went wild.

The three triumphant fighters ran to join two others, who were trying to fend off a wounded lion. The group joined them and finished it off quickly, bringing the count to six men against three lions. One man was hiding alone behind a big, fake rock. The other men were limping or holding their wounds, but they knew they had to continue. They chose a lion to pursue, but as they went after it, a different lion attacked them from the rear, taking out one of the hunters and seriously wounding another. As they stood with their backs against the wall, sizing up the enemy, they saw the isolated man behind the rock and took their wounded man to him, ordering him to protect him.

One of the lions was able to jump up on the monkey guard and then leap from it, landing in the stands of people. The Renegades cheered from down below, realizing that they just had to overpower two more lions. But suddenly a lion saw the two men hiding behind the rock and attacked them, killing them both. As it was mauling one of the men on the ground, the three remaining fighters attacked it with their swords, leaving just one lion for them to fight.

The spectators were unarmed as the lion in the stands attacked and killed dozens of men. Nolan, Titus, and Francis ran inside to get a net and find some animal controllers to help, while the men on the floor hid behind the rock and rested.

The lone lion on the floor prowled around, looking up at the crowd. The lion was so gigantic that it put its front paws up on the monkey guard and roared loudly at the crowd. The three fighters saw their opportunity and charged the lion, thrusting their swords deep into its sides. It dropped to the ground and remained motionless. The men hugged each other in joy as they realized they were alone on the floor.

Most of the crowd cheered loudly as the emperor gave the signal to release the prisoners. On one side of the stands, however, a mammoth lion was attacking and killing many of the viewers. Nolan and his men worked their way across the seating area with their net. As they approached the lion to throw the net, it turned abruptly and attacked Francis. Titus and Nolan threw the net over the lion as one member of their group jabbed his spear into its side. They were able to overpower and eventually kill the animal, but they were not able to save Francis. The crowd cheered loudly and poured out of the Coliseum, understanding that the day's events were over.

Nolan and Titus kneeled beside Francis and cried softly. They were approached by two of the emperor's advisors.

"His Excellence has requested that you stop mourning for your friend and attend to the matter at hand, which is moving the battleships into the building," the advisor stated.

"Yes," answered Nolan. "We were just about to take care of that." Titus picked up Francis's body and carried it over his shoulder.

"We are not doing anything until we tell his wife,"

said Nolan. "Francis loved her more than anything, and I think she felt the same way about him."

"How much time do we have until we need to move the battleships?" asked Titus.

"I am half tempted to take off after we leave Francis's home," said Nolan. "I know Ulric is up to no good."

But after the tearful visit with Francis's wife, Nolan went to the building that housed the battleships and gave the order for them to be moved to the Coliseum. The men were all there, waiting eagerly to complete the task. Then he returned to the Coliseum and gave the order for the workers to move the clay-covered strips out of storage and cover the entire floor. The water proofing would be completed just before the ships arrived.

Nolan and Titus were heading for Nolan's office when they heard voices in the hallway around the bend. They stopped talking and listened carefully. Nolan peeked around the corner and saw a big, husky man standing with Ulric.

"He has to come to this office eventually, and when he does, we'll grab him," Ulric said.

"What do you plan to do with him?" asked the man.

"You take him and put him in Room 135, the same one that he once went to and freed my prisoners," said Ulric. "Then we will just forget he's there for a while. The battleships won't be moved here, the water won't be delivered, the floor won't be flooded, and he will get all the blame. When the people have all been sent home without a show, we can pour wine all over Nolan and take him to the emperor, telling him that he's drunk."

"That's a remarkable plan," said the man. "What do you think the emperor will do?"

"I think he will have Nolan killed before our eyes," said Ulric.

⚬

Nolan and Titus slipped out a different way and left the area. "I don't even need to talk to the people who are bringing in the water yet," said Nolan. "They have everything in place. The water will be coming fast from four different sources, and they don't expect me to give them the signal until almost daylight."

"Are you ready to come back to the house now?" asked Titus.

"You go on ahead of me," said Nolan. "I need to find out if anyone has purchased our villa yet."

When Nolan arrived at the man's house, it was late. He knocked on the door, and the when the man opened it, he was surprised to see him but pulled him inside and closed the door.

"I am relieved to see you," the man said. "I took a man and his wife over to see your property. The wife fell in love with the place and purchased right then. I have your money." He went over and pulled out a huge sum of money and put it in a box for Nolan to take. Then he said, "Before we left, someone pounded on the door. When we came out, there was a group of probably eighty soldiers waiting for you. A man demanded to know where you were, and I said that I had no idea and that you did not live there anymore. He looked very angry, and they went down the street in the direction of the Coliseum."

Nolan was speechless. *Is it possible that Ulric went to my villa while I was calling on Francis's wife and talking to the shipbuilders?* he thought.

"If I were you, I would take this money and never come back," the man said.

"What did the man look like?" Nolan asked.

"Short. Heavy set. Dark hair turning gray," said the man.

"I might just take your advice," said Nolan. Nolan paid the man for his service and thanked him for everything. Then he picked up his money and went out into the street. He decided to go straight to Titus's house, get the boys, and leave. When he got there, Titus and his wife had no idea where the boys were. Nolan's stomach burned, and he could barely breathe. He told them about the soldiers who came to arrest him.

"I know how those people think," said Nolan. "They would use Felix and Flavius to get me, and then they would probably kill them along with me in tomorrow's performance."

"Why are they after you?" asked Titus's wife.

"It's probably because they figured out that I let those Christians go," said Nolan. "I have to find the boys."

"No," said Titus. "You stay here. I'll go look for them. I just don't know where to start."

"You don't think they would go to our villa, do you?" asked Nolan. "I told Felix to stay away from the place."

"Can you think of anyone they would want to say goodbye to?" asked Titus's wife.

"Just Francis," said Titus. "But they won't be able to see him."

"Let me think," said Nolan. "Maybe they went to see one of their friends."

"Titus, you can't just go out wandering around the streets, looking for them," said his wife.

Just then, they heard the door, and the two boys came in. The three parents grabbed them and held them, but the boys wrestled out of their arms.

"Something terrible has happened," said Felix. "I went to say good-bye to Miranda, and her mother told me that she has been taken prisoner, along with her sister and her sister's little baby and her husband, and their whole church. One of the children in their church was hiding and got away. The child overheard the man say that they will be featured in a battle at the Coliseum."

"Oh no," said Nolan. "I don't even know where to look this time, and if I go near the place, they will arrest me too. This is all the work of one ambitious man who wants my job."

"Couldn't we disguise ourselves as spectators tomorrow and act like we are going to watch the show?" asked Felix.

"We don't have tickets," said Nolan, "and that would be too late anyway."

"All I know is that Argus and I disguised ourselves as visitors the day we rescued Ravi, and no one even looked at us," said Felix.

"Isn't there some kind of back door we could go in?" asked Titus. "Isn't there a place where that ambitious guy would never go?"

"Of course," said Nolan. "Gate 80. Every dead animal and every dead person is removed through Gate 80. All of the slaves that work in there wear black tunics and masks over their faces. We see them all the time, and it's as if they're invisible."

"You never let us go near that area," said Felix. "Would they be working there now?"

"Absolutely," said Nolan. "They have to get all twenty of those lions out of the place before morning, as well as the twenty-one men who lost their lives. Let's go."

CHAPTER 32

"Let's sneak up to first level and look down at the floor to see what's going on," said Nolan.

"This mask is sure itchy," said Flavius. "How do these people wear them all the time?"

"They're slaves," said Titus. "They have no choice. Flavius, tuck your hair up into the mask better. Your red hair is really noticeable."

They looked onto the floor of the arena, and one battleship was already in place. The second one was just entering the building. "Look over there," said Nolan. "They are standing by to seal off the entranceway with the waterproof covering. Everything is on schedule."

"You four," shouted a taskmaster. "Stop looking at those battleships and get that lion out of here." The four of them went over to the lion. They noticed that it was already loaded onto a wheeled cart, so they grabbed ropes and guided it out, following others doing the same thing. When they got it outside the gate, they left it in place for others who were loading them onto a wagon. They went back into the building and returned to the place where they could observe the floor again.

"The second battleship is in place, and they are waterproofing the entranceway," said Nolan. "Which way will work to our benefit? Should I give the signal to flood the place and float the ships, or should I keep it dry and send the place into turmoil?"

"How are the prisoners getting to their ships?" asked Titus.

"The walkways are being attached right now," answered Nolan. "See them. The prisoners will cross the walkway and then put on the costumes and pick up their weapons. They will be instructed to fight and kill anyone and everyone wearing the other color, or they will be killed."

"Where will the prisoners come from?" asked Flavius.

"They will come from many prisons around the city," said Nolan. "Of course, some of them are probably being held here at the Coliseum, because most of the animal rooms are empty now."

"If you don't flood the place, they won't bring the prisoners in," said Titus.

"That's true," said Nolan, "but then we might be discovered before we can save them. At least this way they will bring the prisoners right up to those walkways."

"Yes," said Titus. "You have to give the signal."

"You three wait right here, out of sight," said Nolan. "I must go to four locations to signal the water flow. Don't worry about me. I intentionally kept this part a secret. I am the only one who knows these people, so no one will be watching for me."

Titus, Flavius, and Felix hid in the seating area out of the sight of the slaves and their taskmasters. They heard a whooshing sound as water poured in on the west side of the floor. Soon the water flowed from the north, and then the east, and finally the south.

Nolan joined them, and they were amazed as the waters rose.

"It can't be," said Felix. "The prisoners are already arriving."

They watched as a stream of prisoners was forced onto one of the walkways. The people were very scared as they walked across a narrow path, holding onto little ropes to keep them from falling in the water.

"Do you see Miranda?" asked Nolan.

"No," answered Felix. "Those people don't look like they are from around here."

"I wish we could rescue more that just your friends," said Nolan. "None of these people deserve to die. It's all my fault. I thought up this madness as a distraction so we could get away. Until recently I thought they only used prisoners who were murderers, thieves, and other evil people who deserved to be punished. But I have no excuse. I only hope God will forgive me. I have asked him to."

"Father, what we need is a miracle," said Felix. "Let's ask God to provide a way out of this mess and then help us escape the city."

The four of them dropped to their knees as Nolan poured out his heart to God.

"Dear Lord, when I thought of this event, I was only thinking of myself and the safety of my own family. But Lord, we need your help to save the lives of these innocent people. Give us wisdom. Help us see the way, and then help us escape. In Jesus's name. Amen."

"We need to believe that God will answer our prayer," said Felix. "I was just reading in Luke's letter[16] that a centurion believed that Jesus just had to say the word, and his servant would be healed. Jesus was amazed at his faith and healed the servant. So we need to act as if he has already answered our prayers."

"Then we need lots and lots of wagons to get them out of here once they are set free," said Nolan.

"Father," said Felix. "There was one thing that Maximus begged me to do on this trip. He said to ask you who your favorite wagon driver is. He said he promised to tell him about Jesus when he found out more. I'm supposed to tell him how to get to that nice church we visited."

He doesn't live far from here," Nolan said. "I'll be back soon."

The other three stayed in their hideout and watched as the waters rose and the battleships began to float.

"Do you think Father needs to tell them when to turn off the water?" asked Felix.

"I'm sure he has everything worked out to perfection," said Titus.

"What if we went over there and cut the ropes of the walkways and threw them into the water?" asked Flavius. "They would have to construct new ones and that would buy us time."

"Shhh," said Titus. "I hear someone."

The three of them ducked down even lower as they listened to a conversation in the seating above them.

"I guess Nolan was able to take care of matters," said the husky man. "I mean the battleships are down there, and the place is flooded."

"Well, I won't be able to follow through with my plan to discredit him, but I will be able to have those Christians slaughtered," said Ulric. "And I want him here to see it. We can get rid of him somehow after that. His defenses will be down, because the emperor will be so happy with the performance. Maybe we will just kill him ourselves and then somehow take credit for all of this." He laughed out loud at the thought.

Please, just say where they're hiding them, thought Felix.

"Where are all the people who will fill the battle-ships?" asked Ulric's companion.

"We moved ten of them here to test the walkways," said Ulric, "but the other two hundred of them are in that Grecian temple next door." He laughed very loudly at the thought. "We have been bringing prisoners in from all over the city and putting them there. Yesterday we brought in those Christians, which made the emperor's advisors think very highly of me." He laughed again and then suggested they go home and sleep for a few hours.

Titus and the boys waited a while to make sure they were gone, and then they headed toward the exit. They saw a giant dead lion on a cart and pulled it down the ramp, leaving it next to the wagon, where other slaves were loading them. The three were able to just walk away, and no one seemed to notice.

"Follow me," said Felix. "I know exactly the temple he was talking about." They went around the Coliseum, staying in the shadows of nearby buildings. They removed their masks but kept them handy in case they had to go back in the Coliseum.

"It looks like they only have six guards watching the entrance," said Titus. "Of course, I don't know how to get rid of those six guards."

Suddenly the earth began to shake violently. They

moved away from the buildings and held onto one another. The tall pillars supporting the front of the temple fell, crushing some of the guards. The other guards ran off, not even looking back.

Just then they saw a caravan of wagons approaching on a nearby street. "That must be Father," said Felix.

He ran and got his attention, motioning for the wagons to follow. Titus and Flavius entered the temple and were amazed that the large room was full of so many people. It was lit by only one small lamp.

"Could I have your attention, please?" began Titus. "We are attempting to rescue you all from a terrible death inside the Coliseum. Our success will depend on how quietly you can all file out and climb onto a wagon. Try to cram as many onto each wagon as you can. If we run out of wagons, I suggest you run away and disappear in the city, getting help from other sources."

Nolan pulled his wagon aside and got out. Then he motioned for wagon after wagon to pull up, load, and take off. The wagons went off in all different directions.

"Son," yelled Nolan. Felix ran to him and explained that all but ten of the prisoners were here in one place, and that the others were inside the Coliseum on one of the battleships.

"If your friends come out," said Nolan, "put them in that wagon over there that I reserved for our own family."

Felix ran back and watched the wagons being loaded and then driven away. Finally Miranda and her family came out, and Felix took them to the wagon and got in with them.

There was a group of prisoners that didn't have a

wagon left for them. A man who they figured was from Africa, since he resembled Ravi, approached them and spoke.

"We are very grateful for what you have done for us, but we are worried about others who were in prison with us for a long time," said the man. "They were taken from here hours ago, and we don't know where they are."

"They are probably the ten prisoners who were taken inside the Coliseum," said Titus. "We must get out of here now, but I suggest you enter the building, look for the battleships, and call to them. Try to get them off the ship somehow and then run away into the city."

Then Nolan, Titus, and Flavius climbed in the wagon and took off. Felix told them how to get to Miranda's house. They stopped in front of the house, and Miranda jumped off and ran to the door. Her parents were overjoyed, and they cried as they took them inside. Felix kissed Miranda good-bye and said that he would come and see her when it was safe.

Titus, his wife, and Flavius soon gathered up everything that meant something to them, and Felix helped carry them to the wagon. Nolan's favorite wagon driver was more than happy to drive them to Naples.

Nolan sat by the wagon driver, and the others snuggled in the back of the wagon with many boxes of stuff that Sonya could not live without. As they were going through the streets of Rome, some chariots went flying down the streets with a dozen soldiers. Nolan put his head down, but as he looked to the side, he saw Ulric in one of the chariots.

Later, when they were safely traveling on the road

to Naples, Titus asked Nolan how he secured so many wagons and drivers in such a short period of time.

"Thousands of people are still in Rome for the big performance," said the wagon driver. "Those wagons and horses belong to those spectators and were stored nearby. I didn't think they would mind if we borrowed them."

"Where did you get the drivers?" asked Titus.

"Those are my brothers, my nephews, and my neighbors," said the driver. "They were happy to help out."

❧❦❧

Nolan and Felix had a tearful reunion with the family and thanked their wagon driver for all he did.

"You look different somehow," said Sabrina.

"With God's help we were able to rescue those people who were supposed to fight on battleships. I feel like a huge weight has been lifted off me," said Nolan.

"And how are you, Felix?" asked Sabrina.

"I'm fine, Mother," said Felix. "We witnessed a miracle of God. I don't think I'll ever be the same."

❧❦❧

A few days after the emperor's birthday celebration, Nolan's friends and family decided to go out in public and enjoy a meal at a local eatery. They had just attended their first worship service.

"What did you think of the church service?" Nolan asked Sabrina when they were seated at a large table in the corner of the place.

"It was beautiful," she answered. "The music was wonderful."

"My favorite part was communion," said Nolan. "I am just in awe of what Christ did for us, and taking the emblems made it seem so personal to me."

"I can't believe the way the people have accepted us," said Sonya, Titus's wife. "I'm thinking that maybe we should just settle here in Naples for good."

Before anyone could respond to her idea, a group of people came in and was seated at the table next to them, so they decided to eat quietly for a while.

At that table, a man had been drinking too much and was talking way too loudly. Someone asked him how he enjoyed the emperor's big birthday celebration.

"Well," he said, "the first several days were very exciting. I don't think I've ever had so much fun. But then we were invited to attend the big finale. Thousands of us arrived at the Coliseum, but we were sent away. I guess the place was flooded somehow. Water was flowing out the sides of the building."

Nolan's eyes opened wide in surprise. "How could I forget to have them turn off the water?" he whispered.

"We were kind of busy," said Titus quietly.

The family continued listening to the loud man at the table nearby.

"Why did it take you so long to come home then?" asked someone at the table.

"Something happened to my wagon and horses," he explained. "I had to stay several extra days at the inn."

"That's odd," said someone. "Do you think the emperor enjoyed his big party?"

"At first, I guess," the man answered. "The whole city is talking about the changes there. I heard that one of his advisors killed the Coliseum manager, and without the manager everything fell apart. The place was flooded, and all of the performers escaped. There won't be any performances for a while, because they have to clean up all the damage caused by the flooding."

Nolan and Sabrina went home, rejoicing and thanking God.

"I know we could still be in danger," said Nolan, "but it sounds like most of the people who would be out to get me think I'm dead. Ulric must have told the emperor that he killed me."

"He knows you are still alive," said Sabrina. "Do you think he will be looking for us?"

"Perhaps he will be," said Nolan. "But God protected us when we were in Rome. Let's trust God to protect us here in Naples."

EPILOGUE

Nolan lost weight and purchased some of the new, modern tunics. He cut his hair and wore it in a style like the teenagers were sporting. Sabrina's hair was naturally turning from black to white, so all she needed to do was wear it a little shorter and fuller.

They decided that all Christians were in danger now, so there was no place where they would be completely safe.

So Nolan and Sabrina were able to live their lives in Naples. Claudia married Flavius, who began to study medicine under a well-respected physician. Argus, Felix, and Maximus opened a landscaping business to support themselves, but their real passion was spreading the Word of God, whether traveling on the land or on the Great Sea with their favorite sailors.

ENDNOTES

1   Romans 8:28–32

2   Luke 2:8–20

3   Romans 15:13

4   Matthew 2:1–20

5   Genesis, Chapter 1 to Genesis 2:1–3

6   Genesis, Chapters 2, 3, and 4

7   Luke 24:13–35

8   Matthew 14:22–36

9   John 11:1–44

10 Matthew 2:16–18

11 Acts 8:26–40

12 1 Kings 7:2

13 Matthew 6:29

14 Acts 27:13- 28:6

15 Luke, Chapters 1–6

16 Luke7:1–10